Maurice Leitch, born in County Antrim and educated in Belfast, began his broadcasting career with the BBC there in 1960 as a radio features producer. In 1970 he moved to London to work in the radio drama department continuing to direct documentary feature programmes. In 1977 he became Editor of *A Book At Bedtime* on Radio Four until leaving in 1989 to write full-time.

By the same author

Novels
The Liberty Lad
Poor Lazarus
(*Winner of Guardian Fiction Prize*)
Stamping Ground
Silver's City
(*Winner of the Whitbread Prize*)
Chinese Whispers
Burning Bridges
Gilchrist
The Smoke King
The Eggman's Apprentice

Short Stories
The Hands of Cheryl Boyd

Audio book
Tell Me About It

Television Plays and Screenplays
Rifleman
Guests of the Nation
Gates of Gold
Chinese Whispers

DINING AT THE DUNBAR

DINING AT THE DUNBAR

MAURICE LEITCH

LAGAN PRESS
BELFAST
2009

Published by
Lagan Press
1A Bryson Street
Belfast BT5 4ES
e-mail: lagan-press@e-books.org.uk
web: lagan-press.org.uk

© Maurice Leitch, 2009

The moral rights of the author have been asserted.

ISBN: 978 1 904652 52 6
Author: Leitch, Maurice
Title: Dining at the Dunbar
2009

Set in Caslon
Printed by Athenaeum Press, Gateshead

for Ian Cochrane
1941-2004

CONTENTS

Hear Me Out *13*

Swan-song for the Nightingale *53*

The Valet's Room *92*

Rancho Notorious *150*

The Good Ship Lollipop *187*

Dining at the Dunbar *216*

Albatross *255*

Hear Me Out

'Now I want you to be a good boy tonight. Behave yourself, you hear me?'

Their little joke, you might call it, something just between the two of them before he put the dummy in the suitcase, closing the lid, then heading out to the car. But, sometimes, too, depending on the mood he was in, he might pursue the conceit simply for the fun of it, as well as the practice, even after, and despite the clasps being in place. And then from within would come that other voice, convincingly muffled and distinctly peevish, *chance would be a fine thing*, followed by a groan, further evidence of a grouchy nature.

The house where he lodged belonged to a widow whose husband had passed away suddenly while watching a gameshow on television, *The Generation Game*, or maybe, *The Price is Right.* Obviously, as far as he was concerned, it wasn't, having paid the ultimate penalty while watching the conveyor belt of toasters, electric kettles, hairdryers, Dust-

Busters and two-speed hammer drills slide slowly past his hardening gaze, as perfect a metaphor for gluttony, and possibly envy, as one could wish for. One of the deadlier sins most certainly, and, indeed, he had often made use of the image when out delivering the gospel message with the help of his little friend.

On the floor directly below Mrs. McNair kept the set tuned to a considerate murmur barely pricking the silence of his upstairs room so, when practising, he felt constrained to employ only the softest of tones in case she might hear him over the chimes of the *Ten O'Clock News.*

Sitting on the edge of the bed facing the mirror with his bright-eyed boy-companion on his knee, he would murmur, 'So, tell me, young Chip, and how has *your* day been?' and the dummy's eyes would roll up, and its painted jaws click before rasping, *Why ask me, you're the one with all the answers around here?*

That was the nature of their relationship, Mister Nice and Master Moody on stage, off, as well, something that had become set like the varnish coating Chip's hollowed-out, glue and fibreglass form, while all the while those would-be penitents sat watching to see if his lips moved or not. But then the experts were in agreement, work at keeping the mouth motionless for the first five minutes and no one will even bother looking at you the rest of the time, all eyes fixed on little Chip, star of the show. And, sometimes, playing on it for light relief, the dummy would growl, *Any more of that out of you, mister, and back in the case you go*, and that innocent revival crowd would rock with laughter before the next more serious evangelising segment of their double-act came round.

'Off to do the Lord's good work, Pastor?'

Mrs. McNair had the door of the lounge open so she could catch him on the way out.

The television was showing a shampoo commercial, a brunette lasciviously towelling her hair while simultaneously managing to leer at him. For some reason he could barely drag his eyes away, even when the bottle and its label expanded to fill the screen.

'Where exactly is it this evening — or is that a wee secret?' smiling, as she said it, lowering the volume on the set with a squeeze of the remote buried in her lap.

'Oh, no secret, Mrs. McNair,' affably he replied, whilst knowing full well what she was getting at. Like the Good Lord Himself, he, too, preferred to move in mysterious ways, once he'd told her in an unguarded moment, hoping to deflect her curiosity, and ever since she hadn't allowed him forget it.

'It's this wee hall, oh, away off in the back of beyond.' And he mentioned a place he felt certain she had never heard of.

But then she said, 'Oh, but I know it well. My people used to visit relatives there on my father's side. The Burnsides are still well known in those parts. That was my maiden name, by the way.'

Trapped there in the doorway, he felt the dry, close heat of the lounge making him lethargic and heavy-eyed already. Cocooned in her downstairs lair like some pale, plump grub, she rarely opened a window, legs stretched in front of her, propped on a leather pouffe facing the blazing electric fire and the television. He could distinguish the outline of bandages through the thick lisle stockings, for she suffered from what she called 'various' veins, relying on a stick her late husband Jim had used himself before his fatal coronary, in this very room, by all accounts, perhaps even in the same petrol blue velour Parker Knoll recliner.

Having her confined to the ground floor seemed more than a satisfactory arrangement, for he dreaded the notion of her being in his room. Even so he kept the suitcase locked at all times with its own five-digit, secret combination, based not on his own birth date, as might be expected, but the dummy's, which he calculated right back to the time he first began fashioning him in that other life of his.

'Oh, if you only knew how lucky you are, blessed with the power of both legs.'

He felt his own tremble beneath him, poised and aching for flight, but she was relentless.

'That new, young, foreign doctor with the funny accent says I should have them stripped.'

She meant the veins, not the legs, and he had this sudden horrific image of someone in a white coat and mask half covering a swarthy face, hauling hard on strings of something unspeakable like bloodied spaghetti.

'But, no, I told him, no, I could never face the knife. Tell me, Pastor, do you think the laying-on of hands might provide some blessed modicum of relief, for I've tried nearly everything else. I don't mean an out and out cure, you understand, just some temporary easement, that's all.'

He hung there looking down at her. At his back squatted the suitcase in the hall, locked and ready for the road, and a voice in his head whispered, *Go on, humour the old bitch. Who knows, it might work ...*

'I tell you what, Mrs McNair,' he heard himself say, 'why don't I offer up a wee personal prayer at our meeting tonight? The positive power of supplication has been known to work wonders for a lot of people in your condition, if not physically, certainly spiritually.'

She looked at him with pity, and he could read disappointment written there tinged with contempt, *why keep a dog and bark yourself*, the expression coming to mind, and suddenly he was seeing himself through her eyes, hovering, twisting his hands together, in his high-shouldered, old suit with the wide lapels, fashion relic from that time when his life had entered cold storage for nearly a decade.

And what about that suitcase, too, going everywhere he goes? her thoughts continued arcing across to him. *What's in it? Bibles? Hymn books?* And then a most terrible, shocking notion came fluttering its dark wings inside her head like a bat in a bedroom — *what if he isn't what he says he is? After all, it's only his word he's a man of religion, a man of the Word. What if — ?*

A programme had been on television barely a week ago, all about what they called 'lily-whites', people, men, women, too, in some cases, outwardly respectable, but like primed charges waiting to go off, ready to spring into action the minute their handlers made a phone call. No matter what, she would just have to see inside that lump of luggage sitting there in her own hall right now like a time-bomb. She would, even if it killed her ...

As *Stars In Their Eyes* started coming back on again after the break, he left her there, surge in the volume telling him he was free to go now she had lost interest in him and his wishy-washy, all-talk, no-action religion.

In the driveway he continued to burn with resentment and

felt like taking it out on Chip by putting the suitcase in the boot, but, relenting, he slid it along the back seat where it always travelled.

Outside it was a fine, clear, settled evening and after the deadening, sickbed atmosphere of Sunnyside the air flowing through the car's open window felt like precious balm. Despite its age the ancient Morris Traveller raced gamely on, and he tried directing his thoughts ahead to the performance an hour's drive away, but the same sarcastic voice inside his head continued nagging at him.

Laying on of hands indeed! Forget the legs, how about that old turkey neck of hers, eh? Just think how good that would feel. If that wouldn't bring about a sudden conversion, I don't know what would. Come on, loosen up. Keep on the way you're heading, friend, and you'll worry yourself into an early grave, and then where would that leave me, eh? Thought of that, have we? No, I don't think we have somehow ...

After a couple of miles of it, nag, nag, he pulled over into the first lay-by and sat there, hands covering his ears, even though the problem was on the inside. Another car came slowly by, and the driver, some fat old codger in a Morris even more elderly than his own, stared across at him sitting there like one of the wise monkeys. Mercifully the voice stopped at about the same time, possibly shamed into it, he suspected, by the look on the hayseed's face.

In the hedge a matter of feet away there happened to be growing a late bloom of some kind, purplish in hue, marooned there like some botanical castaway. Reaching out he plucked it from its stalk, and before threading it through his buttonhole put it to his nose. No proper scent, just a dry, dusty hint of something. Still, it was the colour that mattered, and as he drove off, in his head this neat little segment was already beginning to take shape about the lilies of the field, and red being the colour of blood and, by association, redemption, as well. And back inside his snug, padded case, Chip kept his trap shut as though recognising who was the brains of this outfit when it came to putting a routine together.

By the time he got to where he was booked to perform most of the light had gone and he lost some time peering into the gloaming trying to locate where the gospel tent was pitched, for it was a 'canvas mission' according to what he had been told. But he wasn't unduly worried, knowing from experience country people of the sort who would be coming never hurried themselves if they could help it, trailing in whenever it suited them. Still, there was a score of cars and muddied Land Rovers already in the pasture when he found it, the pale looming bulk of the marquee a shock to the senses in the growing dark of the surrounding grassland.

In a space clear of the rest he parked the Traveller, then sat staring dully at the hedge in front of him. Emptying his mind was how he saw it, and often, too, he would imagine a trickle of water draining off all the residual stresses of the day along with it. There was also this wee prayer he would recite to himself at such times. 'Dear Lord,' he murmured to the flecked windscreen, 'bless our joint endeavours this lovely autumn evening. Fill the pair of us with the fiery breath of Thy Spirit, and give us powerful tongues the better to promote Thy Heavenly Message.' And from inside the suitcase there followed what sounded like a heartfelt *Amen* in anticipation of what was about to take place on stage at the back of that tent over there, already starting to glow from within as the generator got into its stride.

Looking towards the marquee for the first time he saw what appeared to be the outline of a cross above the entrance, and as he watched, it seemed to flicker, before flaring into sudden life, picked out by a generous studding of lightbulbs. Admittedly several were on the blink, but that didn't detract from the display, which must be visible for miles, he reckoned, drawing the faithful and the curious like moths to a flame, or *burning bush*, he thought, and in a mood of renewed fervour found himself calling out, 'Show-time!' to the empty car, even though that was usually guaranteed to enrage whoever was still inside.

Over by the open flap of the marquee a knot of men in dark suits were gathered, and as he approached out of the dusk they turned to stare at him, their eyes going directly to the suitcase. One of them came forward to greet him, hand outstretched, a ruddy-faced, cheerful seeming individual, the others looking about as much fun as a convention of undertakers.

'Is it your good self, Pastor? Tell me, have you had anything to eat yet? I know the ladies have prepared some sort of a wee collation.'

But, no, he told him, no, he was fine, just fine. Something a little later, perhaps.

And then Gilmore, for that was his name, a local auctioneer and cattle jobber, leaned in close as if to shield the humour of what he was about to say from the bunch of mutes over by the tent flap.

'How about your wee friend then? Would he maybe care to partake?'

They regarded one another, the moment hanging fire until

— he couldn't quite get over the effrontery of it himself — down near his feet a voice murmured, *Not just right now, thank you kindly. After the meeting would be more than welcome.*

The holy-roller in his Sunday best stared at the case, then at him, then back again.

'Two speakers for the price of one, eh, Pastor?'

'Well, you know what the good book says. Whatsoever ye do, do it with all thy might. We always believe in giving value for money.'

And the irony was finely gauged, these back-country types notoriously tight when it came to putting their hands in their pockets, collection plate, either. Hard enough to get petrol money out of them. But then he was doing the Lord's work, after all, and he did take pride in being able to live like a church mouse, a phrase particularly applicable to someone in his position. And as he would often tell himself, too, someone who had managed to come through what he had could hardly miss what he'd never had, not for the best part of fifteen years or so. For a moment he felt his eyes go dead as though even thinking along such lines spelled danger, especially with a stranger a matter of feet away, a habit he had become used to by now, like being the tenant of a house with one particular part of it kept permanently dark and closed off. Just like the suitcase, in a way, when it wasn't by his side.

'Let me take that off you. It looks a bit heavy.'

But, drawing back, Kells tightened his hold on the worn handle, and Gilmore stared at him and the suitcase for a moment.

Then he said, 'So, tell us, Pastor, just exactly how do we go about introducing you? From the platform, I mean.' At which point an harmonium inside the tent started wheezing out a hymn tune.

'Gospel ventriloquist will do fine.'

'At the back there's this wee private place where you can relax until it's time to go on.'

And so along by the wall of the tent he led him, steering clear of the guy ropes with an almost dainty, high-stepping action incongruous in someone his size. A pale, yellowish glow filtered through the canvas as they went brushing past. On the far side the congregation was now singing 'Never Lose Sight of Jesus'.

'Tea in the big pot there, cake, sandwiches, too, if you happen to change your mind.'

They were in a curtained-off section at the rear of the tent proper, a crush of trampled grass underfoot, and a trestle table covered with plates piled high with foodstuffs. Gilmore pointed to a row of fold-up chairs arranged in a semicircle as though waiting for a meeting to convene.

'Take a pew,' he said with a grin. 'And put the yoke down on one as well.'

He stood there staring at the suitcase, and Kells just knew he was dying to ask what was inside.

'You don't mind me asking, but it's not black, is it? The wee puppet, I mean?'

They regarded one another, Kells feeling doubly disadvantaged, sitting down, as he was by now, and having to gaze up into the other's broad, sun-scorched face.

'Not that I've anything against dark people, mind, we always collect for the African missions and such, but there's wee weans out there tonight with their mammies and we wouldn't want them going home and having nightmares, would we, now?'

'He's as white as you or me,' Kells heard his own voice

waver, and for the briefest of moments the urge to let that other voice speak for itself from its leather-bound sanctuary was hard to resist.

'So it is a *he* then?'

This was becoming irksome in the extreme. Why should he have to put up with this catechism?

'Mr Gilmore — ' he began.

Someone on the far side of the curtain was now leading the congregation in prayer. He caught the words 'infinite mercy' delivered in a thick, country accent, followed by 'everlasting life', repeated several times as though the speaker had already exhausted his puny, biblical vocabulary. But the real reason he had stopped dead was not on account of the actual words, but because he was thinking of the shocking notion of having something female on his knee, his right hand buried under a petticoat, or whatever it was young girls were supposed to wear in this day and age. It was something he had never considered, but the person facing him obviously had, and irritation turning to downright loathing, the temptation to allow Chip's tongue free rein grew inside like a cry bursting to be let out.

'Mr Gilmore, I wonder if I' — he almost said *we* — 'might have just a tiny moment of private contemplation.'

But the other still made no attempt to move.

'Tell me, do I detect that wee hint of an American twang?'

Closing his eyes, and lowering his head, Kells gave the impression of someone silently joining in with the unseen folk a curtain's breadth away, until, hallelujah and hosanna, didn't the over-friendly ape finally take the hint, parting the curtains and disappearing from view.

After he'd gone Kells continued sitting there with his eyes

shut, feeling drained already without having preached a word. But after a time his energies seemed to revive, and Chip's along with it.

Black, indeed! What does he take us for? Some sort of fairground act? Right, let's you and me go in there and put the fear of God into that bunch of backwoods yahoos.

But, alas, it wasn't to work out like that. Relaxing there, unprepared, suitcase still unopened on the chair by his side, what does he hear through the curtain but, 'And now here all the way from America, please would you welcome our visiting speaker for the evening, Pastor Eric Kells. Over there he's something they call a gospel ventriloquist, but I've no doubt his testimony will still be from the heart, no matter what road it travels, or what name you care to put on it. Now the Pastor has come a brave wee step to be with us all tonight. I don't mean Kentucky or Tennessee, just a matter of a couple of counties away. Still I know you'll want to extend a hearty Tyrone welcome to him, and an attentive hearing to what him and his wee jack-in-the-box friend have to say for themselves.'

Then he went on to say, 'And may the Loving Lord Jesus in His bountiful mercy give His blessing to what we're about to receive,' almost as though he had become bored, confused, or both, and was saying grace.

But Kells was still feeling stunned by the American business. The sheer, fictional effrontery of it had put him off his stroke, so that when he did arrive on stage, Chip was inside the suitcase instead of in the crook of his arm as usual.

In glum silence the crowd sat watching as he wrestled with the locked lid without having uttered a word. But, finally, he was ready and seated on a chair facing those rows of upturned, rural faces, and, as Gilmore had mentioned, indeed, quite a number of youngsters *were* present, clutching their mothers and sucking their dear little thumbs, staring up at Chip with a sort of fixed expression of dread on their round baby faces. Already, it seemed, 'the fear of God' had been put into them. But the adults were another matter entirely, turning out to be as unresponsive a bunch of clodhoppers as ever he'd had the misfortune to preach to.

And so it begins ...

'I'd like all you good folk to meet Chip here,' kicking off in cheery, ice-breaking tones. 'That's his name, by the way, because you might say he really *is* a chip off an old block.'

Usually that got a laugh. But not tonight. Not here.

Still, he persisted. 'Say good evening to the good people, Chip.'

If you say so.

'What do you mean, if I say so?'

Well, you said it, not me.

'Come again?'

Well, it's that word 'good'. It bothers me.

'It does, does it?'

Yes, it does.

'Well, it should, for it's not easy to be good. A lot of people may think so, but true goodness, the sort that comes from deep within has to be worked for. It's not something you can just slide into like your clothes every morning.'

Well, I wouldn't know much about that, now, would I?

'We're not talking about you for a change, we're talking about these good people here.'

There's that word again. Every time I hear it I have this urge to be bad, bad, bad!

'Well, the Scriptures, as a matter of fact, do have quite a lot to say about that, about people who felt much the same way. People who strayed off the true path, because the other way, the good way, the gospel way, felt too stony and difficult. Am I making any kind of sense here ... ?'

But, of course, he knew he wasn't, the words falling like stale, chewed-over crusts instead of the heavenly manna he had intended. And Chip was not much help, either, his features less animated than usual, if that were possible, glassy blink of the eye, action of the hinged jaws doing nothing to bring some desperately needed life to the proceedings.

Earlier than intended he finished with a well-known gospel refrain, 'Coming home, coming home, no longer in the path of sin to roam, I'm coming home ... ' expecting the crowd to sing along, but they sat staring up at the pair of them while he soldiered on alone, not even bothering to bring Chip in on the chorus. Even the harmonium stayed silent, the raw-faced youth who played it staring off into the shadowy, upper reaches of the tent with a contemptuous smirk on his face which seemed to say, *wouldn't count on any repeat bookings, if I were you.* Or, as Chip might put it, *don't call us, buster, we'll call you.*

When the humiliation seemed total and complete, and he was back behind the curtain once more folding Chip's limbs into the suitcase, Gilmore joined him.

'Well, I'll say one thing, it *was* different,' he said, helping himself to a slice of chocolate cake from the trestle table, leaving a dark coating around the rim of his mouth.

'Some of the old-stagers on the committee, I may as well tell you, were more than a wee bit anti to the idea of having you here in the first place. Graven images, all that sort of thing, you follow me?'

Oh, indeed he did, and sensing a caustic one-liner welling up from inside the suitcase, concentrated hard on snapping its brass hasps in place, then spinning the little, numbered, calibration rings that locked Chip in for the night. Or, at least, until they got clear of this awful place.

'Mind if I offer a wee friendly word of advice?'

Was it his imagination or was there a soft shifting beneath the leather lid? Lately he had begun to notice a little too much of that for his own good, a sensation inside of something listing off-balance, the merest tremor, like a minor landslide, all in the mind, of course.

'What people still want is your old-fashioned hellfire and damnation. Now, be frank, they didn't get that this evening. What you came up with, if you'll forgive me for saying so, might be okay for some pokey wee Sunday School class somewhere, or a Mothers' Union meeting, but not here. Folks in these parts still expect to be told they're heading for the hot place. Next time, if there's to be a next time, my advice is hit 'em hard, and where it hurts. Now, we had a preacher here last month, Pastor George Ravendale, his name was — maybe you've heard tell of him — well, he had this place in hysterics, people down on their knees crying out for forgiveness, at least three, maybe more, healings, with the laying-on of hands. Now you know your calling better than I do, I'm only some ignorant old farmer, and the way you work the wee dummy is clever right enough, but, be honest, just exactly how many sinners do you think you brought to the Mercy Seat this night? Hardly an away win, was it, now?'

For some reason the football analogy rankled more than anything else. He and Chip kicking goals for Jesus? Scarcely what he had in mind when he started out on this crusade, when he put that old life of his, the one he preferred not to dwell upon, behind him for good.

But in the car driving home, the suitcase laid across the rear seat like a salesman's samples, his mind veered back to all of that like a dog drawn by the lure of its own vomit.

When he found the Lord that time he was at the darkest, lowest ebb of his life, and it was as if a sudden, shining light had come on, and he was standing naked, bathed in it, as though in front of a mirror. To be truthful, he really was in the raw at the time, he and Winston Mahood both, having just performed their very own baptism ceremony in the shower-block together. '*Hallelujah!*' he called out to the beaded tiles that fateful day, for it was as if he was radiated from within like one of those illuminated anatomy exhibits, every particle of tissue and muscle, every artery, every nerve, highlighted in stunning living colour. Gradually, of course, that inner glow grew dimmer and dimmer as the days passed. But then, he told himself, that no longer mattered so much, now he had been chosen to turn on that same light in others.

Still, after tonight's sorry fiasco, he doubted whether he had sufficient battery power left for the next praise meeting when it came around — *if* it came around. And that thought, arriving so sudden, so final, like that, made him pull over and, leaning into the back, take Chip from his resting place, hauling him, loose-limbed and lolling, into the passenger seat, setting him upright there against the grey and navy flecked upholstery like some frozen-faced, junior hitchhiker.

And so they sat side by side staring out through the windscreen into the dark of a strange countryside, the engine making soft, cooling sounds while he began to talk.

'Remember Myrna Rice? *Ms* Myrna Rice? Glasses? Plucked eyebrows? Hooped ear-rings? The rehab sessions? Having to pay the piper some day, so why not let all of it out now, eh? Alternatively write it down like the rest of the group — nearly all of whom, he could have told her, were only there for the brownie points, Ms Rice, I let her have it ... Oh, call me Myrna, please. After all, I call you Eric, don't I? Very well, Myrna, then. With the greatest respect, I've already come to an accommodation, thank you all the same, with my Saviour, all past transgressions washed away by the wonder-working power of His Blood. Oh? she said, Oh? Then — What exactly is it you're making there, may I ask? Something for a young relative, is it? A doll, she was thinking, a dolly, ah, how sweet! Maybe when it's finished you might allow us to put it in our art exhibition? Imagine it, you in the middle of all those desperate pictures of thatched cottages, sailing boats, wee children? You?'

At which point, the lift of his voice filling the confines of the car in that way, it came to him that maybe he had been living inside his own head far too much of late, and starting up the engine almost came out with, 'Put your seatbelt on, you hear me? Oh, all right, then, see if I care,' only just managing to repress it in time.

The following Monday Mrs McNair speared him in the hallway.

'Oh, Mr Kells, can I have a word with you a wee minute?' before he had time to duck under the net of her radar. The suitcase was upstairs. He had just been slipping out for some milk for a bedtime, hot drink, for he hadn't been sleeping well of late, mind twirling like a top.

'Now, Mr Kells, you know I'm not the sort to lay down rules and regulations just for the sake of it, you are a grown man, after all, but I really must draw the line about certain things.'

He stood looking at her in shock. The television had been turned off, and that dead, dark oblong, with its slight but ominous bulge, seemed somehow to reinforce the seriousness of his offence — which was what exactly? The drying of his underclothes in front of his electric fire? He knew she would be far from impressed if she found out, having a deep-seated dread of being burned to a cinder in her bed some night. She had shown quite a surprising imaginative turn of phrase, talking of bared wires beneath the floorboards and in the dark of attics, just waiting to come alive, arcing and flashing in the small hours like something from some late-night horror film.

'What it comes down to is entertaining visitors in your room. Now you know that was one of the stipulations we agreed on when you first moved in, respecting my privacy in that way.'

He continued staring at her, mind refusing to function, tongue, also, and it was the oddest thing, but it occurred to him how much he missed Chip being by his side right now to talk them out of this situation. From where he stood he could see her mummy's legs supported on the leather pouffe with its vaguely Middle Eastern markings, a souvenir, from where exactly? — for it looked out of place among the rest of her traditional furniture, the settee with its tartan rug, the nests of tables, the display cabinet with its photographs of the dead husband Jim in his bus inspector's uniform. It distracted him, as did the bandages bulking out the surgical stockings, which he found himself scanning for traces of pink, his tongue trembling with the urge to enquire how her operation had gone, that's if she'd decided to go through with it.

But, instead, he said, 'Oh, but there has to be some mistake, surely, for I would never have anyone in my room without your permission.'

She fixed him with the ferocity of her gaze for, like a lot of long-term invalids, most of her remaining energies seemed to be concentrated there.

'Mr Kells, for all normal purposes I may well be tied to this chair you see here, but I'd like you to know my hearing is as reliable as ever it's been.'

And then it struck him what she was on about, the revelation quickening his brain into sudden prevarication.

'Oh, I know!' he cried. 'It's the radio! You must have heard my radio.'

'One of the voices I heard was very definitely your own.'

'Well, then all I can say is there must be somebody on the local station who does a grand impersonation of me,' he said shaping his features into a smile. 'I tell you what, why don't I turn it down low from now on if it bothers you so much.'

But he could tell she wasn't convinced, and as the rest of the week passed he felt distrust and suspicion seeping like an invisible fog up through the floorboards to where he sat facing the mirror with his door locked, Chip mute and expressionless on his knee. All of which didn't help him one iota sleeping, for in the morning he would still be lying there sweating and bleary-eyed after a night of starts and panicky dreams.

It became so bad he took the car out one afternoon and, driving to a town where nobody knew him, went into an off-licence and bought a bottle of something strongly-proofed and alcoholic, barely looking at the label, or the pimply youth behind the counter, so desperately fallen from grace did he feel himself to be.

Back in his room he sat staring at the brandy where he'd placed it on the chest of drawers, trying to face down the devil who had led him to this pass. He was trying to work out when last he'd had the taste on his lips, and much of the reason he couldn't remember had to do with him being such a hard drinker in those awful days before his sins caught up with him and this enormously heavy hand landed on his shoulder. Now, of course, he knew it was the Hand of the Lord Himself resting there and refusing to go away until he had renounced his evil ways, including the abuse of what was in that amber-coloured bottle resting not a dozen feet away on his landlady's hand-embroidered, Irish linen runner. For a long time he wrestled with the dilemma of whether to break the seal or not, but eventually that word *nightcap* with its innocent sounding ring to it overruled his conscience.

First shock of the fiery spirit on the back of his throat brought tears to his eyes, and a hot, searing trickle travelling deep down into the pit of his stomach. Determined to reap the full benefit straightaway he climbed in under Mrs McNair's salmon-pink eiderdown and lay stretched there waiting for the cognac to take effect and lull his body into much needed slumber.

Well, it must have worked, at least temporarily, for next thing he knew it was three in the morning by the outlines of the luminous hands on the wristwatch lying on top of his King James Bible. Pressing the dial to his ear to make certain the watch hadn't stopped, sure enough didn't he hear that soft, slow, remorseless tick. Lying under the slithery satin of the bedspread he debated whether to step up the dosage, but felt far too dispirited and listless to even rise out of bed. However he must have dozed off, for next time he turned his head towards the bedside table it was five.

A knife-edge of greyish light ran along the bottom of the blind and he watched for it to lighten, as stubborn and slow as the imperceptibly jerking hands on the watch face. All hope of sleep gone, he tried not to think of it, elusive and trembling like some shy creature just hovering on the boundary edges of consciousness. Instead he kept fancying he was hearing things, specifically the sound the watch made, even though it lay out of earshot.

But that slow, measured pulse grew stronger and stronger, until presently it was as if the sound was arriving, not from a single source, but from two. Propping himself up on one bare arm he began moving his head from side to side trying to locate where the echo could be coming from. In pursuit of his quest he climbed out of bed shivering ferociously, for the room was chill, as it always was at this hour before the heating came on below in Mrs McNair's cushioned quarters. The linoleum felt like ice but he kept moving around the room, head travelling from side to side as in a game of blind man's buff, and in his imagination a voice did seem to be telling him, *warmer, warmer*, even though his feet were twin, frozen blocks, and then, finally, he came to the suitcase and shock anchored him in front of it.

Bending low, he listened. Then, in a rush, fingers trembling, he twirled the tumblers on the lock and pulled back the lid. From his coffin, open-eyed as always, Chip stared up at him, and then Kells remembered the children's watch he had fastened on that wooden wrist. Neat little touch at the time, he had thought, something to make him that fraction more lifelike, more like the real thing, along with the necktie and the hound's-tooth waistcoat. But it was only a rubbishy trinket of a thing, not a real watch, not a proper going one. He stared at it. Then he lifted up the hinged arm and put it to his ear, just as he had done earlier with his own old Timex. The glass felt cold as if the suitcase was an icebox with a corpse inside. He listened intently, but there was nothing, watch as dead as its owner. In a sort of rage at himself he shook the wooden arm, then listened some more, but, of course, absolutely nothing. Finally, he allowed the limb to fall back slackly and, avoiding Chip's glassy stare, snapped the lid shut ...

Outside a cockerel had begun to crow. It seemed a curious occurrence, for the neighbourhood was solidly residential, and it struck him it had to be connected in some strange, perhaps even prophetic, way with the ticking watch. And at that point a sort of fear started gathering inside as though events were conspiring against him, bunching up like avenging creditors. For an instant he looked at the Bible on the bedside table. In moments of doubt and despair that could always be relied upon to bring him back to some sort of level ground, the slow, monotonous drumming of the antique words lulling and calming. But something told him not to attempt opening it at random as he usually did. It would be a waste of time, nothing coming off the page save the scent of old paper.

Instead, he crossed on bare feet towards the chest of drawers and, twisting the cap off the brandy bottle, drank down a good two inches of the yellowish stuff without pause or barely swallowing. Then, pulling the eiderdown up over his head, he lay curled inside its satin cave until consciousness receded for a second time.

And as though in an echo of one of his own parables, that is how the rot set in.

Over the next week he drifted between light and dark, barely knowing which was which, helped on by the demon in the bottle. Not really caring any more, he slipped out under Mrs McNair's surveillance, for even *she* had to doze off sometime, head back, open-mouthed, on the recliner, while the afternoon cookery television programmes and confessional talk-shows flickered away unregarded.

At the local corner shop a short walk away he bought more drink, strolling in and out as though what was in his wire basket was as innocent as Lucozade. And back in his room the empties started lining up on the chest of drawers, first a single file of dead soldiers, then a platoon, for his old capacity for the stuff had returned as though hovering there in some sort of suspended animation all along.

Then one night he awoke with a jolt, his sweating face prickly as a hedgehog's, no razor having touched it for days, with the feeling there was someone in the room watching over him as he slept, but not in a caring, or solicitous way. He half-imagined a figure sitting in the armchair regarding him, and as his eyes adjusted to the dark, he realised it was Chip, but a different Chip somehow, spare, almost a shadow of his old self, as if stripped to the bare wood, which, as he peered closer, turned out to be true, for all his clothing down to his very shoes and socks was missing.

For a crazed moment the notion flitted across his brain like a wing beat that the dummy must have done it himself — *itself*, he corrected — and it was that tiny, linguistic quibble which brought him to his senses. He tried to remember what had happened the previous night before he fell into bed clutching the bottle. Empty now, it lay halfway across the floor between the bed and this new, vindictive and angry-eyed Chip, like someone who had been put through some humiliating ordeal. Turning on the bedside lamp, he swung his bare legs out of bed and, sitting there, confronted the figure in the armchair.

'Well, say something, damn you! How do you expect me to apologise for something I don't even know I *did*!'

Down below he felt certain he heard a muffled cry as Mrs McNair shifted in her sleep, the sound bringing him back to some semblance of sanity. Scrabbling about on the bedroom floor, somehow he managed to gather Chip's discarded duds together, his socks and his shoes, but found he was unable to dress him on account of his hands shaking so much. And so, in an even more demeaning twist, unable to face that glassy stare, he put him back in the suitcase naked as he was, something he had never, ever done before. Never.

Yet something must have stopped him toppling headlong into the pit. It may well have been the sight of the suitcase on the far side of the room, and being reminded of what it held. Locking the whiskey away — by now he had moved on from brandy and its sickly-sweet, caramel aftertaste — he lay in bed, face turned to the wallpaper, in the grip of a hangover which refused to loosen its claws even after three days, something which he had forgotten was almost the exact duration of that old affliction when he wasn't sliding from one to the next.

On the Thursday, nervy, light-headed, he managed to wash and shave himself and, edging downstairs, successfully evade Mrs McNair's attentions yet again, a trick he seemed to have mastered by this time, despite feeling like a condemned man expecting the call of his gaoler.

About a mile away was a café where men sat smoking and reading the racing sheets all day long in a haze of tobacco and cooking oil, and he went in and sat down at a dented Formica table. The slatternly woman who ran the place took his order, barely glancing at him as if he were no different from any of the other hopeless cases she catered for, and after he had wolfed down a mess of fried stuff, he went into her filthy toilet at the back and threw up the entire foul, undigested load.

Gasping, he ran the tap, trying to rinse the taste of grease from his mouth. Over the basin hung a postcard-sized scrap of mirror and, fitting his features to its proportions, he tried to see himself as the woman might have done earlier. The smell of the cubicle, the tiled walls, the slow, escaping, torturing drip of water, all brought back to him the place where he had wasted such a stretch of his life, and as he hung over the cracked porcelain rim staring at the reflected person he had become, he felt certain he could also hear in his head, too, a distant, reverberating clang, yet another recurring element from that same squandered past.

Backing to leave he saw the reverse of the door was liberally etched and inked with initials, just like the walls of that former place. They were familiar, these initials, one set in particular possessing a powerful and personal resonance, and seeing it highlighted there like a reminder for him and him alone, he shook for a time, before wiping his damp face with a square of torn-off tissue.

But the wound still throbbed, and later that same afternoon, as though intent on further tearing at the scab, he went into a dank phone box — again the same fly-specked oblong of mirror, again the same angry initials — and dialled a number connected with that past which had reared up to claim him, and the voice on the other end of the line, unchanged save for a slight mid-Atlantic intonation along similar lines to his own, reacted as if he had never been away, he and his listener sharing a bond, after all, forged in their place of confinement.

'Winston,' he said, 'this is Eric. Eric Kells.'

And the voice replied, 'Eric!' And then, 'Still sanctified in the Lord?' and when he said, yes, yes, very much so, that was why he was on the phone to him right now, the other launched into what sounded like a well-practised, holier-than-thou, answering-machine message.

Standing on the chill concrete base of the kiosk, staring at the change in his palm, Kells waited patiently until the gospel commercial had run its course, half-expecting to be told to speak after the beep.

'Tell me, Winston,' he said, 'are you still involved with that wee mission-hall of yours in the East end of the city?'

'No longer wee, brother, no longer wee. And we're building an extension, so hungry are the people for the Living Word. I trust you, your good self, are reaping the same sort of harvest. Never forget, we have a mighty debt to repay, you and me, with our labours in the Lord's Workshop. Speaking of which, still got that wee figure of yours, the one you made all that time ago?'

And, of course, then he had to explain about his act with Chip, while watching his money run out, reversing the charges not being an option, for it would have been too much like an admission of his own abject failure in the soul-saving business.

Nevertheless, somehow, he managed to tie up a single appearance at The Daybreak Tabernacle of the Nazarene the following Wednesday — 'for old times' sake'.

The hardest part was getting through the intervening days without a drink, but by dint of burying himself in the Scriptures, and taking long, exhausting walks all over the neighbourhood, the inked crosses on the Advent calendar pinned to the door of his wardrobe edged closer to the time. And throughout that entire week not once did he go near, or even look at the suitcase.

On its chair it lay exactly as he'd left it after that fearful night when something snapped in his head, and which he still preferred not to think about. Yet deep down he continued to blame what had taken place, whatever it was, on the one inside. Chip was responsible, he told himself, in the moments when he wasn't poring over the densely annotated print in his New Testament, or striding head down, preoccupied, along unfamiliar drives and avenues with the names of English and Scottish lakes and rivers. His own particular crescent was called after a mountain peak in Wales.

The day before he was due to drive to the city he unlocked the suitcase and sat for a long time before lifting the lid. He had this strange feeling inside, a mixture of trepidation and, yes, remorse, too, for what he had done had been a form of punishment, as he now saw it, a way of showing just who was boss around here. A fresh start was what was called for, a return to the way things had been in the beginning before he had allowed doubt and depression to sneak back into his life. Somewhere along the line he had let himself be drawn towards the very edge of the pit that social-working creature with the hooped earrings had said was waiting for him as sure as night follows day — why should *he* be any different? But, then, he was, oh, he was, he told himself, and felt a fierce delight in continuing to prove her wrong.

What was called for was a revivifying jolt of spiritual electricity for them both, and The Daybreak Tabernacle of the Nazarene would be the very place to reveal to the world their newly-charged partnership.

'Hallelujah!' he cried aloud to the room, the house, Mrs McNair herself, snoozing downstairs in her airtight retreat like some geriatric dope fiend — the entire godless neighbourhood — and lifted the lid.

Chip was lying face down, rumpled and misshapen looking, as if he had been flung there like a discarded toy.

Instantly his heart smote him, and gently lifting him out, he began rearranging those boy-sized limbs, twisting the head about on its wooden stalk of a neck, straightening the joints of legs and arms, finally dressing him from top to toe, sliding on the checkered pants, the shirt, the tie, the waistcoat with the pearl buttons. When all was complete, socks and shoes on the correct feet, varnished cowslick rakishly in place, he sat him in the armchair, the pair of them confronting one another across the expanse of thin, Indian patterned rug.

Nothing was said for a long time, the noises an old house makes gradually reasserting themselves as though holding breath until all the turmoil was over, which it was, as far as Kells was concerned. It was.

Softly, so as not to mar the mood, he said, 'Now I want you to be a good boy tonight, you hear me?' and there seemed to him to be a reassuring response there, a new humility in the eyes, posture, too, of the little figure facing him.

The Daybreak Tabernacle of the Nazarene, when he found it, was this narrow, tin-roofed structure tightly bolstered between two ordinary looking houses as though someone had built it where a common right of way might once have been. Situated in a sea of relatively recent red brick — the address was Coronation Gardens — outside it had a wayside pulpit. 2000 YEARS OLD AND STILL UNDER THE MAKER'S GUARANTEE, it read, and underneath the name Pastor Winston Mahood in gold script as if the quote was his creation and not some nameless, evangelical copywriter. Every dwelling in the street had a flag of some description flying from its own angled foot of tubing, protruding from the brickwork like a defiant, stumpy finger. The symbols and initials on the red and purple flags registered with Kells with sudden, chilling familiarity, as though he had never been away.

Sitting outside in the car, for the first time he felt real curiosity about the man he had once known so intimately, the pair of them lobbing Bible quotations at one another across a chill expanse of cement floor like a couple of theological tennis players. He wondered if he had changed much. He recalled he had been brought up in a street similar to this one, and had now returned to minister amidst the same rash of slogans which had branded them both, literally, in his case, because of the tattoos on both arms as well as torso. Kells wondered if they were still there under the clerical vest, that's if he wore one in his new life. But then, of course, they had to be, he told himself a trifle impatiently, reminding him each time he took a bath of everything he had turned his back on when he found Justification and the Lord's Sweet Forgiveness.

But if he'd had a mental image of ministerial garb, dog collar, even, he couldn't have been more mistaken, for Winston had on a white sweatshirt with JESUS SAVES across the front. He also wore trainers and had his hair gathered in a ponytail, and good God, was that an earring? It was. Kells didn't dare look too closely in case it turned out to be in the form of a crucifix.

'Welcome, Brother,' boomed Mahood advancing to meet him like some gym-instructor instead of someone who promoted the Gospel, when first he entered the hall. It was empty save for a trio of teenagers in matching sweatshirts who were energetically sweeping the floor.

'Am I too early?' Kells asked, feeling not only premature, but conspicuous as well, on account of his suit and tie.

'You can never be too early, or too late in the tabernacle of the Lord, brother. We have no opening or closing times here. So, tell me, brother, how has your own wee ministry been progressing?'

For the first time he glanced down at the suitcase as though Kells' 'wee ministry' might be contained in that battered antique piece of luggage in comparison with his own extensive parish. The teenagers, Kells couldn't help noticing, were following Mahood's every word as though on a leash and licence from their master.

'Can't complain,' he lied, but then got the feeling they might be playing the same game, warily circling one another as in the old days. Even when they shared that same small space together, always there was this competitive edge, the pair of them locked together head to head in contention over the finer detail of the Scriptures, while all about everyone else in the place pursued their own profane concerns.

'Will you join me in a moment of silent prayer, brother? For old times' sake?' said Mahood.

And letting slip their brooms, the young sweepers slid to their knees in what seemed a single, synchronised movement. Mercifully the floor was clean thanks to their efforts, but Kells still felt uncomfortable, for there was something obviously rehearsed about the entire thing, as though the performance was for his benefit and his alone.

And so they knelt there in a semicircle with closed eyes breathing in the smell of floor polish. One of the teenagers, the only girl, was right next to him, and he could sense her embarrassment leaking across like a moist, invisible mist. Beneath his lowered lids he could make out the plump contours of her upper thighs under her jeans and, incredibly, felt himself aroused, instantly invoking a text in his head at random, something he always did when lust trembled on a hair-trigger as now, repeating it over and over until he felt composed once more. After Mahood had said, 'Amen,' the girl smiled shyly at him as though in gratitude for his forbearance.

But, still unsettled, and in spite of that silent mantra from Saint Luke, Kells now did a foolish thing. Excusing himself he went to the toilet in the back recesses of the building and, locking the door, from the suitcase took out the half-bottle of Famous Grouse he had brought along in case of dire emergency, just as this seemed to be turning out to be. After a healthy snort he ran the tap to rinse away the taste, hopefully, smell, as well, then, sucking ferociously on a Polo mint for extra protection, he made his way back to the body of the hall.

Music — some New Age rubbish — was drifting along the passageway towards him, and when he came out into the glare of a sudden, almost theatrical barrage of lighting he saw that Mahood was on stage with the three teenagers. They were fluttering tambourines in the air, and already the hall was packed with eager worshippers all singing and clapping to the beat. Kells stood there, the whiskey not doing the job it was supposed to do, any confidence he possessed in his own capabilities draining away before this almighty display.

And then, even more unnerving, Mahood was beckoning him up on stage to join him and the young songbirds. Stiffly, as though in a dream, Kells began to climb the wooden steps by the side of the platform, lugging the suitcase along like some affliction he was fated to carry, and gazing out on all those joyously mouthing faces saw, to his surprise, quite a few coloured ones dotted in among the more homely, indigenous variety, the sudden shock of it registering as a deep pang of personal failure, making him realise, as if he needed further confirmation, that he never should have come here.

When the hymn came to a close, its air and words something you might hear on some children's TV programme, Mahood raised his arms proclaiming, *'Glorify! Glorify!'*, the congregation joining in. Kells felt the sound and emotion enfold, then wash over him, like a wave beating on some stubborn, encrusted balk of wood. Bowing his head, he bore it, for that was how he saw it now, all this directed at him and him alone, standing there waiting to be converted in his out-worn sixties suit and paisley patterned tie, the suitcase alongside like some apparatus of punishment attached to one leg.

Another hymn followed, then another. Then a haggard looking individual stood up to testify, rising from the rows as though primed to detonate at this precise moment. He spoke of a combination of drink, wife-beating and child neglect with what looked like real tears in his eyes, and those in his immediate vicinity moaned and swayed in sympathy, even some of the darker complexioned ones who looked far too professional and respectable in their smart, Sabbath clothes ever to have been driven by such raw urges.

More penitents arose, with much the same histories, before finding Jesus and the Mercy Seat, and gradually Kells edged back from the limelight to where a solitary chair sat in a pool of shadow. In a moment of crazy wish-fulfilment he saw himself sitting there all by himself in the emptiness of the hall long after everyone else had departed into the dark of the street outside, yet knowing, at the same time, he was trapped with nowhere to go, all this fervour drawing him towards one conclusion and only one, being called upon to open up his pathetic box of tricks for these people.

And at the thought a heaviness seemed to be gathering inside, a great, undigested lump of something. He could feel it lying in his stomach and on his chest and, lifting up the suitcase, he laid it across his knee. Staring out past Mahood and his three young disciples into the fierce glare of the hall, under cover of the open lid he twisted the cap off the bottle inside, then, ducking swiftly down, put it to his lips, finishing off what was left in a single swallow, the heat of it hitting him, then racing through, dulling brain and senses. And so he waited, willing the effect to last until his moment came.

And eventually it did when the atmosphere was at a peak of frenzy, people rolling their heads about bellowing for *mercy, mercy, mercy*. Kells sat where he was, still centre of all that turmoil, the drink lazily uncoiling in his veins. But already he could sense it starting to lose power. It seemed to have settled somewhere below the waistline as though he were encased in lead down there — deep-sea diver's legs, he thought — and he was wondering how he would get them to function in a reasonable manner when Mahood suddenly threw up both arms like a prophet, crying out, '*Redemption in the Power of the Blood!*' above the clamour. A woman in a purple hat took up the call, then another, and another, echoing the cry as if reacting to something deep-seated and essentially female.

But then the mood began returning to a murmuring calm, occasional little sighing eddies rippling, breaking out, people glancing shyly across at one another as though to reassure themselves they hadn't been behaving too outrageously moments earlier.

'Brothers, sisters,' intoned Mahood, 'the Redeemer looks down on our humble gathering here tonight and He thanks you from the bottom of His Heart. Believe me, no one ever gets turned away from His House. No one. Whenever a sinner comes forward with repentance in his heart and on his lips, He listens, oh, believe me, He listens, and takes heed.

Now, a friend of mine happens to be here with us tonight, an old comrade from those distant, troubled days before the Saviour seared the pair of us with the laser beam of His Holy Word. Tonight, at my request, my comrade and colleague in Christ would like us all to share some of that same message of Love with the help of a little friend of his. Not magic, dear friends, not music-hall trickery, but something new in worship from the far side of the water.'

So, here it was at last, the big moment. But the tongue in Kells' mouth felt numbed as well as frozen. For a brief, demented instant he thought of pleading sudden illness, a seizure of some kind, brought on, perhaps, by the debilitating Power of the Spirit, not such a far-fetched occurrence in a place like this. But already he knew it wasn't in him to carry it off, things had gone too far. *Too far*, the words kept ringing in his brain, *he* had gone too far, been pushed too far, and as if that actual refrain was the trigger, he took Chip out of the suitcase and set him on his knee.

Sitting there on his moulded plastic chair in a fresh pool of light he felt calm suddenly, skin cool, hands steady. The little figure, too, felt reassuring to the touch, even its scent, with its mixture of glue, hobby paint and leather from the inside of its case, acting like a sedative. For what seemed an eternity they remained mute and motionless, he and Chip, gazing out over the craning heads of the crowd as though at something private only they were privileged to see.

But in the stretching silence Mahood could be heard to cough then clear his throat. He looked both impatient and nervous at the same time. But before he could intervene Chip murmured, '*Hell's bells*', and instantly there was a quickening in the hall even though Kells was the only one able to make out the actual words.

'Now I want you to be a good boy,' he heard himself say, 'behave yourself,' and a woman near the front tittered and smiles began to break out.

Painted head slowly travelling from side to side, and a beady glint in his eye, Chip said, *Hands up all who believe in miracles*, in tones that everyone could hear.

At which point Kells closed his eyes, feeling relaxed, as if all the fret and tension was draining out of him like waste water from a bath which had been much too full far too long. His hidden hand continued operating instinctively, but the rest of him had handed over all responsibility to something as disembodied as a ghost. He could feel it all right. More importantly, hear it, but it was as if he himself was floating at some high and distant remove from everything about to take place.

Now that's what I came all this way to see, the voice

continued, gaining strength as well as authority, *some of that good old-fashioned trust in mind over matter*, gaze roving across the sea of upraised hands and eager faces like the beam from some small, carved, unblinking lighthouse.

Never thought I could talk, did you now? Be honest. Still, here I am, your very own livin', talkin' doll, and have I got a treat in store for you, all you good people who came along here tonight hoping for someone to inject a little jolt of spiritual excitement into your drab and boring lives.

No, no, don't look at our friend here. Poor thing, cat's got his tongue. And not before time. The nights I've had to sit here like this keeping my trap shut. Except, of course, when he's decided to put words into it. Take it from me, you don't want to hear any of that. Not tonight, you don't. Anyway, it's my turn to get a few things off my chest for a change.

Now, confession they say is good for the soul, and we've heard quite a lot of that here tonight. We have, haven't we? You, sir, now don't tell me you don't feel a whole lot better for letting it all out.

The head had stopped revolving, eyes settling on the man in shirt-sleeves who had broken down earlier recalling his destroyed marriage, health and job, all because of drink and an addiction to a well known, over the counter painkiller. The man looked agitated, dropping his head, so the beady stare homed in on someone else, a thin young woman this time with dark circles under her eyes who had thrillingly confessed to being 'a fallen woman'. She, too, allowed her head to sink.

Throughout, Kells sat staring at the back wall where there was a panoramic rendering of The Wedding At Canaan. In his head, hypnotically, almost, he found himself counting the faces in the mural as if everything going on in the hall around him was unimportant compared with getting the guest-list right. His lips moved quite openly now, mind floating free.

Let me tell all you good folks here a little parable. Well, maybe two halves of one. For actually it concerns two people, who, believe it or not, just happen to be here with us tonight. But I won't point them out to you. Not just yet, for they might just feel it in their hearts to be moved to provide their own testimony, like the way some of you have been doing, letting it all hang out for Jesus.

The voice paused, Chip cocking his head to one side as though waiting and listening for a response. However, none came, and the silence seemed to curdle, broken only by the heavy sighs of one of the coloured women near the front.

No? Very well, then, I'll continue, shall I?

Once upon a time, not a million miles from where we're sitting here tonight, there were two young men, and like a lot of young men of similar age and background, they smoked, they drank, they gambled, they followed the lusts of their loins.

Now where they grew up there happened to be these other older men who preached hatred and animosity towards people of a different faith to their own, although in no way could it be said they were particularly God-fearing themselves. That was just their excuse, you see, for these older men, they badly needed to blame others for their own ugly, empty, pointless, angry lives.

Well, very soon the two young men in our story started believing everything the older men told them. They didn't need a lot of convincing, mind. So one dark night when they'd been drinking they went out looking for someone they could take out all their anger and frustration on. And they found someone like that. He was hitchhiking along a lonely country road and when they got him into the car it didn't take them too long to find out his name. Just an ordinary, everyday name, you might say, to a lot of people in some other place. But not there, and not to our two young men, and it was just the excuse they needed to blindfold him, tie his hands behind his back, then drive him to an abandoned quarry where, after they'd had their cruel, torturing way with him, they left him there like a bloody, punctured sack of butcher's meat.

Well, when they got home, burned their stolen car and clothes, and washed themselves scrupulously all over, they went out drinking some more, and when they told the older men what they had done they found they had become heroes. So much so they went out again the following night, and the next, finding out something else about themselves, namely, that they were beginning to get a taste for it. In other words they enjoyed it. But because this happens to be a parable, their sins eventually did find them out, and so they ended up in prison.

But now, here comes the miraculous part. Just a very short time afterwards they found the Lord together in that place of captivity. They did. And you know something else equally wonderful? They began telling everyone around them that their sins had been forgiven them, washed whiter than white, just like one of those soap powder commercials. Now, wasn't that truly miraculous and inspirational? Wasn't it? Well, I certainly think so anyway.

Oh, and I forgot to mention that when they got out of prison they started this brand new career telling other people not so fortunate as themselves about the wonder-working Power of the Lord and what He could do for you, too, if you just got down on your knees like they did and asked Him for a *blank cheque to pay off all those bad debts of a vile and sinful nature.*

Now doesn't that make you want to rejoice? Doesn't it? Have you ever encountered anything as wonderful as that? Even had the good fortune to run across two such remarkable individuals in real life? You haven't. Well, stick around, folks, for the good news is this might turn out to be your lucky night.

Throughout, Kells continued feeling as though he was in a sort of dream. He could hear someone speaking all right, and the voice did sound familiar somehow, but it was as if it was travelling from very far away, even, perhaps, from that distant, mythical place of rocks and pale brown hills depicted on the back wall where people in brightly coloured robes congregated under a blazing sun and a piercing cobalt sky. In the dream someone appeared to be telling a story, a long, involved account of some kind, maybe even the man in the brightest garment of all, but who or what it was about his brain couldn't quite take in.

But then, to his dismay, he found himself beginning to falter in his careful calculation of all the people present in that Bible picture, for the man in the pale sweatshirt nearby with the words across the front was shouting something suddenly and waving his arms in the air.

'*Doll of Satan!*' he seemed to be yelling. '*Doll of Satan!*' while the people in the hall began shifting on their chairs with startled faces as if shaken out of some kind of deep sleep.

And then the shouting man, he did this most shocking thing by far, for he threw himself across the stage at Kells sitting there. But, instead of going for him, as it looked he might do, instead he dashed Chip from his knee, sending him flying to land in a corner all mashed up and broken looking.

'*Doll of Satan!*' he kept on yelling. '*Come out of him, Beelzebub! Leave him, I say! Leave him!*'

Down in the hall men were on their feet shouting too now, their womenfolk in hysterics, while the three teenagers huddled together at the side of the stage like infants trapped in the grip of a horror film.

And throughout, Kells sat where he was silently counting away, back to the beginning of his tally all over again, while that other distinct and separate part of him, the part that lay broken, head twisted back to front, legs bent under it like two checkered pipe-cleaners, continued babbling away as though no power on Heaven, hell or earth could close its mouth now it had begun.

Swan-song for the Nightingale

When the phone rang the boy was in the darkened sitting-room, one low watt light bulb the house rule on account of his mother being this twilight creature of late, soaked rag permanently lapping her temples, topped-up glass of something amber close to hand, smoke curling upwards from a Rothman's King Size. In the weak pool cast by the Anglepoise, his homework book sat perfectly aligned, important to get it just so, because this was how he did everything these days. *Meet my son, thirteen, going on seventy*, she would say, but he was used to the sarcasm and, anyway, he got the impression she secretly enjoyed having her very own 'personal pensioner' around, as she liked to call him.

The phone in the hall continued to ring until he heard her cry out, 'Whoever it is, tell them I'm dead!' and getting up to answer it, silently he mouthed, *and far as I'm concerned, might as well be*, knowing the dialogue off by heart.

'It's Ollie,' he told her, sticking his head into her tobacco, whiskey-tainted den.

'Tell him you can't get any more blood out of a corpse.'

He looked at her. Bandaged brow. Chinese silk robe. Bare, mottled stick legs resting on the Moroccan pouffe, a word which made him uneasy, which she must have realised, otherwise why keep on using it all the time *Seen the pouffe anywhere ... ? Move the pouffe a bit closer ... Did I ever tell you that old pouffe came from Morocco ... ?* The word had another meaning, as well as spelling, nothing to do with a stuffed, embossed cube of camel leather, and one which he didn't appreciate hearing, especially from that pig Murnaghan at school, who he also felt convinced had been the one to scratch it into the door of his locker with a pair of compasses.

'He says he has some terrific news.'
'Like I've gone platinum in Patagonia or Peru? Tell him to drop dead. Join the six-foot-under club.'
Sometimes he relished the way the things she said, not like other more normal mums at school sports and things, hair washed and set and smelling of proper perfume instead of camphor and Southern Comfort. *Say hi to my mother, folks, the washed up, alcoholic country singer.*

Murnaghan's mum was totally glam, a six foot blonde who wore leather trousers and drove a cherry red Mazda Sports coupé, parking it in the Head's own parking bay on Open Day. All the boys fantasised over what she had on under those skin-tight, glossy drainpipes — if anything.

Once Murnaghan had said to him, 'Know something, Quinn? My Granny's got one of your mammy's LPs. Some folksy, fiddley-dee crap about peat bogs or something.'

He meant 'Footing the Turf on Tory', her first big hit, of course, with that deeply embarrassing photograph of her barefoot on the cover with the donkey.

'Look, I think he means it this time.' he told her and, groaning, she took a sustaining draught from the tumbler close by.

'Okay, put the gangster on,' and he carried the phone in to her, trailing it by the long flex from the hall.

Ollie used to be her manager, might still be, for all he knew, Ollie MacManus, this big, bald slob in a teddy-bear coat and canary-coloured, horses' head scarf. He had this faint recollection he might actually be his god-parent or something, one of those half-forgotten memories from babyhood associated with all-night parties ending up with his mother face down on their kitchen table out of it amid a turmoil of half-emptied glasses, bottles and overflowing ashtrays.

Back under the glow of his lamp once more, he tried to concentrate on his quadratic equations, but kept listening instead to the one-sided conversation taking place next door. She was giving Ollie hell, that was obvious, but then as he continued to eavesdrop, the tirade began to falter, then peter out, as though the person on the other end had weathered the storm and was now the one doing the talking. And so he cocked his head, hoping for some rejoinder on her part but her tongue seemed to have lost all its power as well as bite.

Eventually the receiver dropped back in its cradle, and there was this other extended silence, somehow more disturbing than the one before, and he concentrated even harder in case she was crying. *God, please, not the water works, please* ... face raw-red and ugly the way it used to get.

Looking at the checkered page in front of him he saw he had made a blot. *Shit,* he thought. Now he would have to tear the page out and begin afresh, damn it, and damn his pathetic mother along with it, her and her fraught passage through 'the change', Murnaghan's expression, his own mother being much too young to be afflicted that way, so he said. More like a glamorous big sister than somebody's plain old mum. Murnaghan's father was overseas much of the time, something big in oil in Dubai. Sometimes he thought he took a seriously unhealthy interest in his horrible classmate's family life, not having much of one himself, he suspected, just him and The Lifford Linnet, or Newtown Nightingale, as she used to be known before her career took a nosedive along with a corresponding header into the whiskey bottle.

Five minutes later as he faced a blank page for the second time, he heard her heading upstairs, not groaning and sighing to herself, but sprightly, almost, humming, too, which segued into this full-blown recital in the bathroom, something else he hadn't heard in an age.

Next morning she had his breakfast ready waiting for him on the kitchen table, again something of a first.
  'Hello, my own wee man,' she murmured, kissing him on the back of the neck, and smelling of toothpaste instead of stale Jim Beam. 'How would you like to go on a trip?'
  He turned to look at her. Same old red silk kimono, but her hair was actually combed, amazing, and fresh lipstick applied, matching the contours of her mouth for a change.
  'What do you mean, *trip*?' he said, getting this uneasy feeling in the pit of his stomach.
  'Oh, you know,' she said, 'just a wee tour, that's all. You'd really love it, you would.'
  'But the half-term doesn't come up for months!' he protested.

'Oh, school, school, school, that's all I ever hear out of you these days. Turning into a right boring old bookworm you are.'

This from somebody constantly harping on about the near life or death importance of 'book reading', having been denied her own education for a life of drudgery in that fish factory before being rescued by Radio Eireann's big 'Voice of the West' talent competition.

'Anyway, it's not as if it's next week. Ollie has to set everything up, although he says the bookings are as good as in the bag already. Oh, darling, darling, just think of it, your mammy back in front of all her old fans again. Know what he said to me on the phone last night? Do you? The Girl From The Banks Of The Finn has been away far too long. She owes it to her public to make their dreams come true all over again.'

Shovelling in the soggy dregs of his Sugar Puffs, he left her there gazing mistily at the spice rack, 'Encores!' already ringing in her ears.

Over the next week she stopped smoking — because of her voice, she said — rehearsing non-stop in her favourite location, their bathroom, its acoustic as flattering as a Greek amphitheatre, even if the mirror mightn't have been quite so flattering. Drinking, of course, remained another proposition entirely, him making his usual after-dark trips to the bottle-bank, enough clear, green and amber glass to stock a small re-cycling plant. And Ollie was on the phone as well, sending her blood pressure even higher.

'He says I could be sharing the bill with Daniel O'Donnell, can you believe it? Now tell me, should I hold out for equal billing or not? What do you think?'

He was in the middle of his Latin unseen at the time,

Caesar's Gallic Wars taxing him to the utmost without this deranged creature reeking of throat lozenges bursting in on him from beyond the lamp-lit circle of his concentration.

'I'd leave that side of things up to Ollie if I were you,' he told her, genuinely surprised at his own improvisation. 'After all it's what he gets his ten per cent for, isn't it?'

For an instant she froze before cupping his cheeks in two hot, clammy palms.

'Oh, I should listen to you all the time, so I should! What a combination. What a team. Me with my voice, and my brainbox of a son with his … his … ' the words tailing off, rather taking the shine off the moment it did somehow strike him.

After that he tried putting the entire business into some dark, unused corner at the back of his brain somewhere. Why couldn't she see he had much more pressing issues to contend with, for she was right, school, that's all he ever did think about, all those subjects bunching up, clamouring for priority. He couldn't wait for the time when a mere handful was all he needed to concentrate on. Already Murnaghan talked blithely of university, Oxbridge, naturally, even though that had to be at least four years away. *Four years*, he thought, groaning inwardly. A prison sentence. How could he survive the hell of it under the same roof as this rejuvenated songbird reliving her past triumphs? By now she was playing all her old LPs again, the house reverberating to the sound of her younger voice on crackling black vinyl, many of the sides having been badly scratched from all those late night into early morning boozing sessions.

There was one great big gaping hole in all of this, and that was the absence of Ollie. Where was Ollie, for he still only existed as a hoarse voice on the end of a telephone. 'And how's our young Mastermind today then?' that customary, tedious greeting of his each time he went to lift the receiver, another major gripe, for why, in God's good name, could she never answer it herself, almost as though she were this barefoot colleen still, like the one on that awful LP cover who had never seen, let alone heard a phone or a ringing tone.

Then one evening just after he had finished his latest batch of prep and was in his pyjamas brushing his teeth — mercifully she had vacated the bathroom for once and was below sorting through a pile of her old stage outfits — the mystery man himself showed up. His car, an ancient Mercedes, made a noise like a World War II tank, and although he had never seen, or heard it before, he knew instantly it could only belong to one person.

Turning off the tap, he listened intently at the open door to the two voices below, the one, familiar, excitable, and to his deep disgust, *girlish*, and the other, deep, rumbling, scarily masculine.

He heard the first one say, 'Well, well, well, and if it isn't the invisible man himself.'

But he could tell by her tone she didn't mean anything nasty or accusatory by it, and a sort of disgust welled up in him at what he saw as a betrayal of all those old grievances she had unloaded on him, and now to be behaving like some flirtatious teenager.

He was creeping along the landing to his own room, fingers crossed he might have been forgotten in all the starry gush going on below, when he heard her call out, 'Sweetheart, oh, sweetheart! Are you up there?' and he froze in his too short, plaid dressing-gown and Bart Simpson bedroom slippers. For an instant he thought he might just be able to get away with the fiction he was already snug under the covers, but she was not to be denied, that whiskey voice hounding him.

'Come and say hello to Ollie, pet! He's dying to meet you!' *Sweetheart. Pet.*

Well, there was no escape. It was only a modest suburban house after all, a corny old movie line, *you can run, but you can't hide*, entering his head like some pointless incantation to ward off fate as he padded downstairs.

When he got to the sitting room all had been transformed by sudden bright lighting, and she was posing for Ollie's benefit, clutching a spangled, emerald green evening gown to her chest. Under it he could see she was wearing a slip and little else, his blood running cold at the sight, and, mind reacting once more in deeply irrational fashion, the thought, *thank God Murnaghan isn't here to witness this*, broke surface like a shark's fin before sliding off into other waters.

Ollie, for some reason, he couldn't care less about, which was curious, for he was sitting there enjoying the floor show, a fat grin on his fake-tanned face, a grin which said, *Well, what do you reckon, kiddo? Pushover, eh? Putty in these two hands*, covered, incidentally, by a stretched pair of chamois leather driving gloves. The boy could see the ridged outline of rings breaking the yellow hide across the knuckles, and it was this that really turned him against him, not so much the rings, more the fact he hadn't even bothered taking the gloves off on entering the house.

Moments later, if further ammunition was required, it arrived when he called him by his own, very private, greatly loathed saint's name.

'So how's our young Bosco then, eh? Your mammy tells me

you're the right little font of wisdom these days, a regular juvenile t'ink tank. Eh, Dolly?'

Dolly, for frig's sake! Bosco and Dolly, like some awful kids' TV puppet act.

'The name's Kevin.'

'Oh, really? Since when?'

They both laughed at that, the golden complexioned slob on the sofa grinning up at him, and his own mother, treating him like a figure of fun, which in their eyes he supposed he must appear, in his shrunken, shortie, plaid dressing-gown and TV cartoon slippers.

'Bosco, I think, somehow suits him better than Kevin. You know, when you were no bigger than a ... ' making a gesture with one banana-coloured hand, as though saving himself, too lazy to even make the effort.

The boy wondered how much more of this nauseating crap he was supposed to put up with. Couldn't they see he was an early riser? People like his mother and Ollie MacManus were the type who lay in bed until late afternoon after staying up all night carousing, which, in fact, turned out to be the case.

Upstairs in his room he lay listening to the sound of their laughter, and then the records began, on and on in an orgy of old times, an entire six-inch batch threaded on to the spindle of the radiogram as an accompaniment to their merrymaking.

When finally he got to sleep, some time after two, he reckoned, they were still hard at it, but he couldn't be certain as the dial on his Baby Alarm had started losing its luminous powers of late.

The following morning, when he descended to a whiskey-stale ground floor, he saw the Mercedes was still in the driveway squatting there like some great screaming, metal advertisement for all the neighbours to see and speculate about. Clearing a corner of the kitchen table, he got his own cereal and bowl and tried not to think of what was upstairs, eyes fixed instead on the long list of additives on the back of the packet. But, try as he might, he still kept thinking of Murnaghan as though he might be waiting for him, a grin on that sly face of his. *Well, well, well, so just what went on in your house last night then?*

Of course no such thing occurred, but as the day crawled through into late afternoon, he found himself manufacturing a new dread for himself as to what might be awaiting him when he arrived home.

The good news was the Merc was gone. The not so good his mother was still in bed. He sat in the living room too het up to allow himself to feel annoyed about the mess. Strewn across the carpet, half the LPs lay missing their sleeves, while the radiogram hummed faintly still, and he counted at least half a dozen dirty glasses, which could only mean they must have been switching drinks, and even he knew the kind of hangover that could induce. For a moment he had this cheering fantasy Ollie might get pulled over for drink-driving in broad daylight, but then, recalling what Murnaghan had said about the pigs in their jam-jars never flagging down big or flashy looking cars, concentrating instead on old bangers, or likely looking joyriders in back to front baseball caps, that had to be too good to be true. Murnaghan said his mum charmed her way out of half a dozen speeding tickets a month at least.

At six o'clock The Lifford Linnet still hadn't surfaced from her nest, so he took a pizza out of the freezer compartment, zapped it in the microwave, then ate the lot, even though it said for two people on the box. He watched the News on television, turning up the volume deliberately, and, yes, it seemed to do the trick, for soon after he heard movement upstairs, followed by the toilet being flushed.

Next day happened to be a Saturday, forty-eight hours of relative freedom — there was still an essay to write, bloody Jane Austen — and so he sat there waiting, pretending interest in a sports quiz on BBC One. He had every intention of making her suffer when she appeared. It was his right, he told himself, one of the few remaining consolations of this lousy home life of his, and so he started stoking up the fires of resentment in preparation for the door opening. He knew she would be contrite, which would allow him roughly fifteen minutes or so of silent recrimination, before eventually, caving in, which he always did, despite all those mimed tongue lashings to his reflection in the bedroom mirror upstairs.

As he sat there staring at the screen, above the studio laughter he thought he heard this soft moaning noise coming from the far side of the closed door, like a dog, or a cat, or something, certainly an animal of some sort in pain. Then it ceased and for a time there was silence before the door was pushed open.

'Sweetheart, what time is it? Sweetheart, did you get something to eat? I've got the most awful, terrible migraine.' *Shorthand for hangover, you mean.* 'Thank heavens it's the weekend. I'll clean this entire place up, top to bottom, you'll see. I will, I really will.'

He continued glaring at the TV, some blonde airhead creasing herself at everything the two brain-dead footballers were saying, but inside he was counting off the minutes before he finally relented and acknowledged the mess in the dressing-gown on the settee. He could smell the after booze fumes with her every breath, but then it wasn't morning, was it? Practically evening. Night, for God's sake!

'You wouldn't be a dote and get your poor suffering mother a Nurofen, would you? A couple? Please?'

When he got back from the bathroom cabinet — enough remedies to stock a small pharmacy — he placed the capsules on the coffee-table alongside the glass of water, then dropped down in front of the TV again. She sighed, but just sat there looking at the painkillers as if incapable of movement.

Then she said, 'In case you're wondering, Ollie slept in the spare room. I couldn't let him drive home in *his* condition, now could I?' and once more he felt aggrieved, her jumping the gun in this way before he could bring up the subject. Which, of course, he never would, letting it lie festering as usual.

'I'm going up to my room,' he said, rising, and she waved a hand weakly in the direction of the two Nurofen and the tumbler of water. He handed them to her, waiting for her to wash down the pills.

'Don't be cross,' she said.

'Who's cross?' he said, but it was in his voice.

'Don't go,' she said. 'Not just yet. It's early still,' and grudgingly he fell into the armchair again, turning the sound down on the television a couple of notches with the remote.

'Ollie says you're all grown up. Wouldn't have known you for the shy wee chap he used to buy sweeties for. *God*, he thought, *this was going to be even worse than he imagined.* Yet at the same time there was something desperately pathetic about the way she was sitting hunched there, half-dead looking, with the glass in her hand, that made him stay where he was.

'I know it's hard for you to know what it's like at your age, but it's not been easy, no man around to take care of things.'

Suddenly he felt this rush of heat suffuse his face and neck, trapped in his armchair, with all these horrible secrets about to tumble out, things that were supposed to remain unspoken where they belonged, frozen, like all those faces in the photograph album he avoided asking about in case he might learn things about himself and that mysterious, featureless father of his, the one he had never known, didn't want to, either, not ever, full stop. Once a long time ago she had called him 'a love-child', whatever that was, although he suspected it might well be one of these expressions meaning something else not quite so charming or attractive-sounding.

'Ollie left this for you,' she said, taking something from her dressing-gown pocket, holding it out to him in her clenched fist.

'What is it?'

'Come and see for yourself.'

The hot sensation in his head seemed to have subsided a little, but further down the knot in his stomach still felt hard and compacted. Sometimes, inside, he felt as though there was this mechanism measuring out the time it took him to get over things.

She opened her hand and he saw it was money, a note folded the size of a postage stamp. He took it from her, but refused to open it out, laying it on the arm of his chair instead.

'He's really fond of you, you know.'

'Is he?' he said, watching the TV.

'Yes. He wants you and him to be friends the way it used to be when you were little.'

He looked at her. 'I don't remember any of that.'

'Well, you should, for he's been very good to the pair of us over the years. Like a — '

And she stopped as if the word had got stuck in her throat.

'He'd really like you to come along on this trip. He says he feels bad about not keeping in touch.'

He sat there listening to all this. Saint Ollie. Now what part of the woodwork had he emerged from all of a sudden? And just exactly what had these two been cooking up last night together, the records dropping down the spindle, while they went through every combination of hard stuff in the cocktail cabinet? *Ollie and Dolly,* suddenly he thought, *Dolly and Ollie.* And seeing him smile, and scenting weakness, she came lurching forward on the settee.

'Look,' she said, 'it'd be great fun, it would, really. Just the three of us. You never did see your mother knockin' 'em dead. She can still do it, you know. She can.'

Even her complexion seemed to have taken on a new and healthier tinge.

'Anyway there's no way I'm leaving you here on your own. No way, José. Don't want to be had up for child neglect, do I?' *God, she was even cracking jokes now.*

'Okay, so we all know you're a teenager — just — but that's not the point. And I meant to tell you, if you're still so concerned about that old school of yours, Ollie can fix that as well, doctor's line, anything. You've never really seen Ollie in action, have you? He'll talk to Mr. O'Neill, explain to him how important this is, and you can bring your work along with you. Now how does that sound?'

Then she said, 'Even bring a wee school friend along, if you like.'

And that was when he caved in, the notion of Murnaghan and him together in that way just far too appalling to imagine, everything else sounding suddenly reasonable, bearable, even.

And so it was, a week later, he found himself on a Goldliner coach with his mother, along with a complement of other more normal passengers, bound for Donegal where the famous concert tour was scheduled to kick off. She tried to explain away their manner of transport by telling him Ollie would be following along in the car with all her stage gear later, making it sound like some sort of penance on his part, while they slummed it in a blue and green tour bus.

They sat together at the back and already he imagined he could detect an uneasy current as if she, too, might be having serious doubts regarding their mode of travel. She was wearing a silk, polka-dotted headscarf and a pair of goggle-sized dark glasses like some incognito glamour queen. Staring straight ahead, for a good half hour she didn't speak while he read *The Mayor of Casterbridge*. Outside it was a fine, bright day to begin with, but gradually the farther west they travelled the more the weather seemed to deteriorate.

Just before they got to the Irish border the bus driver pulled in to a roadside pub to allow everyone to get out and 'stretch their legs', as he put it, and there was an immediate rush for the toilets, the women in particular racing towards the low white building at the far end of the car park. He and his mother sat on in the empty bus together. Even the driver had disappeared. He wanted to say something, for the silence was beginning to hum in his head like air-conditioning. And then for the first time he noticed someone had carved the words FUCK OFF in the imitation leather of the seat in front. It could have been something a lot worse, of course, but he still moved his book forward to cover it in case she spotted it.

'Sure you don't want to go now? It might be your last chance,' she said. He shook his head.

'Well, I am. I'll be back in just a tick,' and she rose and made her way along the gangway to the front of the bus.

From his window seat he watched her cross the barren car park, holding on to her headscarf, even though there was no real breeze as far as he could make out. Like a grounded air hostess, the image came to him, because of the scarf, as well as the boxy, navy two-piece, plus matching shoes, half-high in the heel.

She disappeared through the pub's glass doors. For the first time he saw the name of the place under the eaves. The Ponderosa, even though the P was missing.

He tried getting back into Hardy's Wessex again, but those two landscapes, the one, period, lush, romantic, and the other, the one he could make out beyond the ramparts of cement-filled oil drums to dissuade car-bombers, warred too much for supremacy in his head for him to concentrate on the paperback in his lap. Instead he kept waiting and watching for the doors of the roadhouse to swing back open again and the first passengers to re-emerge, but they never did.

Sitting there at the back of the bus all on his own with his knees up to his chin he started getting this feeling of having been abandoned, as though one of those old nightmares he used to suffer from when he was younger had taken on an element of reality. He looked at his watch. Four thirty-five. Only a week ago his mother had told him it had been a secret birthday present from Ollie, a Sekonda, with a luminous dial like his Baby Alarm, but he hadn't checked it against the time the bus had pulled in and emptied like that.

Outside it seemed to be getting a lot darker suddenly. A flock of crows swept past, blown about haphazardly on high like a sudden flurry of burnt paper. He started counting in his head, and on the stroke of one hundred and thirty-seven the door of The Ponderosa swung open and the bus driver emerged. He appeared to be in high spirits, laughing and glancing back over his shoulder.

Then the others materialised, equally animated, and to his horror the boy saw that the object of their merriment was his mother, hemmed in by a small knot of jolly looking women and one stout, red-faced man in an old-fashioned tweed suit. For an instant the man stumbled and looked as though he might fall, a roar going up as he was grabbed and kept upright. *Christ*, the boy thought, *she's drunk already* — he couldn't care less about the guy in the herringbone suit — and so, taking cover, he shrank down in his seat quivering with shame.

Sliding open the door of the bus, the driver called out, 'All aboard the Nashville Express!' trying to sound American, and not bothering to hide the booze in his voice, a new and additional horror, and then his mother climbed in, looking more like an air hostess than ever, advancing, as she did, up the aisle, sunglasses pushed high on her head. With a bump and a sigh she dropped into the seat at his side. He could smell peppermint on her breath. Then the other passengers piled in, laughing uproariously as though they'd known each other all their lives.

'Guess what?' his mother whispered, but he was in no mood for games. He had been right, she *was* tipsy, along with nearly every other person on board judging by the look of them. But how had they all managed to get so smashed?

'Oh, stop sitting there like a stewed prune. For once in your life cheer up. You're on your holidays. Remember?'

And then she did this most appalling thing, standing up, clapping her hands like that same air stewardess about to order everybody to fasten their seatbelts, only announcing instead in a loud voice, 'Everybody, I'd like you to meet my precious wee son who's keeping his mother company on this trip!' and they all turned around to get a proper look at him, the freak sunk as low as he could get behind the last but one window seat with FUCK OFF etched into its sloping back, the exact sentiment he wished on everybody present at that moment, but especially his own mother in her latest, starring role as Miss Singing Airline Employee of the Year.

Honking his horn, the bus driver crashed the gears, the coach lurching forward, nearly sideswiping one of the green, white and yellow car-park oil drums, at which a tremendous roar went up, and the red-faced man in the tweed suit, who was swaying dangerously in the door-well, broke into sudden song, the boy recognising the ballad as one from his mother's own repertoire.

But before he could get going properly, cries of, 'No! No!' rang out, followed by chants of, 'Dolores! Dolores!' and for the boy suddenly everything fell into place, realising, as he did, what had taken place back there in the bar already disappearing behind them.

Rising to her feet in an updraught of perfume and mouthwash, for a second time his mother planted herself in the aisle to face the front of the bus. Coyly, for the briefest of moments, she fingered her headscarf, as if to say, *well, now, if you really all insist*, and realising what was about to take place, the boy opened his book, the print as unreadable as Finnish or Romanian, everything going downhill fast from that point on and him not able to do a solitary thing about it.

For a solid hour, it seemed, she entertained that bus load of pensioners for free, face flushed, eyes bright, responding to their cries of, *'More! More! More!'* while he suffered in silence. By the time they reached their destination she was tottering on her feet with fatigue, sweat beading her face and neck and staining the underarms of her jacket, that earlier band-box-fresh air hostess now looking as if she'd come through a hijack.

The boy stared out at the sparse lighting signalling the approach of a town, *their* town, and felt relieved in spite of all he'd endured inside the bus, for outside everything had been dark, remote and forbidding, more like a foreign country rushing past than one of their own cosy Six Counties. He thought of his corner of the sitting-room back home and his Anglepoise and its comforting spread of light, all the life he knew confined within that one pale yellowish circle, and he wondered how he was going to get through the days and nights ahead.

At their hotel — it looked deserted, as though closed for the season — the driver pulled up with a melodramatic screech of the tyres, calling out, 'Your stop, Dolores!' in overly familiar fashion, and they made their way down the length of the bus being simultaneously pawed and congratulated, although the boy couldn't help noticing that quite a few of the older grey heads were now slumped against the seat-rests with the reading lights switched off. The entire bus, he realised, stank of stale drink and tobacco, and when he got outside the air smelt fresh and damp, with a hint of windborne turf smoke, something he hadn't expected.

'It's been a pleasure and the rare privilege, Miss Quinn,' announced the driver after he'd taken their suitcases from the luggage compartment under the bus, setting them down on the pavement side by side.

He sounded respectful now, sober, too, his mother reacting in regal fashion with, 'Would you have a pen handy, Eugene?' after the man requested an autograph.

'I'm sorry I haven't a photograph,' she told him, signing the back of an envelope. 'My agent Mr MacManus takes care of all that, you know.'

'Well, the best of luck with the big tour, Miss Quinn. I've got all your records. My wife and me are your greatest fans.'

'That's lovely to hear, Eugene. Thank you for getting us here so safely,' and for one further incredulous moment the boy felt convinced she was about to offer the man a tip, hand imperiously held out for change to Junior Flunky here to Ireland's Premier Queen Of Country, as one faded newspaper cutting once described her.

Inside, the hotel foyer was dark brown and dead, desk unattended, but after his mother had banged a bell on the counter a girl came out from behind a curtain licking her fingers as if interrupted at her supper. She stared at them like they were a couple of refugees from a foreign country.

'Quinn's the name,' announced his mother briskly, looking about her at the dreary furnishings. The boy smelt boiled cabbage, or at a guess, cat's piss.

'Have youse booked?' enquired the slatternly girl, and the boy sidled off to study a revolving stand of postcards to avoid the inevitable opening salvo of hostilities.

'*Dolores* Quinn?' his mother repeated with a rising hard inflection, emphasis on the Christian name. Then she said, 'Isn't there a poster anywhere? There should be a poster.'

The girl continued staring at her. She had greasy, reddish hair with twin corkscrew ringlets hanging down either side plump, freckled cheeks.

'What's your name, girl?' her mother asked, softening her tone.

'Teresa,' the girl replied.

'Well, Teresa, honey, be a pet and go fetch the manager. I'm sure *he'll* know who's staying at his hotel and who isn't.'

'He's not here. He had to go to Letterkenny on business.'

'Business? *Business?*'

The boy couldn't help wondering just why that particular word should be the one to push his mother over the edge. The postcard he was examining at the time was a picture of a mournful looking donkey. It reminded him of the infamous LP cover, although this one happened to be laden with matching creels of turf. He leaned closer trying to shut out the sound of the tantrum taking place at the desk. He heard the words, 'en suite', then 'Inishowen Room', but already he knew nothing that was going to be said here had the power to cut any ice. He wondered how long it had to take before his mother accepted that fact. The thing about adults, well, the one he'd had so much bitter, personal experience of, was they seemed to expend an immense amount of time and energy in such situations, arguing, protesting, generally hitting their head against walls of stolid indifference, or just plain stupidity, as now. The donkey in the photograph seemed to agree with him, its sad eyes a mute testimony to the essential mulishness of every human it had ever posed for in a hard and thankless life. On a sudden whim the boy removed the postcard from the rack, slipping it swiftly into the pocket of his anorak, a souvenir of hell on the road with Mommy Dearest. He would build up a little archive of such things, he told himself, that's if he ever wished to be reminded in later life of what he had been through.

'The place has gone completely downhill. Rack and ruin. I never would have believed it. Never.'

They were in their room at last, the fat girl having humped both suitcases up three musty flights of stairs all by herself as in some form of penance, puffing like a train, then going back down again, sighing heavily.

His mother was sitting on one of the beds, the double with the salmon pink eiderdown. His was in the corner under the window. Nothing he could do about it. He saw that now.

'It was never like this. Roger Moore once stayed here on a fishing holiday. It's all my fault, being sentimental like that. There's a new Ramada five miles up the road. But, of course, I would insist for old times' sake. *Me.*'

It was obvious tears could not be far off, so he asked, 'What about Ollie?'

'What about him?'

'Well, where is he?'

She looked at him. 'Well, he must have had a puncture or a breakdown or something. Still, just wait till I get my hands on him, that's all.'

But she continued staring into space with that silly, half-baked expression on her face. The boy wondered what it would finally take to have Ollie shown up for the rat he was. He still could do no wrong in her eyes, it appeared.

'Are you hungry?' she asked, coming all over motherly for

an instant, and he lied, for he knew there was no earthly chance of getting anything to eat at this hour in this place. She seemed relieved at that, and shortly after told him to undress and get into bed while she disappeared into the curtained-off alcove where there was a bath and a hand basin. No toilet — that was down the hall — which reminded him of something out of a black and white horror movie. He heard the sound of water begin to flow and gargling and she came back out again in a pink velour dressing-gown with cold cream all over her face, hair a mass of flesh-coloured, rubber curlers, making her look like the Bride of Frankenstein from that same vintage scary movie.

The boy had never slept in the same room as his mother before, or if he had, he would have been much too young to remember. He lay there pretending sleep, waiting for the snoring to commence. Back home he could often hear that low, choking rumble proceeding from the room at the far end of the landing. But a far worse dread was that he might have one of his wet dreams and the damp patch down the front of his Batman pyjamas would be noticeable in the morning.

Sure enough, some time in the early hours, he did have a sleep sequence of an erotic nature, but luckily no sticky residue this time. Before its details floated off into deep, dark space, never again to be retrieved, as invariably they did, he half-recalled it had to do with Murnaghan's mum in the front of her red Mazda, with her doing the kind of things to him her son had often elaborated upon in the showers after sports. But then just as it was getting to the serious, eruptive stage, the ringletted girl from the hotel joined in, despite the car being only a two-seater.

Deep in the throes he must have called out a name, for next morning at breakfast in the mausoleum of a dining-room, his mother enquired, 'Who's Alison, then?' and he went rigid with embarrassment.

'Wee girlfriend, is she?' she pursued coquettishly. 'Well, you're at that age, I suppose, even though I still think of you as my baby boy.'

Luckily there was no one around to overhear this, for her voice was booming away at the time in the emptiness surrounding their solitary set table, the redhead from his fantasy having dumped two piled plates in front of them, then gone off yawning, never to be seen again. As he toyed with his eggs and bacon it came to him just how lucky he was not to have cried out 'Teresa' instead of that other name.

After they'd eaten his mother spent the entire morning trying to get through to Ollie on his mobile. 'Either engaged, or unobtainable,' she kept saying, until, finally, 'That fat bastard, how dare he!' which cheered the boy up considerably, for now, perhaps, she was coming round to his own unshakeable opinion that Ollie MacManus was indeed an underhand, overweight, fat bastard and had been all along.

Outside a drizzle cloaked all to be seen through a rubbed circle in the hotel lounge window while he waited for the calls to end. At long last she came out of the glassed-in kiosk.

'Well,' she said, 'he knows where to find me if he wants me. Dolores Quinn has never been the one to chase after anyone. Never.'

The boy said nothing, didn't dare look up from an old *National Geographic* he was rapidly leafing through in case someone caught him lingering over all those bare-breasted native women with pots on their heads.

'Let's you and me take a wander as well as gander to see if there's any life in this one-horse dump, though I very much doubt it. Talk about getting this comeback off with a bang.'

'More like a whimper,' the boy said, for it was the first time he'd ever heard her use the expression 'comeback', up to now almost as taboo as 'farewell performance'.

She looked at him. 'Well, well, *you're* starting to come out of your shell. Maybe you won't be so much of a wet blanket on this trip, after all.'

Oddly enough he felt cheered by that, and when they ventured out the rain seemed to have cleared as well. They passed over a bridge with a foaming torrent rushing through stone arches to the distant sea. Gulls were blowing about in the wind, and he could smell turf smoke much more strongly now. The few people hurrying to work along the damp streets stared at them as though out of long habit, and he could sense the change in his mother already, head erect, with that odd, half-welcoming smile on her face, getting ready, as he saw it, to be recognised. It was a habit he had grown to loathe when they were out together, yet this time, for some weird reason, it didn't seem to grate so much, or have him cringing with embarrassment. This was her town, after all, he told himself, and these were her people, too, in a way, he supposed, and so she had every right to indulge herself, expect a little adulation. With something of a shock, also it struck him, he was starting to feel more of a grown-up than someone who, not so very long ago, had been worried sick about a damp patch on his pyjamas not drying out quickly enough.

Walking on he could sense his mother's gathering frustration, for even though the looks kept on coming in their direction, no one, as yet, had accosted them. She was, of course, wearing her movie-star shades, which may have drawn attention, but at the same time disguised who she was.

In leisurely fashion they proceeded over the bridge with its rushing flume, past the big clock, hour hand drooping slightly like a faulty finger, the monument to some dead old Fenian, the Munster Bank, the Post Office, the three denominational churches, countless shuttered pubs, and then in the window of a newsagent's, amidst all the postcards advertising local services, he saw the poster. He saw it before she did, in lurid Day-Glo orange, leaping out at him like a shout, with its heading, WHERE ARE THEY NOW? GONE BUT NOT FORGOTTEN. IRELAND'S STARS OF YESTERYEAR, his eyes homing in automatically on his own surname. For him, the shock was bad enough. Still, he had this vain hope the impact on her mightn't be quite so brutal because of reading it through dark glasses.

She stopped dead, and he halted alongside her, for there was no way of pretending it wasn't there. He watched her lips move, but the rest of her face gave nothing away, eyes hidden behind those great tortoiseshell, round-rimmed Ray-Bans.

'Let's go,' she said, taking him by the arm, hauling him back to the hotel, not uttering a word until they were inside their room with the door closed.

The room smelt rank and airless. The beds hadn't been made. Never would, if that girl downstairs had anything to do with it, he suspected.

'What are you doing?' he asked. He was sitting on his own bed watching her dragging clothes from the wardrobe, the clash of wire coat-hangers like a sudden tinny thunderstorm going off inside all that oak-finished Melamine.

'What does it look like? I'm packing.'

'Packing?' he repeated like a parrot. 'What for?'

'What for?' Now it was her turn.

'You think I came all this way to be insulted, humiliated, laughed at? Do you? Do you?'

'Who's laughing?'

'Oh, yeah? Sharing billing with a singing priest? And how about all those other showbiz household names? A twelve-year old tap-dancer. Somebody who beats his own head with a tin tray to 'Mule Train'. A comedian who should have been dead and buried yonks ago. A bunch of beardy, fiddle and banjo merchants the age of Methuselah in Aran sweaters? Pass me the suitcase.'

In spite of everything the boy felt impressed at how rapidly she had absorbed, then translated the small print on the poster, and after what seemed like only a few seconds of perusal.

'What about Ollie?' he stalled, watching the pile on the bed opposite grow. How had all of that gone into one suitcase? A feat worthy, surely, of The Great Mulvani himself, another name on the dreaded poster.

'You keep on asking me that. I've told you. Ollie's dead. Or would be, if I was able to get my hands on him. Well, what are you waiting for? Start packing.'

But the boy continued sitting there unable to move. This was everything he had been praying for, the pair of them cutting their losses, heading back home, back to his cosy corner of the sitting room and his ordered stack of school books. But for some inexplicable reason it seemed it wasn't what he really wanted after all. Not right now anyway.

'Well?' she said again, placing her pink corduroy toilet bag on top of the layered edifice like a cherry on a cake. 'You like this dump, is that it?'

He shook his head.

'Well, then?'

'I think you should do this one concert,' he told her, summoning up all the powers of persuasion he never realised he possessed. 'People have bought tickets. The hall's booked.'

'Yeah, the parochial hall. I've never played a parochial hall in my life. Never. Well, maybe just once a long, long time ago.'

To his amazement he realised he was starting to wear her down, something he had never been able to do before, all the pleas for thing he'd craved, like new trainers, or a skateboard, or an electric guitar that time, falling on deaf ears. Unlike Murnaghan who said he could twist his own mother around his fat little finger just by subjecting her to the silent treatment. She couldn't bear that, he told the boy. 'Even when I asked for the Play Station.'

They were still silently fencing with one another across the disorder of the room when there came a knock at the door, a development so unexpected she collapsed on the bed in a heap alongside the mountain of clothes, stirring up a perfumed eddy as she did so. The boy rose and crossed to the door to discover the red-haired girl curtseying there like some bit part character in a bad period drama.

'I beg your pardon, and sorry to be interrupting youse, but there's a gentleman in the Rosapenna Room asking for your mother.'

At that the heap on the far bed stirred as though recovering some of her old verve. 'If it's a blackguard by the name of MacManus,' she rasped, 'he can drop dead,' directing her ire, not through the girl, but through him, relegated, as always, to the role of scapegoat to the royal household.

'Oh, but I'm sure it's nobody like that. It's a clerical gentleman. A father, so he is.'

The boy expected another comeback, possibly along the lines of, 'Well, tell *him* to get lost too,' but, instead, she got up and, going to the dressing-table, began touching up her make-up in front of the oval mirror while he and the girl watched, for she hung on in the doorway open-mouthed and saucer-eyed as ever.

'Now,' said his mother, 'we'll go down,' sounding composed as though the prospect of meeting someone of the cloth had calmed her down, even though the boy knew she never went near a chapel or a church if she could help it, nor did he, despite attending a fiercely Catholic school.

Following her downstairs he wondered just what she was about to throw his way next, but, oddly enough, while not exactly starting to enjoy it, he didn't feel as apprehensive as he might have done.

The Rosapenna Room was a lounge bar within a lounge, oak-panelled and cosy with a coal fire in the grate. On first entry the place looked lifeless, his mother gazing around with a suspicious expression at the maroon leather bucket chairs grouped about the walls. But suddenly they heard this loud cackle of a laugh and a head popped out from behind a massive, leafy pot plant in the corner. The head was crowned by a skewed, helmet-like covering of fleecy white curls like a sheep's, above a bright red, grinning face, and the joker in the cleric's collar, for he was, indeed, wearing such an item, tight as a tourniquet about his bulging neck, broke into song.

'Oh, sweet Bunbeg, my sweet Bunbeg,' he serenaded them in a high, trembling tenor voice, 'Your leafy glens, your mountain streams. I rue the day I left your charms ... ' and a lot more of the same old folksy rubbish besides, while they stood there like a couple of surprised victims at their own birthday bash.

Despite the shock the words somehow did register a chord of familiarity with the boy, and then it came to him where he had heard them before, coming from the speaker of their very own Ferguson radiogram back home, to be precise. This old nutter of a pulpit-thumper was actually singing one of his mother's hits straight back at her.

When he'd finished, not the entire nine and ninety verses, thank the Lord, he advanced on them with outstretched arms.

'Dolores, mavourneen!' he cried. 'Macushla!' Close up he looked drunk, sounded it, too.

'This is Father Dwyer,' his mother introduced him hurriedly before he could embrace them both.

'And just who is this charming young man?'

'Kevin, meet Father Dwyer.'

'Och, sure, call me Dixie. Everybody does,' boomed the priest, clasping his hand in a damp, mottled paw. His breath smelt of onions with an overlay of whiskey. While his mother watched nervously he led him across to one of the red leather armchairs. For the first time the boy noticed a glass of something on a table beside his chair.

'Well, Dolores, and how are you at all? I must say you look the same wee colleen I first sang with in that Strabane hall all those years ago. How many was it now? Ten? Fifteen?'

'Closer to forty. Cut the cackle, Dixie.'

The boy felt shocked by the sudden belligerence in his mother's voice. She was pacing about the room flinging glances at the unattended bar in the corner, and it came to him the call of the drink must be making her behave in this way. The black-suited figure sunk in the armchair at his side must have recognised her crying need for a stiffener, for he bellowed, 'Teresa! In here, pronto, there's a good girl!' and to the boy's amazement the redhead appeared as if from nowhere, racing over to the bar with its shelves of different coloured bottles and rows of upturned glasses.

After she had dispensed large drinks for the pair of them, his mother said, 'Dixie, would you do me one gi-normous favour and be good enough to tell me just what we've let ourselves in for here.'

The old woolly-headed priest stared up at the ceiling for a moment before sighing deeply. 'You might well ask, darlin', you might well ask.'

'I have to say,' said his mother, 'it's not exactly what I had in mind.'

'Me, neither. Let's just say we've all been badly let down. Or left, you might say, holding the proverbial babby.'

His mother took a fierce swig from her glass.

'Promises were made,' she retorted angrily.

'Indeed they were, but, sadly not worth the paper they were written on. Or *not*, as it turns out, in this particular case.'

The boy was watching and listening avidly to all this as if some absorbing piece of drama was unfolding in front of him. On no account must he allow himself to miss a solitary twist or turn in the plot, he told himself.

Again the old priest sighed, easing the action a little further towards a resolution, that's if there was to be one. 'Dear, dearie me, wouldn't you think by now we'd have learned something of the wily ways of the viper.'

His mother stared at him. There was silence in the little snug for a moment. Behind the bar the girl had stopped pretending to wipe the surface in front of her and was concentrating as achingly on the action as he was.

'You mean you haven't heard? No one's told you yet?'

'Told me what?'

The priest raised a plump paw and the girl came running across with a full bottle.

'To put it crudely, Ollie Mac Manus has done a runner. By now he should be in the Cayman Islands with all the tour advance money in an offshore bank account. The rest of the concerts have all been cancelled. We'll be lucky to get our travelling expenses. By the by, how did *you* get here?'

His mother got up and sat down a few times, her face approximating to the colour of the leather chair she'd been sitting in.

'The low-down, back-stabbin', dirty rat, and after all he promised me.'

'*Us*, darlin', *us*. We've all been had. Even that sweet wee dote of a tap-dancing juvenile, Little Mary Of Dungloe. But, then, you do know what they say about 'the chosen people', don't you?'

Behind the bar the girl gave a sharp intake of breath as if she'd just overheard something unspeakably sacrilegious and the three of them turned to stare at her. Suitably chastened, she sank from sight below the level of the bar.

'Ollie a Jew-boy?' exclaimed his mother. '*MacManus?*'

'The mother was a Weinberg from Dawson Street. Sure the line always follows the distaff side.'

Again there was silence in that over-heated little room. For the first time the boy realised there were no windows of any kind. It felt like they were in a box within a much greater box, maybe a larger one beyond that again, like one of those Russian dolls, everyone present engaged in some sort of private ritual all their own, making him nervous, yet excited, at the same time.

'Nevertheless,' continued Father Dixie Dwyer in a low and mournful voice, 'and despite the position that blackguard has put us all in, we owe it to the public, if not ourselves, to still put on a show.'

'Buckshee, you mean?'

'More like a charity event.'

'Well, you can include me out. I've never worked as an amateur in my entire life and don't intend starting now.'

The boy looked at her as she said it, the face red and rigid, the mouth and chin determined. She caught his glance.

'No,' she said again, shaking her head for emphasis. 'Dolores Quinn has always kept her professional dignity. No way does she sing for nothing more than her supper. No way.'

But, of course, she did, as he knew she would, along with all that other little band of stranded entertainers, their very own singing priest with his medley of Count John McCormack favourites, the comedian with the nose like a radish, the tap dancing waif, the skinny character banging his head in time to a cowboy record, the middle-aged folk-singing trio, not forgetting the pianist who supplied the musical backing for all of them, the great Eddie 'Fingers' Stacpoole himself, who had once accompanied Johnny Mathis on the Ireland leg of a European tour when his own MD had dropped out sick, or too drunk, at the last minute.

The concert was due to be held in the Saint Xavier African Missioners' Hall, a grey stone, drear-looking building near the head of the town, at eight o'clock. But his mother ensured she would arrive at half past.

'Let them wait,' she told him, as he fidgeted in the room watching her put her war paint on. 'In a dump like this, they'll be wandering in like Brown's cows right up till the last minute. I know them.'

Sitting on the bed the boy realised he had never seen her like this before. In fact he'd never heard her sing in public either, and that sudden realisation brought on a feeling of sweating agitation that she might be awful, a complete and total embarrassment. He wasn't sure he could handle the horror of that, not just for himself, but her, as well.

Still, the good news was she looked and sounded sober for a change, applying lipstick and eyeliner with a slow and steady hand. Her hair, too, never looked better, puffed out in a great helmet-like effect with a burnished sheen to it, thanks to a visit to a hairdresser in the town that afternoon with young Teresa from downstairs. She, too, must have undergone some kind of make-over in Siobhan's Salon, for when they got to Reception she was waiting for them, unrecognisable in a fuchsia pink trouser suit, made up to the nines, and with her ringlets gathered back in a tight, sleek, gleaming bun.

Seeing her that way, smelling her, too, for she seemed to be drenched in some sort of powerfully floral scent, the boy had a sudden flashback to his nearly but not quite wet dream of the night before. He sensed himself going all hot and sweaty again, and when she winked at him, it felt like she, too, was recalling what they'd been up to together in the front of Murnaghan's mum's Mazda with the gearstick pushed all the way forward. Sitting alongside her in the back of the taxi taking them to the hall, he continued feeling feverish because of her lively breathing presence, while his mother's great lacquered head cut off his view of the road in front.

The driver, an old bloke in a bobble hat, kept up a steady stream of chatter, while his mother stared silently in front of her as though conserving all her energies for the performance ahead.

When they reached the hall it looked deserted, even though the doors were open, and lights showed somewhere inside. In a perfumed rush Teresa leapt from the taxi and paid the driver. Climbing out, the boy continued to be amazed at her transformation, not merely her appearance, but her entire personality, as though some form of female conspiracy had been hatched under adjacent hairdryers that afternoon. Despite all the odds, he felt he was starting to develop a distinct crush, with the added embarrassment of a definite boner in his pants as well. Just how was he going to sit through an entire evening of song and dance with that pink trouser leg pressed close to his own?

But he needn't have worried about distraction, even one of an arousing nature, for that night his mother was an eye and an ear-opener, a revelation, no other word for it, when her turn came to get up and do her stuff. That was the expression she used, 'doing my stuff', as though what she was about was as ordinary and mumsy as baking a cake, say, although she happened to be a hopeless case in the kitchen, always had been, nervous about touching the pots and pans as if they might give off an electric shock to someone of her delicate constitution.

Spellbound, the boy sat near the front alongside the new and invigorated Teresa, for she, too, was enraptured, he could tell, at one stage entwining damp fingers in his, as if the sight and sound of the big-haired goddess on the platform above them was just too much to bear.

The other acts passed in a blur, even Father Dixie Dywer with his drawing-room ballads, but it was obvious the audience felt much the same as he did, for they kept calling her back, stamping their feet with cries of *'Dolores! Dolores!'* that made the hairs stand up on the boy's neck like trimmed wires.

When it was all over and the Irish National Anthem was being played, the boy realised just how much he had missed. He was thinking of what she had actually sung, of course, the famous repertoire, for he couldn't remember any of it, the songs, or their order. They had all seemed to flow into one another, the little pianist with the gammy leg smoothing their passage, key perfect, seamlessly.

Back at the hotel an end-of-show party of sorts took place with lots of hugging and kissing and 'didn't it go well?' comments, but as the drinks started jostling for more and more table room his mother whispered to him, 'Let's get out of here while we're ahead, before the bitching starts, for it always does,' and so, gradually, discreetly, they edged for the door.

No one seemed to notice their departure much, if at all, and looking back the boy saw Teresa was now sitting on the pianist's knee, a glass of something pink in her hand, with what looked like a tiny umbrella sticking out of it, while Father Dwyer was in another corner deep in conversation with the tap-dancing waif still in her traditional pleated kilt and green and orange knee socks, his kindly old paw tousling her elfin locks.

'Well? And how do you think it all went then?'

They were in their room and she was swabbing her make-up off with a load of cotton balls. He knew she was looking at him in the dressing-table mirror as she spoke, and that *it* really meant her.

Over on the far bed he trembled for a moment on the brink of telling her what he really felt, but, instead, replied, 'Pretty okay, I guess.'

She turned to look at him, face a puttied mass, eyebrows suddenly, startlingly non-existent. She laughed. 'Well, don't get too over-excited, whatever you do.'

And suddenly he felt himself relax, knowing in that moment she didn't really need, or want to be told, how well she had done, but was teasing him, and the mood between them continued to grow for, laughing once more, she said, 'So what did you think of our Father Dwyer then? Come on, tell the truth now.'

Before he got a chance to reply she said, 'How about that wig, eh?' and they both laughed.

'He didn't touch you, did he?'

The boy stared at her.

'Never mind,' she said, rubbing cold cream into her cheeks.

For a long time there was silence, but then the boy screwed himself up to ask the question which had continued to plague him like a troublesome itch.

'What about Ollie?' he asked.

'Oh, fuck Ollie,' she said. Then, quickly, 'Sorry, sorry,' and it was his turn to laugh, not just at the unexpectedness of the f-word escaping from her like that, but her clown's face as she said it. Rather, her expression as she swivelled in his direction.

Shortly after they both turned in and, lying across from her in the dark, he heard, 'Are you awake?' even though it must have been obvious he was.

'Not too old to give your old mum a goodnight cuddle, are you?'

So, rising up, he groped his way across to her bed, the unexpected chill of the satin eiderdown making him draw back momentarily, and then it was really weird lying beside her in that way, conscious as he was of all that white stuff on her face a foot away from his own, not to mention all those scary rubber rollers. Strangest of all, after a time it began to feel totally natural to be that way, and soon they began talking softly as though having the light off had somehow made all the difference between lying stiff and wary together and letting all sorts of private, previously unmentionable things creep out in the dark.

Like for instance, 'Is Ollie *really* Jewish?'

For a moment he couldn't believe he had said it, but then in a rush, 'Doesn't that mean I might be just a wee bit Jewish as well?'

For a long time there was silence. Then he heard her say quietly, 'What do you mean?'

'Well, if he's really my — '

Suddenly she snapped the bedside light on, sitting upright in the bed. Lying alongside her staring at the ceiling he saw it was papered in the same floral pattern as the walls, and waiting for the storm to break started counting pink and white stemmed rosebuds.

But instead of erupting she began to laugh.

'You think Ollie, you think Ollie's your — ' unable, it seemed, to bring herself to use the word either, even though it rang silently in their heads like a gong. 'Me? And Ollie MacManus? You?'

He could feel the bed shake and suddenly felt angry and made to pull away, but she held him close, putting a bare, skinny arm about his shoulders.

'Listen, listen,' she told him, 'one of these days, soon, very soon, I promise you I'll tell you the full story. You deserve to know. You're old enough. My very own wee man,' and to his utter disgust she planted a great wet, sloppy kiss on his cheek.

'It happened a long time ago. Well, just over thirteen years to be exact. Look, is that enough to be going on with? For now?'

He lay there for some time before answering, with a definite urge to make her suffer, counting off the minutes in his head until it was time to give in.

But, instead, this time he heard himself say, 'Okay, but just as long as you don't forget. Promise?'

'Girl Guide's honour.'

He went back to his own bed after that, and in the dark it felt warm and cosy just like his own bed at home with its Road Runner duvet cover.

'Sleep tight, don't let the bugs bite,' he heard her whisper as sleep began closing in.

Then she said, 'Maybe I'll take up golf when we get back. Join a club or something. Be a proper mother for a change. How about that, eh? What you reckon?'

This time he pretended to be asleep for real. Maybe she would, he told himself. Stranger things had been known to happen.

Even so, he wouldn't be holding his breath.

The Valet's Room

The first time me and Noonan ran across one another we didn't exactly hit it off, leastways not after that stunt he pulled on me with the teabag, but then it would have been hard to keep up a frosty demeanour anyway, the pair of us sharing that tiny place, and of course I was under him, or supposed to be.

'Welcome to the Master Bates Motel. Care for a cuppa?' says he, stretched out lazily in one of the two grease-laden, old armchairs, an open magazine covering his lap, accent Irish like my own, but with more of a brogue, and if that comes across as condescending, I don't mean it to be.

Well, while he was away off next door humming along with the kettle I had a good old shufti around. Just enough room for the pair of ruined, once-brocaded easy chairs and an ironing board, and suspended around the walls on wire hangers, the shirts, trousers, jackets that come down the laundry chute for pressing and minor repairs. And while we're at it, the pile of magazines stacked all over the shop in warehouse quantities.

Like the one Noonan happened to be reading at the time, face down, split open at the centrefold, across the arm of his chair, and even though the title looked foreign, the picture on the cover most definitely was not, all that baby-oiled, shaved flesh dragging attention straight to the pubic pouch in wet-look Lycra like an arrow to a bullseye. Or glory-hole, as Noonan would refer to that particular nub of desire. Lucky bag, butcher's window, trim, snatch, a dozen more, at least, I had never even heard of before. But then that was his area of expertise. A pity, he'd often say, they didn't allow it on *Mastermind.* Or *University Challenge.* Gerry Noonan reading Minge.

When he came back out from the little scullery place, mug in his fist, he caught me with my head still cocked, eyeing up — or was it down? — Miss Euro-Torso's bare bumpers.

'Not one of them easy shocked ex-altar boys, I trust, are we? Still, if you get turned on by that class of thing, there's plenty of pics of young shavers in and out of surplices filed away back there somewhere.'

He held the mug out to me, tea-bag still in it, string dangling over the rim.

'As opposed to proper pussy, of course. Right, then, take a pew and tell me all about yourself.'

And so we sat regarding one another with the tea cooling in its Man. U. mug, although Noonan somehow didn't strike me as being much of a football supporter. Not in all the time we shared that underground cubby-hole did I once spot a copy of the *Sun,* a racing sheet, any paper, for that matter. No radio either, just his precious, X-rated library of glossies. They came whistling down the laundry chute from the bedrooms above like the devil's own manna, along with the occasional sex-aid, or unused sachet of rubbers if the guest happened to be over-ambitious the night before. And if the evidence sometimes got left behind after they checked out, along with the stained sheets, which didn't really count, of course, the little Filipino maids with their Catholic guilt gnawing at them could always be relied upon to consign them to our own personal hell-hole below. It became a race to see who could get to that hinged trap first to discover what fresh goody had come racing down to our basement depository of filth. But, then, one man's filth is another man's university of life.

Still, that first day of my posting from porterage to valet services, it never entered my head Noonan would have me as bad as himself, especially when I started drinking the tea he had so considerately brewed for me, realising after a couple of sips that the *thing* steeping at the bottom of the red and white mug wasn't really a teabag after all, but something else unspeakably vile.

'Don't worry, it's not a used one!' he called out as I dashed for the sink next door, then ran the tap as I greedily drank to rinse the foul taste of bile away along with any lingering traces of that last cottage pie I'd had in that workman's caff off the Edgware Road.

'Sure and I only wanted to see if you could take a joke or not. You can, can't you?'

And nodding weakly, I allowed him to guide me back to the facing armchairs.

'No hard feelings? Shake on it?'

His hands felt soft and unused to labour as any girl's, for, as I was to discover, any serious pressing or needle and thread repair work was done by this old half-caste bloke Percival who sat cross-legged and mute in a hatch affair off the washroom next door like an extra in a bazaar in some Sabu movie.

Noonan called him Percy Sledge to his face all the time.

'Ach, sure, would you ever give us a bit of an oul' number, Percy!' he'd call out merrily to the old guy, bald head brown as a nut bent over his Singer sewing-machine. 'You know, that platinum hit of yours — or was it gold? 'When a Man Loves a Woman'. Ach, come on now.'

But the old bloke would just smile and get on with his work — and lovely work, it was, too — while Noonan and me, we sprawled out leafing through the last *Club*, *Mayfair* or *Razzle*. A cushy number in duplicate, if ever there was one, even though, officially, I was supposed to pitch in with Percy in the next room.

'Sure don't be ever worrying your head over the likes of that,' Noonan would tell me whenever I expressed a twinge of conscience, more to the point, apprehension, that somebody from management might drop down unannounced with a stopwatch and a clipboard. 'Old Percy loves his job. Has half a village to support back in India, haven't you, Percy?'

And if this doesn't comes across as hopelessly clichéd, much later I was to discover Percy, it seemed, had two degrees after his name, one in biology, and another in animal husbandry, and really had an extended family to take care of, not in Uttar Pradesh or Gujarat, but Wembley Park. But then who were we to be tuned into another's cultural wavelength, especially if they happened to hail from one of the 'dark continents', as Noonan liked referring to such places, whilst stabbing a finger at the latest *Asian Babes* or *Black and Beautiful* to support his thesis. Just your bog standard pair of paddies, were we, and, boy, did we ever work at it, as though that cramped, steam-laden cellar with its twin armchairs and stalactites of porn had somehow become this far-flung, little outpost of all we'd left behind along with everything crude, backward and provincially pig-ignorant.

But then the phone would ring and Noonan would stretch a lazy hand towards the old-fashioned, cream receiver and coo, 'Valet service here. And how may we be of assistance, sir?' Or madam, as the case might be. And for an instant my companion in sloth would become this accommodating servant figure with a manufactured accent a million miles from his own, even though sitting directly opposite me, unshaven, in a stained vest and old, faded blue, polyester tracksuit bottoms.

'Some fucking Frog in one-o-seven wants his cuffs and collars well-starched. I'll fucking starch them for him, so I will,' making a jerking-off motion over the stapled centrefold of the Pet of the Month spread across his knees at the time.

Now although this dual personality business was hardly a new thing to me — we all had, after all, to put a different face on it upstairs each day for the punters — I still found it unsettling. Subconsciously, I suppose, I kept waiting for him to unleash another side of his character on me and one, which in all its raw nastiness, would last a damn sight longer than the time it took to engage in a phone call with one of the guests. I'm pretty sure he must have recognised this, for I remember him reaching across one day and patting me on the knee. 'Young Downey, sure, don't we make the grand little team together, you and me. How long have you been here anyway? Two? Three months, is it now?'

'Percy!' he called out. 'How long has young Declan here

been helping us wash the dirty linen of the lazy and leisured classes?'

'Five weeks almost exactly, Mister Gerry. Come next Monday!'

'Okay, if I want a fucking white paper on the subject I'll ask for it!'

Then, coming back to me once more, 'Short a time as that, eh? Seems like the pair of us have been soulmates a good while longer somehow,' tightening his grip on my kneecap, and I remember thinking, *one of those as well, is he?* for by this time he had me thinking the way he did, sex, sex, sex on the brain morning, noon and night, even travelling back on the Tube, mentally undressing every female in the carriage.

To and from the station, as well, sometimes, all those magazine images seething in my head as in some kind of lust-driven tumble-dryer, how long could it go on, me thinking to myself, as though the rotating drum in the washing machine that was now my cranium might eventually explode on fast cycle. As for that other part, well, I was hand-polishing that up to three, maybe four times a day by now — how could I not be? And often I wondered about Noonan in that respect, for he liked to boast he never abused himself, was saving it all up, with a laugh, he said, for Ms Right when she came along.

'Like one of them fakir fellas of yours, Percy! I've heard tell they can have up to a dozen comes at a time and never shoot the once. All of it going back inside to be recycled or something. Goolies on them the size of coconuts. Like young Declan here in his extra tight Wranglers, dressing to the left, as he does.'

At which point I would feel myself colouring, face a match for my hair, crossing my legs like some prissy young PA opposite on the Bakerloo Line, paperback held high like a shield, and me across from her with my X-ray eyes lasering in on her every erogenous zone.

On more than one occasion, if we happened to get off at the same station, I'd find myself falling in behind, still intent on some set of sweetly munching young buttocks, and quite a few times, as well, found myself tracking my prey all the way to wherever she lived. Once, I recall, as far as Dollis Hill, before turning back, spent and depressed, towards my own bedsitter off Dyne Road and the consolation prize of a spreadeagled Playmate named Candy, Trudy or Heidi. So you might well argue that even though Gerry Noonan had a lot to answer for when it came to involving me in all of that business later, even then I must have had leanings that way myself to make me such a willing partner in his subsequent 'campaign of terror' as the *Willesden Times* put it.

But before all of that came about the routine in our overheated basement underwent a new and different phase. For the worse, you might say, as far as Noonan and his general appearance went. Day in, day out, it was singlet and tracksuit bottoms now, and the eye-watering scent of BO kept wafting across in acrid eddies every time he shifted in his armchair, a low rampart of glossy pulp about his feet in their old, unlaced, Converse trainers. When I first arrived at least some of the time he would actually change into a uniform — it hung on the back of the door, drip-dry white shirt, clip-on tie, black Sta-Prest trousers — when called upon to perform the public part of his duties upstairs. Now he sent me up instead in my own junior edition outfit kept pristine by old Percy, so that every time I came out of the lift carrying a sheaf of freshly laundered shirts, or a suit jacket and pants in polythene, I looked like it was my first day on the job. It felt like it, too, for the air smelt freshly perfumed up there after the monkey house atmosphere I'd just left.

Noonan made it sound like a promotion of some kind. Of course I knew it wasn't, but I welcomed it nonetheless, for it did seem to still the sexual turmoil in my head. At least, for a time, it did. I would bring back reports of my adventures on the upper floors, and at first they were pretty tame in the telling. A fat foreigner in 204 naked save for a hairnet and a pair of tiny, polka-dotted underpants. A woman silhouetted in the shower who called out to me to extract a single dollar bill from her purse on the bedside table. Two young blondes tucked up in bed together with a Great Dane — the canine kind. This last seemed to excite Noonan no end, more than all the rest of my encounters put together. For a week he had been deep in a fresh addition to the library, something called *Farm Girls Just Love To Get Their Oats*. At least that's what he said the translation from the Dutch was, it being a language, he also said, very close to our own. Did I know, for instance, the Dutch word for cock? Go on, have a guess. Inside it was all dumpy blondes being seen to in hay barns by Shetland ponies and sheepdogs — in one instance a billy goat — something I had never even dreamt of before, not even in my most overheated imaginings, and even though I hail from a rural background just like Noonan. Some place in the bogs of Kerry, in his case.

Seeing him so stimulated by my account of the two animal-lovers on the third floor, I began to embellish, then invent from scratch other of my bulletins, always adding a strong, sexual element to the mix. God forgive me, but it wasn't long before I was being invited to join total strangers in showers, strap businessmen to bedheads, consent to blow jobs out of sheer good manners, dole out whippings just short of drawing blood. If only ...

Most of the scenarios came straight from the pages of our reading material, but hearing them recounted in that way with my own added flourishes had Noonan in a lather. Current magazine forgotten, he would lie back, hand buried beneath the waistband of his tracksuit bottoms, while I indulged a talent for story-telling I never knew I possessed, often arousing myself, too, on occasions, I'm bound to admit, and sometimes, in full flow, would hear Percy's old Singer falter in its stride, then stop altogether, and knowing he, too, was in thrall in spite of himself made me even more ambitious.

Then one fateful afternoon, when summoned by phone to pick up a bag of stuff from the fifth floor, I found myself experiencing the real thing, but with a twist in the tail not found in any of the magazines, or my own blue fairy stories. And in some ways they were a bit like that, the handsome young prince with his trusty weapon, succouring, if that's the word, assorted damsels in distress, forgoing their vibrators for the proper article, and what an article, growing as it did with each encounter like Pinocchio's nose. And if I was Prince Charming, what then did that make Noonan? The wicked stepmother, perhaps, waiting expectantly below stairs for reports back from the ball?

Well I knocked on the door, and a voice, recognisably female, not young, but not old, either, called out, 'Come!'

'Valet service!' I, too, cried, pushing open the door and waiting just inside.

No one was there, at least not in the main reception area. It was a suite, you see, one of only four in the hotel, relic of better days when visiting celebrities patronised the place.

THE VALET'S ROOM

Close to Marylebone Station, it had once, so I was told, been on a par with some of the big three and four-star jobs on Park Lane. That was then, now was now, and the entire place sighed with neglect, no fruit baskets in the rooms, no mints on the pillows, no one even to turn down the covers. People who had got hold of an out of date guidebook stayed once and never came back, it was that sort of dump. Why else would Noonan and me be able to hang on to our lousy jobs otherwise?

There was a powerful reek of perfume in the room, musky, heavy, befuddling almost, and instantly I visualised *brunette*, Christ, maybe one of those Arab bints, face completely covered except for the eyes, oh, a thousand times sexier than a flash of something much further down, according to Noonan the result of centuries of harem life, a single laser-like glance piercing the brushed cotton of your Y-fronts to what lay beneath. What lay in mine perked up no end at the thought. But before I had time to caution, *whoa, boy*, even if I'd wanted to, this hatchet-faced blonde with cropped hair, in white shorts and a polo shirt appeared as if all fired up for the tennis courts.

'Call yourself a valet service,' straight off going into the attack, in harsh, forty a day tones. English, not American. 'I've put on the full outfit just to let you see what I'm paying good money for. Look at it, would you? Just look at it.' Spreading the box pleats on her short skirt — good legs, tanned, toned — then the front of her Fred Perry, tits like baby pears, pert being the operative word, even though she was way past the pert stage.

'Well? I think I deserve *some* satisfaction. Can't you say something? Very well, don't move, you hear? Wait right there,' she commanded, disappearing into the bathroom.

So I stood where I was, ardour cooling. For the life of me I could see nothing wrong with the old bitch's two-piece, but then I'd come across chronic complainers before, humping bags for pricks whose religion in life seemed to be giving other people grief, especially those poor sods depending on tips for half their living. Say goodbye to that in this particular instance, I told myself.

More grief, for just then she came back out of the bathroom, my jaw dropping, for she had changed into this see-through negligée number, lacy, heart-shaped motifs strategically appliquéd over all three crucial zones, but drawing my eyes, of course, like filings to a magnet.

'What do they call you anyway?'

'Declan,' I told her. 'Declan Downey.'

'I suppose that's Irish, is it? Well, for starters, Declan Downey, you can put the laundry down, and don't stand there with your mouth open as if you've never seen a girl in her scanties before, although, Christ knows, you must have washed out enough of them.'

We stood there looking one another up and down. The simple truth was Noonan and his mags hadn't prepared me for this, whatever *this* was, and now that it was here I felt like an actor benumbed with stage-fright just before his big scene.

'Oh, fuck!' she said. 'Don't tell me you're gay.'

I shook my head.

'Look, I've a game booked for three. Mind if we get right down to it?'

Well, I followed her into the bedroom, and already my head was in a turmoil over what version of events I was going to take back to Noonan, and even after I had my pants down and was dutifully grinding away, face buried in the hotel's best linen, breathing in the combined scent of its freshness and her perfume, I kept my eyes closed, mentally leafing through as many magazine spreads as I could recall in the time it took to shoot my load.

'So, is that it, then?'

She was lying back, fag in mouth, barely a bead of sweat on her whilst I was drenched.

'By the time I've smoked this Marlborough would you mind awfully not being here? I'm a real fast smoker, by the way. Mind you, not nearly as fast as you, young Declan, when it comes to popping your cork.'

And closing the door behind me into the corridor, I heard her call out, 'Leave the whites! Next time I'll remember not to get a junior to do a man's job!'

Opposite the lifts there was a linen closet, and taking one of the keys from the bunch I carried with me, I locked the door from the inside, sitting down on the floor with my head up against the shelves of sheets and pillow-cases trying to take in what had just happened. My brain felt like it had been bombarded by meteorites, still was, and hunkered in that dry-scented cubby-hole, I tried reversing and slowing down the stream like it was on video, but the rewind wouldn't work. Sensations kept piling in on me, confused, out of synch, the room, the woman, her naked body — what I could remember of it, that is — all scrambled together in the wrong order like a human jigsaw spread on a sheet. Then me and my body, ghastly pale and freckled against the sunbed perfection of hers. For an instant a tiny pubic wedge, auburn, not blonde, swam up out of the chaos, as though somehow hugely significant. Then it, too, was gone, like all those other flying rock samples from outer space invading my head. For a good thirty to forty minutes I must have crouched there — just about the time, I imagine, I should have lasted with Mrs Robinson back there instead of my humiliating quickie.

Going down in the lift my knees felt wobbly, and the tip of my dick had started throbbing, but before that development had time to take its toll on my already over-taxed brain I was concentrating instead on what to tell Noonan — old Percy, too, come to think of it. The truth was I had no stomach left for yet another of my fairy tales, hadn't the desire, or the energy to conjure up something fictional out of the shocking reality of what had transpired back there in the Brunel Suite.

Incidentally, had I come or not? I felt sure I must have done. Then, again, had I?

Boy, was I confused, and when I walked into our snug little den of iniquity it must have been written all over me. Instead, of course, it was the still lingering scent of perfume, something I had forgotten about, that gave the game away and made Noonan straighten to attention in his chair and lay aside his copy of *Readers' Wives*.

'Fee, fie, fo, fum, I smell the whiff of an Irishman's cum,' he greeted me, grinning like a chimp.

'Well, funny you should mention it—' I began, then stopped, remembering my pledge to myself coming down in the lift with my damp, shrunken, tail between my legs.

'Well? *Well?*'

In the next room I heard old Percy's Singer stutter, then stop.

Now, on the facing wall, there happened to be a calendar, not a Pirelli, or a Page Three, but one of those seasonal snow scenes, for it had got stuck at December for some reason — it was now summer — and starting to get my voice back I concentrated hard on that furry white landscape, topped by a deep blue sky, as if it was me and not that distant, small, bent figure trudging through those drifts with a staff and a pack on his back as though on some sort of quest instead of down here where I happened to be in a cave with my two goblin friends.

Alas, the bedtime story they were expecting was not the one they had grown accustomed to, for, still ploughing in my head through all that white wilderness, for the first time I heard myself telling it as it actually happened, not the way it was supposed to in the magazines knee-deep all around, and when I had finished, every last humiliating *i* dotted and shameful *t* crossed, Noonan just sat there.

He looked stunned for what seemed a very long time, before coming out with, 'Just your bad luck to get picked by some tennis-playing lesbian. Or, bi, maybe.'

I stared at him taken aback by his reaction. Rather, lack of the one I'd been expecting, for his voice sounded low and compassionate, and may I say, fatherly, even. And in the next room the invisible sewing-machine remained silent as well, as if old Percy, too, was commiserating with me.

'I never told anyone this before, but I was married the once.'

Letting out a deep sigh, Noonan allowed his head to fall back on the grease spot the size of a saucer imprinted on the headrest of his chair.

'Back in Tralee town, it was. Ten years ago this very month, come to think of it. Dolores, her name was. A June bride, everyone said. And myself, wasn't I the right masher. Big pointy-collared shirt, kipper tie, suit lapels the breadth of your palm, flares, Cuban heels. Not to mention the hair, as near a Kevin Keegan Afro as you could get at the time in Kerry.

'Anyway, the reception was held in this big hotel out on The Ring. Oh, very plush, with lashings of drink, needless to say. Well, about two in the morning, the worse for wear, I went roaming the corridors looking for her, it was that sort of a shindig, out of our skulls we were. To cut a long story short, didn't I find her with her bridesmaid, her best mate, big Fiona McGlynn, both of them in bed together at it like something out of *Girls Only*.

'Maybe they were drunk. Well, they were, I suppose, but was that any sort of excuse? Sure I wasn't riding my best man Padraig down the hall, was I?

'Well, there was hell to pay, I have to tell you, me going ballistic and beating two shades of shite out of the pair of them. In the morning the priest was brought in to smooth things over, but how do you talk away something like that? Anyway he didn't want to hear the sordid details, being into wee lads himself, the whole affair too close for comfort and home, I suppose.

'That taught me a lot, that particular episode, not just about same-sex in Kerry, which was going on a hell of a lot more than people might imagine, but women in general, for you're in a no win situation there, son, every time. And I'm not just talking about that one bad experience back in '87, for there've been others. Oh, yes.

'Take it from me there's no such thing as Ms Right, they're all of them Ms Fucking Wrong. Like that bitch upstairs. Another lesbian. Look, one of them admitted it to me once. Only another woman, she said, knows what it takes to turn one on. And after me at it like a rat up a drainpipe banging away a good three quarters of an hour not getting anywhere fast, she tells me that, so she does! Just like you and that Natrilanova bird. Tiny Tits.'

I looked over at him in the armchair. Had I told him that, about the boobs, I mean? I must have, mustn't I, otherwise he wouldn't have brought it up, which came as something of a shock, me going into physical details like that, when what I had thought I had done was simply provide the bare outlines, as it were, to the encounter. And suddenly, seeing her through his eyes in that way, I started getting angry as well for the first time.

'Fucking feminists!' he was yelling. 'My wife was one before she could even spell the fucking word. Kiddo, they're all dykes at heart, believe you me, and the ones who don't know it yet are only deluding themselves. So welcome aboard and join the losers' club,' hurling his *Readers' Wives* across the room, it colliding softly with the wall, slick pages unfurling in what seemed slow-motion, showing off glimpses of pink flesh and plain faces pleading, *take me, take me* ...

Next door I heard the Singer start revving up again, equivalent, I suppose, to old Percy clapping his hands over his ears, not wishing to hear any more of this. But it felt good to be hard done by for a change, even if it was only at Noonan's prompting, and soon the pair of us were in the middle of a paper storm, magazines flying like multi-coloured confetti, 'What room is the bitch in anyway?' Noonan yelling.

'The Brunel!' me yelling back.

'Well, let's go up and give her a proper seeing to, then. See how she fucking well likes it!'

And for one heady moment I actually believed him. That's what we would do together, bursting in like a pair of avengers from below stairs with our dicks out. I could see it all in livid, high-gloss colour suddenly, her, submissive before our combined ardour, spreadeagled, thumb in mouth, like Mandy, 42-32-38, the reader's wife from Telford with hubby working night-shift. It was a great moment that, heady, with me feeling I would follow Noonan anywhere, anywhere, no matter where or what.

But in the middle of it all the phone went and the madness evaporated as abruptly as it had arrived. Suddenly Noonan looked drained, eyes closed, head back once more in its usual patch of hair oil, and so I took the call. Routine, male, someone enquiring about a dinner-suit and dress shirt.

Old Percy came in then, wringing his skinny, tea-stained hands.

'Oh, Mister Gerry, oh, Mister Gerry,' he wailed. 'All your lovely picture books. You'll never get them back in any kind of order, never, never,' and he started picking them up off the floor while we watched with dead eyes.

About a week or so after that, I think it was, I got turfed out of my digs. No notice. Nothing. The landlord, Mr Ali, Indian, like Percy, but no gentleman, was getting out of the property game, he said, and moving to Doncaster to start a new life for himself. The juxtaposition struck me as hilarious for some reason, knowing Mr Ali, as well as Doncaster by repute, but the result for me wasn't a bit funny, out on the street with my stuff in a bin bag. For a couple of nights I dossed in the local park among the wildlife — it was July, after all — and then Noonan said I could sleep in my armchair in the valet's room, temporarily, mind, until I found a roof over my head again. But, of course, I couldn't, could I, not without a deposit, which I didn't have.

I have to say things were looking pretty bleak, and every time I passed some rank-smelling lump of humanity huddled under a blanket in a doorway, I thought to myself, *that's*

THE VALET'S ROOM

going to be me, see if it's not, and soon there but for the grace of God etc.

Then one afternoon, unable to stand the sight of my miserable mug a minute longer, Noonan said, 'Here you'd better move in with me. It's only the one room, but, sure, can't you kip down on the sofa. More of a bed-settee, actually.'

And my heart leapt visualising something a lot more luxurious than the broken down, old, slatted, futon number it turned out to be. Still it was somewhere to stretch out on, and now there was a roof over me as well. And below that, a ceiling, which I studied intently like an upside down aerial map as Noonan moaned in his sleep and the light crept in around the edges of the burgundy and puke curtains, a colour combination designed specifically to bring down anyone's soul, not helped by the bare forty-watt bulb, either, hanging from the mid-point of my ceiling map like a fly-specked marker buoy.

The rest of the place was pretty Spartan as well, but reasonably clean for an Irish bachelor. I suppose I must have expected a facsimile of where we spent our daytime hours together sunk in our armchairs like a couple of elderly, debauched clubmen, especially with those stacks of blue material. But, and here comes the unsettling part, not a single one, not even a solitary pin-up on the wall. I say unsettling, for here was yet another unexpected side to the man who in his own way had taken over my life. Being married once upon a time, I don't know why, had been the first crack in the glass. Now, this.

And while we're at it, how about the Sacred Heart over the sideboard? Out of politeness I never referred to it, not once, as though it never existed and didn't give me the creeps first thing when I awoke, those sorrowful eyes fastened on me like some amnesiac hippy oblivious to all that half-finished, open heart surgery on his chest. Noonan never mentioned it either as if it was simply part of the wallpaper, or had come with the room when he moved in. But then if he'd hated it as much as I did he would have taken it down. He would, wouldn't he? No, no, it belonged to him, I decided, and then I had this other even more disturbing image of him going into one of those religious repository places and coming out with it wrapped under his arm.

My brain wouldn't cease humming with such fixations as I lay on my thin Japanese mattress and studied him buzz-sawing away across from me in the other single bed, mouth open catching flies.

We didn't talk much, if at all, as I also recall, when we actually were awake in that room, which seems bizarre now, looking back on it. No TV, no radio, no record-player to break the silence, just the pair of us munching on takeaways and snapping open cans of Kestrel, whilst staring at the walls, making a change, I suppose, from the ceiling. Ask me anything, anything, about the décor of that attic room facing out on to Willesden High Road and I will be able to catalogue every last detail of colour, pattern and texture, early fifties style, that being the last time it had seen either paint or paper.

And in the morning we would go in to work on the Jubilee Line, still not talking, then, more and more separately, an arrangement arrived at mutually. But then the instant we dropped into our armchairs and opened our first meaty picture-spread of the day, bingo, it was as if my dour room-mate was this different person altogether, wisecracking, running commentary on Miss Muffette of the Month's claim to her title, teasing old Percy about his one gold disc, counselling me on the wicked ways of our 'fucking hotel' as he described it, 'because that's what people do here'. Everybody except us, I remembered thinking.

A pattern was being set here, a routine, it seemed to me, as unvarying and monotonous in its trajectory as whatever it was that kept old Percy's foot pressed to the treadle of his antique sewing-machine. But horrified as I was at watching my life slip by, there didn't seem a lot I could do about it. Reminders of exactly how I might end up, I could see for myself in the park every Sunday, the paddies sprawled on the grass, beer cans piling up around them, whilst listening to the football, or the hurling, high-pitched ebb and flow of commentary travelling all the way from Athlone, then magically out the other end of a transistor. Mooching past, part of me wanted to join them, but another and more powerful instinct held me back, just like Noonan, loners in our own way, something shared, a bond, unspoken, between us.

Looking back on the thing that came to take us both over so addictively, I often get the feeling it might have been that very selfsame bond that made us do what we did do, and then for so long afterwards, knowing in our heart of hearts we were only minutes away from getting caught each time we succumbed, and if I were to pinpoint the actual event, the occasion, which started us off on our joint descent, it might well be that party we went to in that girl's place in Harlesden. Or maybe it was Stonebridge Park.

Then, again, the entire business was probably long in the coming anyway, a bit like a slow train, maybe, picking up speed and racing to hit the buffers at the terminus, except that, unlike the train, Noonan and me, we just kept on going, didn't we, railways and railway lines, as you will hear, playing an important part in our story. So I don't suppose that particular image just floated up out of the blue from nowhere like that.

The girl's name was Majella, Majella Brady, and she worked on Reception, a freckled redhead like myself, but plumpish with it, and sloppy in dress and manner, which probably accounts for why she invited Noonan and me in the first place. Those other snooty madams sharing the front desk wouldn't give you the time of day, not two below-stairs losers like us. Over-confident, convent-educated types, all going out with reps or foreign blokes working in the hotel, they wouldn't be caught dead with a culchie.

Noonan had a particularly bad word for them. 'The Sisters of No Fucking Mercy', he used to call them. 'Except for some young dago with a moustache, or some git wearing a blazer and rugby club tie.'

But, as I say, Majella was different, would always go out of her way to speak to you if you happened to be crossing the lobby.

'I'm having a wee party this coming Sunday. My twenty-first.' Blushing as she said it, all those sunspots on her fat, round cheeks joining up to form one big, hot, pink mass. 'Why don't you and Mr. Noonan come. It'll be great crack.'

She made Noonan sound like my father, or an uncle, maybe, but, of course, I didn't tell him what she'd called him, otherwise he wouldn't have considered going, smelling a rat that everybody there would be around my age, even less. Still, I was determined to persuade him, for that top room in Utopia Mansions was really getting to me by now, night after night trying to avoid the disapproving gaze of Our Unseen Guest on the wall, His Holy Haemorrhage.

Right up until the last minute Noonan wouldn't say yea or nay, and I didn't want to go on my own, for I had this irrational dread that if I did it might somehow endanger our relationship, that he might hold it against me in some way. All those homeless, hopeless blanket cases I passed in doorways with a mongrel on a rope still exerted a grip on me.

We were drinking full-strength lager at the time, what else? — drinking, I mean — and I had upped the tempo considerably, hoping he might follow suit, mellowing accordingly. And it seemed to work, for after about six cans apiece, the pair of us awash and full of gas, he said, 'Fuck it, why not? We might just get a rub of the relic, you never know. Where did you say it was again?'

Well, we decided to walk, the distance between our place and the address scrawled on the piece of hotel stationery a matter of only a few miles away as the crow flies, the night being balmy with a sort of domed, rosy glow overhead, which I pretended was natural, and not the effect of all the city's joined up street-lighting. I was in that kind of mood, elated at the idea of having escaped that room, and now here we were off on a night-time jaunt together, a load of drink in us, just the way it might have been once upon a time back home in the dark of the country somewhere instead of under the sodium lights and shadows of NW6.

And like a couple of seasoned midnight ramblers too, we headed for our destination in as straight a line as we could given the built-up terrain in between, according to some buried map in our heads, at one point climbing over a wall into Willesden's Jewish Cemetery, as I recall, then traversing those half-toppled headstones with their weird Aramaic inscriptions. Even in daylight it's a strange and eerie place, and often on my Sunday walks to the park on the far side I would pass through it, pretending to be visiting a grave if ever I saw someone there, although, as I think I may have mentioned, with my complexion and hair colouring, no one would ever take me for one of the chosen people. But it was all part of my own private, little weekend world, and having Noonan share it, despite his being unaware, made me come over all warm and comradely.

And so we reached the block of flats, this sprawling, run-down, thirties-style complex, threading our way past the overflowing communal bins and rusting Cavaliers and Datsuns, its name a most unusual one, Frontenac, exotic, even, as though the architect might have suffered from delusions of grandeur, or a yearning for faraway places. But then our dump was called Utopia Mansions.

Anyway, thank God, the lift was working, and we ascended to the sixth floor in the usual dented bare metal box, silently scanning the graffiti as to the racial mix of the neighbourhood, that dread word 'posse' happily appearing not once. Big Tracy Loves It Up The Bum, however, did figure strongly, not only on the walls, back of the doors, but ceiling, as well, we noticed, leading to the conclusion that someone owning a purple felt tip hadn't been one of the luckier ones.

Noonan grinned at me. 'Knock three times and ask for Tracy, eh?' our good humour lasting right up until we reached the door of sixty-seven and rang its bell.

There was a noticeable absence of noise coming from the flat, not the hubbub of raised voices and music I was expecting somehow, and, indeed, I took another quick look at the writing on my piece of hotel notepaper in case I'd got the number wrong. But then the door opened and Majella stood there all togged out in a pink, PVC sort of jumpsuit looking as if she'd been poured into this jumbo-sized, but still far too tight, Durex.

'Come in, come in, Declan. Sure and I see you've brought Mister Noonan along as well,' she cried, looking half-cut already.

I could feel Noonan stiffen at my side on hearing the *mister* part, but before he could hesitate or turn awkward I got him shunted into the flat with the door safely closed behind us. There was a short hallway up ahead with a kitchenette off it, the draining-board thick with bottles, which was a good sign.

Well, the only one, for when we got to the lounge, only four other people were present besides ourselves and Majella, all sitting on a settee staring mournfully at a birthday cake, pink, again, on a coffee table, with a cluster of unlit candles sticking out of it.

In a haze of perspiration Majella stood swaying in the middle of the mushroom fitted carpet, which had quite a few stains on it as well as cigarette burns.

'This is Teresa and this is Paddy and this is Claudette and this is wee Tyra,' she announced in a blur of introductions as we hung by her side, all our hard-won alcoholic buzz evaporating, Teresa and Paddy being a couple of rheumy-eyed, near-to-death pensioners, and Claudette an enormous West Indian lady in yellow and green with diamanté-encrusted glasses on a chain, with the thumb-sucking five year-old clinging to her and staring at the pair of us as if we were a couple of potential, honky child molesters.

'So, how's everybody's glass then?' Majella said brightly, as though the room was packed with partygoers in paper hats instead of it being like a surgery waiting-room. The three adults stared back at her, not speaking, not drinking, either, by the look of things.

Then Noonan croaked, 'Would you be ever having any whiskey?'

And after that things took a dip downhill even more rapidly. Of course we should have cut our losses and ducked out then, I know that now, but instead we went into the kitchen feeling like two hit and run victims badly needing a reviver and got stuck into the bottle of Paddy, still virginal, cap intact.

The rest is far too dispiriting to recount in full. Perched on two stools with our knees under the draining-board, we tore into the hard stuff, dead eyes fixed on the falling level in the bottle with its yellow and gold label. Every so often Majella would stumble in herself to refresh her own glass from her supply of vodka and Russchian, saying things like, 'What kind of music do youse like? The Chieftains? Van Morrison? Planxty? Daniel O'Donnell?' then heading back to the dead room again, which remained like that, not a peep, nor a note out of the stereo either.

At some point we heard the door close and the silence become even more intense. There was about an inch in the bottle by now, Noonan had his forehead pressed to the stainless steel of the draining-board, and I was, well, starting to steady up, the truth being I had drunk myself sober.

'Gerry,' I murmured, shaking him, 'Gerry, let's go,' but he only groaned, face down on the ridged metal.

So I left him to it and went into the living room to find Majella all on her own sitting on the carpet, legs splayed apart, her back up against the front edge of the sofa.

'Happy Birthday,' I said for want of something to say.

The candles on the cake still hadn't been lit, yet it looked as if someone had taken a bite out of it, not a neat, triangular slice, but a bloody great bite. All around her mouth Majella had what looked like a rime of pink icing, so no guesses as to who the culprit was, and she must have been crying too, for there were black mascara snail tracks down both cheeks.

'Did you see my cards?' she said, not pointing, just staring into the glass in her hand. Propped on top of the TV I counted three. 'The rest haven't arrived yet. There's a postal strike on at Kilburn sorting office. Did you know that?'

I shook my head, content to let her talk, for by now I just knew she would. Anyway it was the least I could do in the circumstances, lend a listening ear, I mean.

Well, lucky me, didn't I get the entire family history, the mammy, the out of work daddy back in Derry, the eight brothers and sisters, youngest brother Dominic knee-capped by the Provos, sister Bernie, autistic, another running off with a British squaddie, and the latest update, her best friend Dympna falling out with her over a month's back rent money.

'That's her bed in there next to mine,' pointing off to another room. She began to cry again, the tears coursing down her plump cheeks in inky trickles.

'Look, it's getting late,' I said, 'and we've a fair old bit to travel.' A lie, but who was to tell? 'Can you catch a night bus around here?'

Suddenly she was panic-stricken, her glass spilling over on to the carpet. 'Sure can't you take my bed, and Mr Noonan, Dympna's? I don't mind the couch, honest.'

Next thing I knew she had struggled to her knees, pulling down the zip on her jumpsuit halfway to the navel, no bra, exposing a freckled cleavage awesome in its expanse, the shocking truth being that even though she was as tightly packed into all that pink PVC as sausage meat, not once had I tried visualising what might lie underneath, I don't know why.

I stared at it, at her, then backed off. It was only a little way really, I have to say that in my defence, instinctive rather than anything else, but she seemed to take it personally.

'What's the matter, something not to your liking?' she said, yanking the zip down the rest of the way to the elastic waistband biting into her belly. 'Girls, women, not your thing? You and your boyfriend back there?'

And at that point Noonan came lurching in looking like death, eyes bloodshot, hair all over the place, left cheek still bearing the imprint of the draining board.

'Let's hit the road,' says he, yawning, 'I'm knackered.'

Majella gave a nasty laugh, gulping down the remains in her glass. 'Sure you've only just got here, what's your hurry?'

Noonan just stood there, I swear not even looking at all that naked frontage on display.

'Come on, Dec, time to make tracks,' he said, and with a curl to her lips Majella mimicked, 'Yes, run along, Declan, there's a good lad, sugar daddy's calling you.'

Well, that stopped Noonan in his tracks like nothing could, for drunk as he might have been, even he couldn't miss the calumny there. Face darkening, he took a step towards her. 'Now listen to me, you fucking wee huer—'

And then she was up on her feet spitting out more venom. 'Sure everyone knows you're only a couple of queers anyway!' and in two strides Noonan was across the room taking her by the throat.

Now I don't think his grip was overly-exertive or anything, but her eyes seemed to roll back in her head, the glass falling dully from her hand to land on the carpet, which for some reason transfixed me, that dark spreading stain, I mean, more than what was taking place further up.

Next thing she had keeled over, almost in slow motion, it looked like, landing on the sofa like a floppy pink doll, out cold. At least I prayed it was no more serious than that. But before I could find that out for myself, Noonan slapped her once across the face, not a hard or vicious slap, more a firm, determined pat, and she gave a moan, a dribble of saliva trickling from the side of her mouth.

'Leave her,' said Noonan, 'leave her to sleep it off. She won't remember a thing in the morning, or if she does, she'll regret it,' and as he said it I knew we were both thinking the same thing, the room suddenly still, as if holding its breath, like we were. Reflectively we stood gazing down at those bared, puppy fat breasts, with further down a hint of black underwear, the zip on the jumpsuit — or catsuit, who knows? — that crucial six inches still to go, distance between prick-teasing and the full bounty of the promised land.

'For fuck's sake zip her up and let's get out of here,' Noonan growled, turning and heading for the front door. I could hear him cursing and swearing as he fumbled with the security chain, but I still couldn't drag myself away, eyes fixed on all that raw, naked flesh compared to what I was used to, a row of staples dividing its midriff.

'Come on!' called Noonan, and not knowing why, dutifully I bent and pulled on that little metal tab, when what I yearned to do, I suppose, was ease it down in the other direction.

Closing the door behind me I heard this low rumble of snoring begin, not a bit delicate, or feminine-sounding, and I remember thinking that might well have been the real reason for the flatmate's baling out — Dympna, wasn't that her name?

Going down in the lift, Noonan zombie-like by my side, I got this belated hard-on visualising what she might have looked like flouncing around the flat in a see-through, baby-doll nightie the way bachelor girls are supposed to do. Brunette, most decidedly brunette, I decided, with firm, smallish tits and backside to match, unlike the mountainous Majella, and I was really getting into it, her, as well, when Noonan seemed to emerge from his sleepwalking coma and started giving off as if finally the cork had come out.

'Fuck them!' he raged. 'Fuck the whole fucking lot of them!' and I knew he was referring to women in general, but Majella, specifically, and what she'd said concerning the two of us back in the flat just before she passed out on us like some great lump of human salami.

We were stumbling across a patch of rough ground at the time. It seemed we had taken a wrong turning somewhere along the way, maybe more than one, given the state we were in, whether because of the booze, or the anger which was eating us up, for I had become infected as well by now. Trudging along by his side I feasted on Noonan's resentment, felt it wash over me, with a powerful urge to turn the clock back and with a strong emphasis on retaliation against someone who had let loose a vicious tongue on us for no apparent reason other than her own fucking inadequacy and unhappiness at being who and what she was.

You're right, I thought, *fuck her, and the lot of them*, which is what one or both of us should have done at the time, so saving us all that aggravation. That, I suppose, was really Noonan talking. Still, it sounded pretty convincing just then.

'Where in the name of Christ are we?'

He had halted and was gazing about him. To our right the bare bones of a gasometer were outlined against the skyline, and just yards away, a canal, of all things, running ruler-straight off to parts unknown.

'I think we're near Ladbroke Grove,' I told him. 'If we follow the towpath back there we should come out Kensal Green Way.'

'Fuck, fuck, fuck,' he groaned, collapsing at the base of a broken wall, and we both stared at the oily black ribbon of water, for the first time, I don't know why, becoming aware of the steady hum from the Westway, even though it must have been two, maybe three in the morning.

'Next time some fat, young, lesbian prick-teaser invites you up to her place and then pisses on you, include me out, okay?'

I threw a stone in the water, followed by another, then another.

'Bitch,' I said, the word punctuating each splash, and then the ripples hitting the bank and causing the floating tins and plastic bottles to bump and grind there.

'So maybe you'll listen to me when I tell you they're all the fucking same. Okay?'

'Okay,' I told him, throwing a last lump of brick.

It must have disturbed a nesting coot or something, for there came a screech and a flurry of wings beating the dark water.

'Let's go,' said Noonan as the thing took off. 'Call it a day,' and that seemed to be that. End of story.

Only it wasn't, was it, for who were we to know it was actually going to be the start of something which was to take us over like a craze, or a curse, or both, in the weeks and months ahead, all sparked off on that cindered stretch of towpath, or Molestation Mile, as we came to call it. And it's important to get all this down exactly the way it *did* begin, as it happened. I have a thing about it, for there's been so much fictionalising and downright speculation on the part of the papers, even TV, which you might expect, wouldn't you, to be a little more scrupulous when it comes to such things.

Anyhow, as we were heading along the towpath in what I hoped was a westerly direction, suddenly ahead we saw a figure materialise, travelling in our direction, and a recognisably female one at that. In that instant I felt Noonan grip my arm.

'Walk on the grass,' he hissed. 'Let's have a bit of fun.' And to my shock and surprise he pulled out a handkerchief and tied it over the bottom half of his face western baddie style. I stared at him, at it, paisley patterned, something I had never seen before, him with a proper hankie, that is.

'Go on, go on,' motioning me to follow suit, but when I spread my hands, signalling no go, he mouthed, 'Well put your fucking hood up then,' for I had on a new Umbro sweatshirt, fondly imagining, I suppose, it to be the cool thing to wear to a party where everybody would be young, laid back and listening to U2 and Take That with the red on the stereo up to max.

Well, we began striding out fast and soft-footed together along that grassy, inner strip, eating up the distance between our quarry and ourselves. Whoever she was, she seemed oblivious, with a definite list to her gait, first to the left, then to the right, a couple of times nearly going over into the canal itself, and I realised she must be either drunk, or disabled, which, of course, would have taken all the fun out of it. But, no, I told myself, no, she was definitely pissed, and a lot further down that road than we were, which, of course, we weren't by this time, having nearly sobered up by now. Noonan was breathing hard and heavy at my side, not on account of his lack of fitness, but because he was excited. I could feel it as well, a fizz of adrenalin surging through me the closer we got.

A blonde, I could see that now, bareheaded, with a close crop, jeans, and a tight, sleeveless top. No handbag, but clutching fags and lighter. That last part pure speculation, by the way, but I felt convinced in my reading of her, building up this profile in my head as I ran. Caught-out partygoer praying for a familiar landmark, civilisation, anything, but having landed up God alone knows on this canal bank, staggering on like a lost soul in a desert hoping for an oasis, but oblivious, as yet, to the pair of masked bandits, us, gaining on her hand over fist.

Noonan kept muttering to himself as he jogged. 'Pro ... prostitute ... ' it sounded like, and I had this irrational burst of irritation with him for being so crass regarding something, someone, I already knew, oh, so much more intimately than he could ever to hope to do.

But, of course, we never got around to finding out who was right, for suddenly she stopped, turning to face us, some instinct warning her of impending peril, even though at that stage, I, certainly, intended no real malice. Noonan, I couldn't vouch for, but something about the way he was breathing through his handkerchief made me think differently.

Well, she continued standing there paralysed like a rabbit in a car's headlights, mouth opening and shutting — even at that distance, I could see it — with no sound coming out. But then a scream at that stage would have been unbearable, and I caught myself praying, *please don't yell, for if you do, we'll only get confused about what to do next, not having thought that far ahead.*

Then I heard Noonan mutter, 'Let's get the bitch,' and I realised I was on my own, along for the ride, so to speak. And, so, finally she began to run, ungainly and veering, at first, then, miraculously picking up a surprising turn of speed as if the shock of seeing the two of us gaining on her like a couple of avenging Touregs had sobered her up, giving her the jolt she needed.

'Fuck! Fuck!' cried Noonan racing flat out now and leaving me behind, but then I was slowing down anyway. I watched him take off, arms pumping like a sprinter's, head back, shoulders straight, the years falling away, although I suppose he was still only in his thirties then.

Leaning against a low wall, breathing hard, I continued to watch Noonan closing the gap. The girl was beginning to tire, I could see that, her former spastic wobble returning, and it was just like one of those wildlife programmes on TV. Would the impala escape the cheetah or not?

And then just within biting, clawing distance, the chase was over, for Noonan seemed to falter in his stride, losing pace, as well as interest, coasting to a halt, and his prey broke clear. Hanging there, hands on hips, he watched her go. I heard him shout something after her, then he stooped and seemed to pick up something from the path before turning and walking slowly back towards me, taking the handkerchief off his face as he came.

'Well,' said he, 'so much for all for one and one for all.' His face looked sweaty and pale in the reflected glow from a distant street lamp.

'I was knackered,' I told him, 'honest.' But I knew he didn't believe me.

'Chicken,' he said. Then he began to laugh. 'Tell you one thing, she'll need a fresh pair of panties when she gets home, that's if she's wearing any. Christ, did you see her go, the state of her! Talk about the fucking paralympics. She dropped these,' opening his palm to show twenty Silk Cut and a lighter, not cheap, not throwaway, but expensive looking metal. So I had been right, I told myself, about the fags and the lighter. He lit one for himself, and offered me one as well, the closest we would ever get to her, suddenly it came to me, as we stood there watching our smoke funnel straight up into the chill night air.

'Well, what did you think?' he said.

I looked at him. 'About what?'

'Her,' he said, '*it*. What the fuck do you think I meant? Wasn't it the great crack? Seeing her take off like that? That bitch? Wasn't it? Thinking she was for it?'

He started laughing again, and I joined in, reliving that tremendous spurt of exhilaration, the rush of blood, the perfumed scent of her panic wafting back to us. Noonan was right, it *was* great crack, and we rejoiced, re-running the video in our heads, one, I felt certain, we would play back over and over together, many, many times.

Still, there was that one unanswered question, and I put it to him as we retraced our way homewards. 'Why did you stop like that? At the last minute, I mean?'

He looked at me before speaking, cigarette pale in his mouth, a souvenir of our first chase together, along with the Dunhill lighter.

'Sure there'll be plenty other nights. That was only for starters,' as we came out on to the Harrow Road with the first early car speeding past taking some poor wage slaves into work.

Well the rest is history, as the saying has it. Once blooded with the fresh, sweaty smell of real terror in our nostrils we kept on wanting more of the same, as opposed to what we constantly reviewed and talked about, not in the valet's room with old Percy hovering over his silent Singer just feet away, but back in Noonan's place, the empty beer cans piling up under the sink. Of course it may have been because Noonan didn't want Percy listening in. Still we had our own silent code of nods and winks, and Noonan would pass across some photo-spread, as much as to say, *imagine running into that some dark night.* And later, when we were both involved in a big way, he would say, 'Fancy a spot of fishing tonight?' and, 'How's that rod of yours?' and I would reply, 'Just fine. How's yours?'

'Needs a spot of oiling to keep it supple.'

And I could just imagine Percy shaking his weary old noggin in disbelief at two such armchair cases out on an angling expedition together.

As a matter of fact, I recall Noonan one time actually being serious about kitting ourselves out with some of the proper gear, as a cover, he said, and sitting opposite him in that attic room plotting our next outing I watched his eyes take on a glow as he outlined how the scenario should develop. He got me excited as well listening to him, and even when we did go out and nothing happened, not a nibble, I still looked forward to the next time for, 'Don't worry,' he assured me, 'you've got to be patient at this game. You'll see, you'll see.'

Saturday night into Sunday morning was when we went on the prowl, that being the best time, he said, to go tracking careless stragglers who had given up on sighting a cab's yellow light. He talked like that, like we were a couple of big game hunters sniffing the wind for the scent of human unease, only in our case, so far, there was no game, large or small, except maybe the one playing in our own heads.

Then, one night, I sensed a change come over him as we kept heading on further and further down the towpath away from our usual beat. Near Little Venice he started kicking tins in the water, and passing a moored canal boat — it looked unoccupied, even if it was late and no lights showed — he picked up a stone and broke one of the portholes, or whatever they're called. The instant I heard the glass crack I got ready to run, but Noonan stood his ground and, taking aim, calmly blasted two more before strolling on as if nothing unusual had occurred. It was as if we were invincible, like he said we were, invisible, too, in some weird way, and then one night coming back to the room in Willesden after work I found he had carried the invisibility thing a stage further.

'From now on we'll wear these,' he said, pulling some stuff from a carrier bag. War surplus, it looked like, various shades of blotched khaki. But when I saw the balaclavas I realised something far more serious than angling was intended.

'Go on, try it on.'

So I did as I was told, pulling it over my head, with that momentary spasm of blind breathlessness before getting it in place. I sat there looking across at him in the other chair out of my new eye-holes. The thing itself itched, smelling faintly chemical, which I sincerely hoped wasn't Gulf War toxic. Then he pulled his on, both of us facing one another like something out of a video nasty.

'Boo!' he cried, darting forward in his chair, and then we

laughed and laughed at the sight of one another like a couple of Hallowe'en trick or treat freaks.

The following weekend we got set to hit the canal bank trail once more. But after trying on the jungle-jim outfits and seeing ourselves reflected in one another's appearance, hilarious, really, like a couple of extras in some war movie, we went back to our old gear, hooded sweatshirt for me, navy fleece for Noonan, tracksuit bottoms and trainers. Two joggers out for a midnight run seemed to be what we had settled for and was to become our preferred style from then on, the balled-up balaclavas in our pockets the only hard, or, maybe, soft evidence, I suppose, as to our true intentions. But then a word like that, *evidence*, I mean, never really figured much, if at all, in our vocabulary, not at that stage anyhow. As far as we were concerned it applied only to other people, read about, or glimpsed briefly on TV, a blanket over their heads. And, as Noonan kept saying, anybody out there that late in those places was either asking for it, or didn't much care either way if it happened to them anyway. *It* being something which, as yet, was still only this half-fantasy in our heads. At least in mine, it was.

But getting back to that particular night which was different — not because our luck changed, it didn't — but because of Noonan and that thing he did which was not supposed to be part of the plan.

We were on our way home, a moon was out, something of a rarity in NW6, and I was staring up at it, high and buoyant over Kensal Green Cemetery, when Noonan threw away his cigarette and started pulling on his balaclava. I stared at him, then up and down the towpath, which was as bare and bright as noonday. Incidentally, as a footnote, from then on we always consulted a paper in advance to make certain there would be no moon, full, new, or otherwise, that night being the exception, which may well have upset Noonan, for he liked to think he had covered every angle and eventuality.

Well, he started walking faster, and whatever was on his mind stayed a mystery to me, for I could see nothing breaking the line of the path ahead. I don't know why I did it, but I followed suit, dragging on my own balaclava as well, losing half my hearing in the process, the dark wool acting like a set of ear-muffs. Like being submerged in a knitted diver's helmet, I can only describe it, and not all that unpleasant, either, after the first few times. In fact, and here comes another footnote, sometimes we would sit with them on for upwards of an hour, drinking, before going out, some sort of kink, I suppose, you might call it, developing there.

By now Noonan was sniffing the air like a beagle, and just maybe he had some form of extra-sensory thing going for him denied me for, sure enough, off in the distance didn't I see something interrupt the unbroken line of the path. Close to the water's edge it was, a dark shape, but still, not moving.

'Slow down,' I told him, hearing my voice muffled by the woolly helmet, 'it's only some bloke fishing.'

'At this hour? Don't be fuckin' kiddin' yourself.'

'No, no,' I insisted, 'look. See his rod?'

But Noonan kept moving faster, his breath coming hard the way I remembered it that first time. Yet, by now, it had to be perfectly plain to anyone, even him, that I was right, it was some lonely geek with a deranged belief in something live and lurking beneath those dark, polluted waters among the stolen BMXs and supermarket trolleys.

'Calm down,' I told him again, 'take it easy,' getting panicky at being dragged along in his wake like that. And for what? Why?

We were about fifty yards away now and closing fast, and still our angler prey hadn't looked up, not once, head bent over the handle of his rod. Pulled down over his ears was some kind of knitted cap, so maybe his hearing was as impaired as my own. But then, with the force of a slap, it struck me the poor sod was fast asleep, hunched and oblivious to everything, including his float, round and red as a radish, dead upright in the middle of the canal.

Breaking my stride, I allowed Noonan to pull away, and it was like I was viewing something on a screen with the sound turned down, for didn't I see him two-handedly shove the guy into the canal, barely pausing, as if an invisible tape was still waiting to be breasted somewhere off in the distance.

For an instant I froze, watching the poor sucker struggle and splash about in the stinking water, shocked out of his wits, no doubt, for he turned a look on *me*, not after the retreating back of his attacker, and I suppose seeing the balaclava must have put the kibosh on it for him, for he began striking out for the far side in a sort of desperate dog-paddle, rod, line, hook, sinker, all forgotten, in anticipation of something infinitely more deadly.

Luckily a path ran parallel along the far bank, and I watched as he tore off along it trailing streams of water back the way we had come, not that he would have known that, having a kip at the time. He wasn't an old bloke either. He could have put up some sort of fight, if the shock hadn't done for him, a lesson that Noonan and me, we learned from then on. Sudden paralysing surprise, that was the secret. But none of that might have come about, our careers of sexual bogeymen stalling right there and then on that stretch of the Grand Union Canal the way I felt just then.

'Just what the fuck was that all about?' I tackled Noonan the moment he came strolling back, balaclava off now, I noticed. So I tore mine off as well, half a mind to pitch it in the canal.

'This is *our* turf, fuck him,' replies Noonan calm as you please, bending down and rifling through the guy's gear which, of course, was still laid out on the grass verge as if its owner had simply disappeared off the face of the earth, abducted by aliens, maybe. I saw Noonan pick out something small and silvery, a spoon-bait, then pin it to the front of his fleece. He saw me looking at him and grinned, not caring I had caught him indulging his little weakness, for always it had to be a memento with him.

And, incidentally, that very same cache of trophies, lipsticks, earrings, the lighters, the hair-slides, not forgetting, of course, all those panties — oh, a veritable Knickerbox galaxy, which he didn't think I knew about — was to be what he would live to regret when the knock finally came at the door. Then, again, maybe not, him turning out to be the unpredictable, crazy mess he became towards the end.

'I'm not doing this again,' I told him. 'No more canals, you hear me?'

But he just stood there, that silly grin on his face, looking a little pissed as well, as if the dozen lagers we had downed between us earlier had reared up, biting back.

'Okey-dokey, you're the boss, young Downey,' he said, everything right with his world, there and then even taking a pump, his stream arcing out over the dark water. I heard it hit the surface, as satisfying a slash as a man might wish for, and it came to me Noonan was content now he had got whatever it was out of his system, just like the piss, I imagine, sparkling in the moonlight like a diamond loop.

But, for me, there was no such release. It was going to take something a lot more full-blooded than pushing some poor dope into a canal to get me going. I still felt coiled up inside, Noonan humming to himself as though heading home after yet another satisfying night's work.

Fuck you, Noonan, kept running through my head in subtitles, *fuck you.*

Up to now the two of us had been just messing about, I saw that now, putting scares into people like it was Hallowe'en, masks included, and suddenly I had this hot flashback of resentment, recalling what that fat, young bitch had said at the party about me being Noonan's bum-boy. So, time to up the tempo. No more whittling away the hours in our armchairs wading through acres of faked fucking. This new mood I was in, tingling all over with a surge of electric confidence, I suddenly saw my way clear to doing what *I* had to do, with or without Noonan. If he wanted in, okay. If not, too bad.

He would sit watching me under his eyebrows while pretending to leaf through the latest adult photo-spread, but I knew he had detected the change, even old Percy calling me *Mister* Declan now the way he always prefaced Noonan's name, for I was up and downstairs like a yo-yo, keen, energised, bearing armfuls of chemically tainted dry-cleaning while Noonan slumped lower in his chair getting more and more like some hobo who had wandered in off the street to find a cosy burrow for himself. Back at the flat, too, he was really hammering the booze, coming in most evenings with weighted Thresher's carrier bags.

'Do we really have to have that thing up on the wall

THE VALET'S ROOM

there?' one night I put it to him when he was rightly on, referring to the picture of the Sacred Bleeding Heart, of course, the use of the *we* some kind of indicator, I suppose, of our new-found democratic footing, as I saw it.

He looked over the rim of his Tennent's Export at me. 'Bothers you, does it?'

'It fucking well does,' I told him, 'for I don't care to have something like that staring down at me after I've been out getting my end away.'

'Oho,' said he, 'oho, what have we here then?'

'No more fucking canals,' I said. 'That first time was a one-off, a fluke. We should go for the rail network, last trains, that sort of thing. Look, I got a map.'

I still couldn't take it in, me actually talking in this way, but Noonan seemed to relish what he was seeing and hearing, for he perked up in his chair, first time in weeks, setting his Tennent's down on the carpet. And suddenly it was like the two of us were back in business again, but properly, this time, not half-cocked, a vision of rub-a-dub-dub in the open air unfolding in our heads, the map spread before us with all those criss-crossing, coloured lines and stations on it like threaded pop-beads.

Well, we went for the pale grey of the North London Line — it was, after all, the stretch we knew best, at least the first part of it, anyway, Kentish Town, West Hampstead, Cricklewood, paddy land — before it snaked into Hendon, Millhill, Elstree, and beyond that to even leafier parts.

The further out commuter stations with their badly-lit car parks we would save for another time, even some of those Outer Mongolian reaches south of the river with outlandish names like, Riddledown, Gipsy Hill, Ampere Way, Therapia Lane. Noonan came up with the customary cracks about

Cockfosters and Elmer's End and, puncturing more cans, we made a bit of a party of it, drinking to future conquests. I think that was the night we first put on the balaclavas inside the flat.

The rest of that week we indulged in more of the same, drinking, pulling the map back and forth between us like a couple of kids with a shared comic, all the while offering up wilder and wilder forecasts of what we would do together when the call of the great outdoors became too strong to resist.

Finally, on Friday, in the valet's room, Noonan said casually, 'How about some trainspotting this weekend? The weather looks just about perfect, I'd say. Wouldn't you, old bean?'

And just as casually I replied, 'Why not, old bean?'

The next twenty-four hours it was hard to keep anticipation in check, and when the time drew near for off, I don't know about Noonan, but South of the Mason Dicky Line I felt about ready to explode. Last thing I recall as we left the flat together was the shocking newness of that square of wallpaper where old Bleeding Heart Himself used to hang.

Now although Noonan wasn't exactly being serious about the weather forecast, it really did turn out to be one of the hottest nights of the year, with a sweaty, sweltering feel to everything, the trees in the streets breathing out those little syrupy jets at you as you passed. Every window seemed to be thrown wide with rap pumping out, and every pub had an overflow of whooping, closing-time hooligans piling on to the pavement. Noonan and me, we edged past, two individuals with a serious destination and purpose in mind, and although we'd had a right few ourselves before starting out, the sight and sound of all those other piss-artists gulping last orders down gave us this sensation of being apart, superior beings, if you like, off on a quest much too grave to be delayed or jeopardised by joining in .

Now it's a curious thing, but a lot of people, I've often remarked, when they're getting seriously bevvied themselves, seem to expect, or want, everybody else to be the same, and even though they might be pretty far gone, some instinct stays razor-sharp when it comes to sniffing out what they see as disapproval, or even a reluctance to become involved. Why, I don't know — taking it personally, I mean — and as we tried to circumvent The Case Is Altered, a group of merry revellers outside attempted to draw us into the company, all good natured bonhomie, of course, and maybe we had this deadly earnest air about us that constituted a challenge. I mean, two fellow beings actually *sober* on a Saturday night at chucking-out time!

Anyway Noonan shouldered his way past, and one of the guys slopped part of his pint on the pavement, his big beefy dial altering in an instant, and he yelled something after Noonan, in Irish, it sounded like, his companions breaking into this loud donkey bray, Noonan quickening his pace, and me stepping smartly out behind.

'What did your man say back there?' I asked, after we'd left the scene, my recall of my own native lingo being decidedly ropey.

'Called me a fucking Albanian sheep-shagger,' said Noonan. 'Can you imagine, one of those fucking asylum seekers!'

I tried to calm him down for he was bristling with fury.

'Oh, stuff him and his thicko paddy mates,' I told him. 'None of that crowd'll be getting any pussy tonight, that's for sure. Any night, for that matter.'

'You, as well,' says he.

We were threading a maze of streets just off the High Road by this time, a lot of old bangers up on bricks, and a smell of curry hanging in the air.

'Bombay Mix,' Noonan said, sniffing.

But I was determined. 'He called me one as well, did he?'

'Not quite. More who's your wee, ginger-headed, fairy friend. Well, you did ask.'

I stopped dead, and after a second he did as well, looking back over his shoulder.

'Ach, fuck him,' he said, 'sure he's only a gobshite. They all are. Look, are we going to catch this train, or not?' and started walking on again.

Feeling wretched, I fell in behind, seized by this overriding desire to find a shop-window to catch a passing reflection, to see if, maybe, I did possess some sort of camp demeanour, a devastating thought which continued plaguing me. But was there a word in Irish for *fruit* or *fairy*? Albanian, even? I very much doubted it, but the notion still didn't drag me from my pit. Before it had even got going properly, it looked as if the night was ruined for me.

Now although we didn't know it at the time, that night there happened to be this big open-air rock concert on in Camden — it may very well have been Finsbury Park — and the overspill, the exodus, after the last note had sounded, spread out all over North London, people straggling around lost and disorientated, ears still ringing, in a right old state. Somewhat like ourselves for, after missing that last train we had planned on catching to check out the stations and their late-night revellers, somehow, I don't know how, we landed up on Hampstead Heath. The gay section we got clear of pretty damn smartish. The idea of being mistaken for one of *them* causing a cold shiver to run down our backs even though the night was steamier than ever.

We walked faster, becoming more macho by the minute because of it, and then we saw *her*, coming towards us weaving about all over the road, one of those deathly quiet residential neighbourhoods it was, millionaires' row sort of thing, where somebody yelling would barely raise a blind, let alone cause a light to be switched on.

Dragging me into the shadow of a wall Noonan pulled on his ski-mask, the balaclavas having been junked in favour of something more of the moment, designer gear for ravagers, you might say, less stifling, too, although sticking still to track pants and that manky old fleece of his.

Well, we waited until she was right alongside, singing away to herself, she was, those pop anthems still sounding in her ears more than likely.

Then, out of the dark, Noonan said — and I'll never forget his first words, for they sounded so corny, him with his face covered up and all — 'Care for some company, darlin'?' A line from some hoary old black and white Ealing job, Diana Dors, maybe, in one of her early street-walker roles. *How about some company?* I mean, I could hardly believe it. Was that what he actually *said*?

And she must have had much the same mystified reaction for, instead of bolting terror-stricken, as she should have done, she came to a halt, swaying, peering in at the pair of us in our hidey-hole. For a minute we stared back, and then she started fumbling in her shoulder-bag. Noonan seemed to have stopped breathing behind his mask, and all I could do was gawk as she took out a lighter, snapping it clumsily a few times before getting it to fire. At first I thought she wanted to take a closer look at us. But, no, for what did she do next but start waving it about in the air as if she was still at that fucking rock concert.

'Oh, you can't hurry love, no, you can't hurry love,' we heard her sing. I kid you not, *Phil fucking Collins!* Next thing she just waltzes off humming to herself, lighter still held up like a dancing firefly in the gloom of the avenue as if we were a figment of her imagination, or a tableau of statuary placed there by some millionaire type with a warped sense of humour.

And it was that, the thing about us being invisible, worse, irrelevant, that finally got me going, *fuck you, Noonan, for being no help at all*, and I went after her, my Pumas silently slapping the asphalt, feeling this sudden, terrific rush of blood all through me, but, specifically, in the you-know-where region, up to now marshmallow soft, which, in turn, gave me this really weird flash vision of me sprinting along this deserted road after midnight naked like a pole-vaulter with a hard-on instead of a nine foot caber out in front.

Now that first electric moment of contact can be the most exciting of all. You're on this knife-edge, like which way will it go kind of thing? Will it be the paralysed, catatonic thing, or the biting, kicking, scratching, screaming blue murder thing? Either way you must never, ever hesitate. Grab hold hard, hand over mouth.

None of this I knew at the time, but it came to me instinctively, you might say, like a device just ticking away waiting to go off, although detonation was still some distance off. Well, that's not exactly true. Sometimes it takes place

THE VALET'S ROOM

right there and then. Bang, you've shot your load before things get going.

That night I happened to be lucky, although, looking back, why do I get the notion Noonan might not have been, even though he kept up his gung-ho attitude throughout. And if he was faking it, well, he could have fooled me, just as he'd never be any the wiser, I guess, if I was the one to peak prematurely.

The thing was after I grabbed hold of her and she went limp as a leaf on me — one of the catatonic variety, it appeared — he seemed to get his act together, roaring up and taking over, as if that bit of bad period dialogue back at the wall had been a mere verbal hiccup best forgotten but still something to be redressed. Perhaps, excessively so, for when he got up close, the way he went for her seemed more than over the top, especially as by this stage she was like a sack of spuds. And things then went even more ballistic, for after manhandling our victim across to a patch of woodland between two of those big, silent, white houses, the crazy fucker produced a knife from nowhere holding the flat of the blade against her cheek.

Now I wouldn't want to give the impression I'm some sort of misunderstood victim figure. I know what I am, a danger to women. I accept that. A lot of bad things I've done in my time, but Noonan, with his passion for cold steel and ex-army weaponry, along with handy-sized hanks of washing-line and gaffer tape, all of that to me always seemed more to do with certain screwed up Boy Scout tendencies than being part of a team taking their night time manoeuvres seriously.

Next thing, 'Make a sound and you're dead,' I heard him say. More B-feature dialogue, even though it was obvious she was out of it. The state of her she might well have been tripping, acid, E, magic mushrooms, which would account for her not seeming to care what was happening to her.

Well, what followed I still don't consider to be what other, most people usually associate with forced sex. The actual, well, *physical* part is not something I intend, or need to spell out. Anyway the real bang comes later, as far as I'm concerned, when I get to re-run it back in my head, sort of saving it up for afters, and if that makes me some sort of perve, well, so be it, let the head-doctors make of it what they will.

To be honest the actual *doing* part is invariably messy anyway, so I shut myself off as if everything that's going on is distanced, something taking place between two total strangers, which I suppose it is, really. I mean nobody's introduced anyone. *Like, I'm Declan, and your name is — ? Oh, well, that makes it all right then, let's just get on with it, shall we?* In all of this I can't speak for Noonan, for it was like he was a stranger, too, the sight of his snowy backside probably the most shocking part of the whole episode, for I kept thinking of that dazzling patch of wallpaper where the Sacred Heart picture used to hang as if the two were connected in some weird way.

Well, when it came my turn, in my head I interposed this double pin-up of Dolores Lopez, Mexican Chilli Pepper of the Month, between me and Noonan's leavings. Not that that part bothered me unduly. Later it did, and I started taking over pole position, to coin a phrase, something which Noonan himself had no real argument with. Secretly I think he preferred it that way, getting off more on the S.A.S. fantasies, all that gagging and tying-up lark — a waste of precious time, in my opinion — than the actual thing itself.

The business with the knives was also a worry, for he

would keep on producing some little edged number — well, not so little — as time went on, something I had to live with, for these were certain things we never discussed, like, for instance, the delicate matter of whether we actually managed to shoot our load or not. In Noonan's case I had these serious doubts, for maybe he was still secretly saving it up for Ms Right, as he used to joke in the valet's room. The noises I'd hear I couldn't help feeling might have been staged for my benefit. Even, maybe, for that third party herself.

Anyway, it got to the stage where we rarely spoke at all, before, during, or even afterwards, two dedicated professionals going about their silent business. Noonan did it his way, I did it mine, and, of course, it was inevitable we drifted apart, getting more like lone rangers than two halves of a double-act, something which would have been unthinkable in those early days, nights, too, spent in each other's company thick as two thieves in the valet's room, Utopia House, as well, with His Nibs staring down with that long-suffering, dear-oh-dearie-me expression on his sorrowful mug.

Still we had both broken our duck, that was the main thing, even though it had turned out not to be the mind-blowing experience we thought it would be. Next time, proper out and out resistance was what was called for, mixed with raw fear, biggest turn on of all. No more that sack of spuds business. And it did become more the rule, as opposed to that first druggy exception.

Now we never kept a score or tally, which I understand is customary in our line of work — the nearest we'd have got to that would be the contents of Noonan's trophy drawer, I suppose. But we must have done about a dozen jobs, maybe more, switching rail routes back and forth, the map with its cross-hatching of magic marker colours repaying all those hours of patient study, outer London after dark becoming our playground, all those desolate stations with their unlit cinder paths leading to empty car parks past bushy cuttings. Sometimes I wonder what it must be like taking a train to some of those same destinations in broad daylight. Not near as exciting. No drying of the mouth, no tremor in the legs, followed by that lift in circulation the moment *she* emerges from the underpass heading for the lonely car, or the shortcut past the allotments.

Well we must have been doing it for near enough a year before one of the local rags picked up on it, putting two and two together, or one and one, or just plain one, for the weird thing was they only mentioned a single perpetrator, this solitary, white, serial molester criss-crossing North London. My first reaction was, how could they, meaning all those women, get it so wrong? Why lie about a thing like that? A bout of paranoia then kicked in, mixed with resentment at not being given credit, for it had to be pretty obvious Noonan was the one making the papers with that fucking great commando knife of his, This Man Will Kill If Not Caught, one of the catchier banner headlines.

Incidentally, later, I got to find out, all along, he, Noonan had kept a scrapbook. *A scrapbook!* However the more I pondered the more I put the sheer amnesiac confusion of it down, not to some ploy by the police to flush us out through vanity — mine, I imagine — but to the state our victims happened to be in at the time, not simply terrorised shitless, but plain, ordinary pissed, or stoned, for just, maybe, Noonan and me, we did sort of home in on the returning, late-night, reveller type, hopefully building up in time to riskier game.

And, pursuing that thought, ever notice how they never seem to come out with it in court, or mention it in the papers, about being zonked, I mean? Always this image of Sunday schoolteacher sober rectitude, like the demure, little, black number they wear for the jury's benefit. Just as your friendly neighbourhood mugger never turns up for his day in court in a Tommy hoodie and Air Nikes, oh, no, but a brand new whistle, white shirt and tie like some trainee accountant. I'm not asking for dispensation here. No way. Just merely trying to set the record straight, that's all.

Well, the week Noonan and me officially went our separate ways — I'd got a new job in another hotel, one of the big Thistle chain in Kensington, back to porterage again, but with accommodation thrown in this time — we decided on one final, farewell, partnership sortie. Without ever putting it in so many words we both knew it was to be solo flying from now on, him starting to believe his own newspaper cuttings and all, and me resenting the fact I'd become the invisible man, I suppose. To tell the truth, my heart — dick, too — wasn't really in, or up for it.

Old Percy had just given me this little going-away present, sort of an Indian charm thing on a chain, some god or other who'd look after me, he said, if I always wore it close to my chest. It felt cold there, but inside I was experiencing a warm and nostalgic glow for the old cocoa-coloured bugger. I felt sorry to be leaving him on his own with Noonan and having all that work to do, not that my presence had ever made much difference, the foot-high welter of dirty magazines a reminder of just how little I had contributed.

'Let's give Bushey a go,' I said to Noonan as we set off.

He looked at me suspiciously, for we'd shivered there a good three hours one Autumn night without a sniff of anything female, just a bunch of last train, yuppie-type suits, drunk, screeching and breaking wind as they passed us in our hide in the buddleia bushes. I was secretly hoping, you see, for another washout, so we could go out on an uneventful note, and Noonan went for it.

'Okay,' he said, and all the dozen stops or so from Willesden Junction never spoke another word, just stared out the window at the receding gardens and the occasional lighted back bedroom window.

Stalled between stations once, we had this miraculous sighting, someone undressing close to the glass, slow, provocative, as if to music, while knowing full well she had this train-load of punters avid for her striptease. Black, quite young, oh, a right, dusky little temptress, the pallor of her bra and pants shocking against those skin tones, and, finally, when they did flutter off, for a slow count of ten she stood silhouetted there before pulling the blind down. That was the night we felt convinced we just had to strike lucky, simply had to, for hadn't we been vouchsafed a vision which kept on glowing inside our heads long after like a long-life lightbulb?

Of course we should have known from experience nothing would happen. How many times does the penny have to drop? For the higher you get your expectations up, as well as that anticipatory hard-on, the bigger the come-down. Just like life in general. After that what I always did was empty my mind, tempting fate, if you like, and in a lot of cases, bingo, it actually seemed to work.

Like that night, unfortunately, for creeping along by the

side of my former accomplice in crime, while yearning for my comfortable bed and a good night's kip instead of shivering out here in the armpits of suburbia, what did I hear but the unmistakable, approaching clack of high heels on the chill air.

Inside I felt like groaning as Noonan yanked me into the bushes edging the station path. But there was another reason for my dismay, unconnected with my desire to go home that night a virgin. Something ominously self-confident, aggressive, even, about the sound, told me, forget it, this one was not for us. In a year, maybe. But not yet.

The heels came closer — steel-tipped, quite possibly capable of delivering some serious injury — but already Noonan had gone into his hard-breathing routine, ski-mask on, straining at the leash. I could feel him, *it*, going right through me, then out the other side leaving me limp. Something else, as well, for a branch was digging into my cheek-bone. I wondered how long I could stand it.

She was nearly upon us by now. Already I could smell her scent, Bond Street expensive, and I visualised her car, too, backed up to the wire-mesh fence ready to cough at her approach and the touch of that magic little key-ring in her pocket. Porsche? Saab convertible? And I had this sudden, crippling attack of social inferiority, for no way would a rich bitch like this ever lie down and roll over like some zonked-out, hearth-rug puppy. No way.

I touched Noonan's arm. Hard as iron. Rambo's arm. Like trying to reason with a heat-seeking missile.

And then there she was, for a second glimpsed through the filigree of leaves, bare-headed, tall, swinging an umbrella, one of those corporate, logoed jobs with a deadly, six-inch, metal tip. The pain from the branch digging into me had become too much, so I raised a hand to brush it aside, and, damn me, if the thing didn't snap in half with a dry crack that sounded like a fucking firework going off.

I heard the footsteps falter, then stop, and a voice demand, 'Is anyone there?' bold and patrician as you like. 'If there is, you don't frighten me, whoever you are, you pathetic pervert,' and it was that last bit that shot a spitting, growling Noonan from his lair, while at the same time pushing me further back in. Even so I had a clear view of everything taking place, the pair of them clashing head-on, her whack, whack, whacking him with the rolled-up brolly before he managed to get his hands about that pale, gorgeous throat of hers.

'You fucking piece of shit!' I heard her gasp, as finally she went under, the words shocking in their profanity, but at the same time, supremely arousing, too, with that accent of hers, for I had been right in my surmise, this was top totty, pure *Jennifer's Diary* guest-list material.

They were rolling about in the loose cinders — I could hear the noise they made, louder than anything so far — then I caught the glint of serrated steel and Noonan's voice, low and strangely hoarse, order, 'Give it up, or I'll slash your fucking face!' And at that she went limp, resistance melting, as if into the path below, Noonan's dark bulk on top, and he seemed to solidify as well, and in that instant I was deep inside his head knowing exactly how he must be trying to work out that next move for himself, yet not taking too long over it. I don't know if I can explain this or not, I know it has to sound pretty weird, but it's as if it's happening to you, the rape, I mean, not the other way around, almost, like, *do it, do it, do it to me.*

From my thorny thicket I could make out a glimpse of bare, silk-stockinged thigh, with one expensive looking patent shoe kicked off nearby, and suddenly I got this unexpected touch of the horn, imagining what it must be like further up, rare, untouchable, for toffs' hands only.

Then I heard her say, 'What's the matter, Seamus, not able to get it up?' and into my head floated the memory of another voice, that other tennis-playing cow in the hotel that time, identical intonation and attitude. *Go for it, Noonan, old son, go for it, give her one for me.* And as he finally started bumping up and down, safety-catch off at last, I saw her reach up and pull at his ski-mask, raking his bared cheek with her painted nails.

Noonan roared like a wounded beast and raised the knife. A light from one of the station lamps caught it hovering there, but before it could fall like an avenging brand, I burst from my hidey-hole, scratching face and hands in my haste, bolting from the scene, half-hoping, I suppose, I might just be the distraction to divert the inevitable, but still the act of a coward, a turntail.

Well, I got back to my bare boxroom in the hotel at six in the morning, just an hour before I was due to present myself at the front desk in my new maroon and dove grey uniform with the epaulettes and gold braided loops, like a boy hussar, ridiculous looking, really, but it was that sort of establishment, poncey as hell after the other place.

On the way down I took a detour to the boiler-room and stuffed a bag containing all my clothes from the night before, ski-mask, sweatshirt, pants, trainers, the lot, into one of the furnaces. It probably saved my bacon. Well, I know it did, for when Noonan was collared — in my heart I knew it had to happen, that crazy, mixed-up psycho with his knives and trophy drawer — the DNA did for him, that and the ski-mask he'd left behind, which they traced back to this mail-order place in Leicester he'd sent a cheque away for. A fucking *cheque!*

The Bushey bird's name was Jennifer Combe-Nairn, a City high-flyer, father a judge, boyfriend a stockbroker, so the police pulled out all the stops on that one, forget all those other dozy cows, half of whom never bothered reporting what happened to them anyway, as it transpired. Noonan's smear results were under the posh bird's nails, on the mask, and the tip of her golfing umbrella, but not, *not* inside her, so I guess I had been right all along, all show and firing blanks, and when the time came she picked him out of a line-up, bang, first time, even though he'd spruced himself up along with a number three haircut.

Naturally, they came looking for me. I mean nobody's that stupid, even the police, and at least one of those dopey dames must have reported a two man team somewhere along the line, it stands to reason. They questioned old Percy as well, I found out. Christ, he must have been petrified. Probably thought he'd be deported back to Bangladesh. But, as I understood it, he gave me what amounted to a verbal alibi, clean-cut young country lad, all that, but subsequently developing a stutter, yes, a full-blown stammer, which happened in Paddington Green where they take all the paddies. Nearly three days and nights of it, Messers Nice and Nasty taking it in turns, so like the TV I began hallucinating it really was *The Bill* and not that breeze-block, walled room, one metal table, one metal chair, one full to overflowing ashtray.

A theory grew in my head it was Noonan they were really after because of the judge's daughter, not the other peeping Tom in the bushes. He could wait. He wasn't going anywhere.

I remember the headlines when they came out — Beast of Bushey Caged, Photograph — with a blurry shot of his nibs being hustled to a waiting car, filthy old fleece pulled over his head, an inch of pallid beer gut showing. According to the paper he had confessed to fifteen other attacks, so maybe he was trying to fatten his dossier, that scrapbook of his, although I doubt very much whether he would be allowed to hang on to it in Pentonville.

Right now, you might say, my life is on hold. Maybe the police are just toying with me, who knows, waiting for me to crack, before coming beating on the door. Or, maybe, it will turn out the other way round. Who knows?

Noonan and me, we made a pact, I remember, on one of those nights when we sat guzzling beer into the early hours in Utopia House with our bank robber balaclavas on. If one of us was ever caught, we pledged over the Tennent's Super, he would never grass on the other no matter what. Agreed? Agreed. Of course we never believed it possible, getting caught, I mean. After all we were the Deadly Duo, The Pussy Patrol, The Valet Room Violators. We were, weren't we?

Around about the same time, in fact it might well have been that same night, I also recall him saying, 'Remember that old Tampax I put in your tea that time? That first day? Well, I've news for you, it *was* a used one.'

And the pair of us laughed and laughed until the bitter lager bubbles came frothing back down our nose like foaming surf.

Rancho Notorious

Friday night was when they came riding into town together in their old jeep — not one of your souped-up yuppie wagons with names like Cherokee, Shogun or Pajero, but a proper rust and dung-coloured, army surplus heap — parking it in the same spot across the street before coming in to have their meal. And for a good minute and a half the engine would cough spasmodically like a dying beast, and Sammy Junior, whose father ran the garage and filling-station out on the Lough Road, said retrograde ignition was the problem, at which we would yawn wearily like the jaded junior Rat Packers we persuaded ourselves we were, instead of three out-of-school-uniform, final year, sad cases, knee to knee in the back booth of The Cross Fish, some genius having named it that, not on account of the marine monstrosity on the tin sign outside, but because it sat on the corner where Castle and Market Street converged. But the joke, if there ever was one, had long since run its course, Hostile Haddock, Peevish Pilchard, Crusty Cod, even Exasperated Eel, all having had their day, and so we sat there, spinning out our

Fantas and one shared plate of chips, watching the street beyond for the two women to appear.

Really, I suppose, I was the one, little old me, who had infected the others with an unhealthy interest in the pair, encouraged by our shared boredom as the long summer nights stretched away outside as though we were somewhere inside the Arctic Circle — Thule, or Narvik, say — instead of dull east Antrim, the drawn bedroom curtains red like the glare from a furnace and all that damnably busy bird life refusing to cry off.

During the day I was out delivering mail, a holiday relief job my old man had swung for me because of his connections in the local Masonic. Hedley Porter, the postmaster, was one of the Lodge's higher-ups, and so it was a case of those good old guys with rolled up trouser-legs looking out for one of their own, a connection I wasn't too proud or happy about, but money was money, and I enjoyed pushing that red post bike up and downhill whilst checking out some of the weirder life-forms holed up in our back country parts.

Which is how I came across Marian and her friend the poultry instructor.

'For clucks sake how do you instruct chickens?' was Frankie's reaction when first I delivered that piece of information.

'No, no, you don't understand,' I told him, 'she's a lecturer at the agricultural college, and get a load of this, you'll never guess what her name is.'

'Henrietta? Hetty?'

'Robina. Get it? Marian? Robina?'

Sammy looked blank. Obviously he didn't, never would, or could. But our Frankie did.

'Maid Marian and Robina, eh? Well, don't just sit there, give, give ... '

Which is how I came to be involved in the lives of two perfect strangers with such dire consequences, one large, florid, wild-haired, the other brunette, petite, our own ducktails close together over the worn Formica in the back booth of our local chippy, and me relaying back all those reports laced with pure speculation and a degree of malice hard to comprehend at this stage.

Looking back, I realise I did a terrible thing to those two. There's no excuse for it, and all I can do is tell the story as it happened, even though by saying so I can just see Frankie's face right now, as well as hear his voice. *Oh, ring for the Samaritans, please!* But he was involved as well. Sammy, too, in his own way.

Each morning at six, sticky-eyed and yawning, I would show up at the post office and go through to the back room where the mail was sorted on a big, bare, deal, divided table. Gerry Mulrine was already there up to his skinny elbows in the daily avalanche of letters, packets and tubed newsprint, the heavier items having been sorted the night before and sitting to the side in a graded pile, and as usual he caught me glancing over at the stack. I couldn't help myself. Bad enough a ton of parcels in the front carrier of the bike when the weather was fine, but a total pain in the wet, protecting all that porous brown paper, oilskin cape spread out in front of me like some pregnant woman, for frig's sake.

Eyes narrowed against the rising smoke of his first Sweet Afton of the day, Gerry could afford to be smug. It wasn't hard to tell he resented me. For starters, he had been covering the entire territory in his crimson van for a decade on his own before I showed up and, second, I was everything he loathed, yet another educated Prod sprog with all the attendant privileges he and his sort had always been denied as he saw it. He called me 'the young scholar'.

'And how's our young scholar this morning then?' he'd greet me, keeping his voice down, for old Hedley could be heard bumping about next door like some short-sighted bear in pyjamas and slippers still, under a tweed overcoat despite the August heat.

Normally I would say nothing, waiting patiently until he had finished the sorting, then snapping rubber bands around the thick wads of correspondence. Beside his paper mountain my own puny foothill looked pathetic, thinly scattered on the bare wood of one of the remaining three compartments.

At one time a quartet of postmen had pedalled off in separate directions each morning before modernity arrived in the form of a new Morris van from Cowley making them and their push-bikes redundant. All except Gerry Mulrine, that is, who had been kept on, contradicting all those strongly held beliefs of his concerning religious discrimination. Ever since he had been waiting for someone in authority to rectify their mistake and separate him from his pride and joy, despite the hated royal crest and livery on the side.

'Another parcel for our two Dolly Sisters, I see. Sure, now, mustn't it be grand to be into all that knowledge in such a tremenjous way.'

He really did talk like that, in that corny Barry Fitzgerald fashion, being a blow-in from Cavan or Monaghan originally, or some such down-country place. Books, he was referring to, of course, books, their hard, angular outlines biting through the buff folds of their wrapping, and the dread of my day because of their bulk and weight.

'Och, sure, now, the three of youse must have a lot in common discussing literature and the like.'

'That's true,' I'd say, 'for it's good to talk to somebody half-educated for a change.'

That was pushing it, but he had me nettled, and so the lie sprang easily to my lips, and from that moment on the fantasy became set, me breaking my route over tea, cake and animated discourse with our two lady friends up on Carntall Hill, the reality being very different, of course, for I'd only ever made eye contact and exchanged a word or two, if that, with the big bushy-haired one once so far.

In a boiling sweat, for their lane was long and twisting with a knobbly flint spine which made riding up or down it near impossible, I'd presented myself at the blistered front door, a clamour of dogs greeting me, which was unusual, for I had become accustomed to them lying in wait in the open in the yard, or behind a hedge in ambush, like the collie I'd grown to fear who had nipped me once, twice, then a third time for luck, coming at me under a gate, low-bellied and snakeish, with what I took at the time to be a fawning expression in his eyes.

A shouted command rang out, the barking dying instantly, and the door opening a fraction, I caught a glimpse of this fierce eye drilling me. Then the door swung wide and the big one herself was standing there, hands on broad, corduroy-covered hips, and I felt sure I picked up a damp doggy scent off her, or perhaps it came from the dark cave at her back.

'You're not the usual man.'

Now hearing her voice like that for the first time was something of a shock, the accent, posh, ultra-English, at startling variance with the rest of her, hair a flaming, ragged bush, clothes a disgrace, even if it was out in the sticks where nobody was expected to dress up. But this was *down* with a vengeance, and I found my gaze fastened with a terrible intensity on a saucer-sized hole in the front of her old army sweater through which could be seen a pink, freckled, fleshy bulge.

All the while she kept watching me, raw hands planted on both hips. She wore a man's leather belt, the buckle one of those Western replica jobs. Colt 45.

Without even glancing at it, she took the parcel from me. 'The regular man's unwell, I take it? Will he be away long?'

'No, no, I'm to be your postman all summer,' I told her, the word *postman* sounding like a bare-faced lie.

'What's your name?' she asked, and without thinking, 'Dino,' I said.

'Really? Italian, are you?'

'No, no. It's just a nickname. It's Brian. Brian Ritchie.'

'Yes, you do look more like a Brian somehow. Well, Brian, I'm sure you must have an absolute mountain of other deliveries to attend to,' and with that she closed the door on me, chill, impersonal, as though I was some tiresome, door to door salesman.

Wheeling the old bike, a lot lighter, even skittish now, down the lane again, I heard the clatter of a typewriter start up behind me, in our particular neck of the woods as exotic as a *cicada*, say, and around the first bend I stopped to listen. Whoever was pounding those keys was going at it as though making up for lost time. Time squandered on me, I decided, and for a good five minutes I hung on, head tilted sideways, waiting and listening for some respite. But none came, and the more I craned the more my curiosity burned as to exactly what was being hammered out back there on a seemingly endless roll, as I imagined it, the words spattering the paper in a frenzy.

The rest of that particular day I couldn't get my mind off the business with the typewriter, even visualising the actual instrument, one of those antique black monsters it had to be, totally un-portable. There was one in the post-office gathering dust, a Corona, and sometimes when no one was around I would lightly brush the cool discs of its QWERTY keys, fantasising I was the writer I always dreamed of becoming, the one who'd caused all that stink with his best-seller exposing the scabby underbelly of small town life. Such were the notions occupying my head as, gradually, I emptied the canvas satchel on my back. It smelt of Mulrine's foul foreign cigarettes as if to remind me I only had it on loan. Okay by me, for he could have it back, and his little empire along with it, as soon as September came around.

That was at the start, of course, those first weeks when the sun shone on my face, then my back, then my front again, as the route kept changing course like a restless snake. The early morning stretch was the easy part, making deliveries to the labourers' cottage just beyond town, electricity bill reminders and pool coupons, for the most part, always women answering the door, the men off at work or, more and more these days, hunched in front of a bluish TV screen waiting for the dole Giro to arrive, for it didn't take me long to get to know what was inside those windowed envelopes without having to go to the actual trouble of opening them.

Postcards, always, I read on principle, for if people would put their thoughts down on the back of some seaside view for all the world to see why shouldn't I have first look, most of the messages, as expected, banal in the extreme, food, drink the temperature of the sea, my room, yeah, yeah, yeah. With one exception. The typewriter woman. Hers arrived from exotic locations like Salzburg, Madrid, Portofino, even

Buenos Aires, one time. With the bike propped against a tree, I would sit in the shade with my sandwiches and flask of tea and imagine who Bunny might be, or Guy, or Sholto.

'Marian, old thing, why don't you drag yourself out of that awful damp bog-hole of a place and join us where the red wine flows and the swallows never leave for Capistrano. You'll never guess who's staying at the next villa. Suffice to say, it's one of our very own minor royals, and he and his current *inamorata* still haven't been rumbled by the paparazzi. One swift phone call to one of those dreadful red tops and we could afford to stay on here indefinitely. Love to Robbie. And your gorgeous self. As ever, Sholto.'

Shit, I thought, what if Mad Marian is somebody famous herself. What if she's holed up in that old farmstead back there, her and her companion, on the run from some shocking secret in their past. *Her* past, more like, for the poultry instructor didn't look as though she could ever have had one.

For a week after that I spread the mail for Prospect House, as it was called, on the grass under that old beech tree, turning each letter and card over for clues, holding them up to the light, even sniffing like a bloodhound — some of the letters were scented, the lilac ones, certainly — but afraid to go the whole hog and open the envelopes. What you did was slide a pencil in, then roll it under the flap to loosen the gum, and provided you were patient and careful enough no one would ever know. This, I discovered, when I once intercepted an exam result before my old man could get to it, specs down over his nose and a, 'What's all this, then, young fellow-me-lad?' But at least I had time to get my story straight, or one maybe not quite so implausible sounding.

Sometimes, too, there would be periodicals and magazines

which I would squeeze, then slide from their wrappers to read while I took my lunch break. For the most part these were for the other one, Miss Robina Carruth, according to the name on the stickers, but I quickly tired of *Poultry World* and something equally riveting, *Game Birds Digest*. Obviously she lived for her work, that one, and sprawled on my mossy carpet I contemplated the nature of their relationship, Ms Wild And Woolly and little Ms Wyandot. What had drawn them together in the first place? More to the point, what kept them in that rambling old ruin? There was a gaping hole in my detective work, for not once had I seen them in each other's company.

That was before they started turning up at The Cross Fish for their regular Friday night cod and chips. The Marian one also ordered mushy peas, a curry dip, a double round of bread and butter and a mug of tea, milk, two sugars. Her friend merely pecked at her plate, which struck Frankie and me as hilariously appropriate somehow.

One boring day when not even a single holiday postcard had turned up in the pouch to break the monotony, even 'Robbie's' feathered fowl magazine was overdue, I fell to temptation and opened one of Marian's parcels. This one had already taken some abuse between Mount Pleasant Sorting Office in London and ourselves, so the covering was half-off it anyway — another book, obviously — and a section of the jacket could be seen through a tear in the manila wrapping, some sort of Wild Western illustration, half a guy and the back end of a horse showing, title obscured.

For a long time I studied it trying to get a clue as to what kind of volume it might be. Too slim to be serious — cheap paperback fiction, almost certainly — and then it came to me where I'd seen the type before. Crikey, it had to be one of those pulp cowboy yarns, all gunplay and bar-room brawling, Sammy's dad was addicted to, flattened on the workbench while he tinkered with somebody's alternator or carburettor. After he'd read them they finished up in the brazier in the yard, too wrecked and oil-stained to be of use to anyone. Sammy told us he got through three, sometimes four a week. Some sort of tumbleweed junkie was Sammy's old man, although to look at him you'd never suspect it.

For a moment sprawled there with the ants starting to get to me, I thought I might have somehow got the wrong packet and the wrong address. But, no, this was definitely for Mad Marian, all right. I could also see part of a covering letter, and carried away by curiosity and boredom, I loosened the knots with my teeth, unwrapping the book.

Sure enough, it was a trashy Western novelette, complete with strong-jawed cowpoke on the cover staring off into the misty distance, while his pinto pony seemed equally intent on something the artist had left out. Maybe the clue was in the title, *West of the Pecos*. But was the Pecos a river — or a mountain range? Maybe both? I couldn't remember, that's if I ever really knew anyway.

The author was an Al Cody, but I was much more interested in the letter than what was between the covers, for already I knew what to expect there.

'Dear Marian,' it read, 'please find enclosed the new Al Cody. I hope you like the jacket. We've been able to splash out a little more than usual on an illustrator. Sales of the last have been a lot better than expected, and I'm pushing our accounts department to get your cheque out to you asap. Don't forget we need the typescript of *Empty Saddles* by the end of the month.

Yours, Jonathan.

PS I'm forwarding some fan letters, one of which requested a photograph! Let me know if there's a problem about getting stuff in and out via your local Pony Express. In your last letter you mentioned something about a new 'carrier'. I trust there's no problem delivery-wise. If there is, a word in the right quarter is always a distinct possibility. J.'

Some wiseacre once said you should never pry into other people's correspondence, for if you do you don't know what you might find there, something, perhaps, you'd rather not care to see in black and white, oh, infinitely more deadly than the spoken word any day. Discovering someone I thought might have been a proper writer, a real one, was instead the worst form of despised hack was bad enough, but to have that same old tart actually complaining about me was just too much.

There had to be a certain irony, of course, in that right at that moment I happened to be scanning her mail. I suppose if I'd been a lot older I might have appreciated the subtlety. I know my late, illustrious namesake certainly would, with a shrug of those beautifully tailored sharkskin shoulders, and a rueful twinkle in his dark Italian eyes, all the while shaking ice cubes around in a highball glass. But that was where fantasy foundered. Try as I might I couldn't make the necessary leap between the real me and my dead hero. Still smarting, I re-wrapped the package, then climbed back in the saddle.

Sure enough when I got to Prospect House — already the name was beginning to sound like the worst form of affectation — the clack of the typewriter greeted me long before the dogs did, the sound only rubbing salt in the wound, *Empty Saddles* racing towards its banal conclusion in a blaze of gunfire and men in dark hats biting the dust. I wondered if there would be any love interest, then thought, probably not. Al Cody would be more interested in action of the hearty he-man variety than any lovey-dovey stuff. Just like his readers.

My head was buzzing with all this when the door opened and Al Cody, as I now knew her, appeared. Same army surplus sweater and baggy brown cords, no change there. I saw her looking at the packet in my hand, and right away already knew she was blaming me, so like an idiot I blurted out something about it arriving in that condition from Paddington, England, and she gave me this funny stare as if by mentioning the postmark I had somehow breached her privacy.

Things then got even worse, when she said, 'Well we'll never really know, will we, just how, or where it did happen,' and jumping in again, I told her, 'Sure, it doesn't look too damaged. The book, I mean.'

Slowly she put the packet behind her back. She had these menacing blue eyes that seemed to bore right through you, unwavering, as if waiting for your own to go shifty first, which, of course, naturally, they did.

I remember her parting words. 'It *was* September you did say Mr Mulrine would be back?' and pierced by that word *mister*, all I could do was nod, mumble and retreat, hands gripping the sticky rubber grips on the bars of the bicycle.

Bumping down the lane I kept waiting for the typewriter to resume, but for some reason it didn't this time. Perhaps she was tearing the wrapping from her latest opus to breathe in the intoxicating scent of fresh print. Certainly it would have been what *I* would have done if it was me, but then she wasn't, was she, so I decided then she had to be way beyond that stage by now, after how many pot-boilers, was it? A dozen? More, maybe, given the appetites of readers like Sam's old man for such trash, and suddenly, right there, I halted the bike, wondering if by some remote chance he had ever read any Al Cody, and if so would he have remembered either the author or a title anyway. And, in turn, this got me even more intrigued at the prospect of strolling into our local library and, straight-faced, asking for the latest Al Cody, for there was a row of such things next to the thrillers and romance section, knowing all the while the author lived not a million miles away. Considerably less, in fact.

Needless to say I was bursting to share all this with my compadres in The Cross Fish, well, Frankie, anyway. I could just see him hunched there in his corner seat, that bored expression on his thin face that said, *come on, amaze me, just this once*, and so I would unfold my tale, spinning it out like Rumpelstiltskin, for, after all, that was my prerogative. But then I started getting second thoughts — Frankie again, basically — deciding to hold back until something meatier came along. And even if it didn't, I'd still wait, for I didn't want him to start yawning with that other, *call that hot gossip*, look on his face that just shrivelled you up, and then I thought of the woman again, and resentment really dug its claws into me.

It was shortly after that the two started showing up at our local chippy, the place always empty at that hour, except for the three of us, on a Friday, the town drunks preferring The Peking Flower and abusing Mr. Lee and his three young daughters.

So, there we were, sitting lost in thought, another long

summer evening stretching ahead like a prison sentence. A leisurely walk down by the shore, followed by another up towards the castle, but no short cuts through the old Dissenters' graveyard, for that's where the Junior Head Staggers, as we called them, hung out with their boomboxes and cans of Strongbow and bottles of raspberry Hooch ending up recycled against the church wall. They hated us, and we feared them. And whenever they did come swaggering out of the Loughview Estate into town in a pack in their whiter-than-white Tommy Hilfigers and box-new Nikes, hair gelled forward in that painstakingly separated, juvenile, Roman, rat's tail style of theirs, we would sink down low in our booth and suspend our breathing until they moved on.

Of course they were aware we were in there, and would raise a passing array of middle fingers just to let us know they knew it. Sammy, the only one of us with any backbone for possible rough stuff — Frankie and me being much too refined and cerebral for any of that — would redden, clenching those big motor mechanic fists of his, genetically inherited from his old man, as we saw it, Frankie's being, you might say, a bit like his mother's, who was a schoolteacher who played the piano and collected glass animals. Which left me with mine, neither one thing nor the other, my old man being strictly middle of the road with paws to match.

Well, Mad Marian and her friend came in, the big bushy-haired one heading straight for a table near the door, planking her massive rear end down with a thud that rattled all the condiments in the place. Unfortunately I was sitting facing her and didn't know whether to pretend I hadn't seen her, ridiculous, really, come to think of it, or wait for some form of acknowledgement on her part. There seemed an equal degree of humiliation in either scenario, and I began to sweat sensing Frankie sense my unease, while Sammy gawped, only worsening the situation.

Concentrating on the plate in the middle of the table, I speared one, then two fries, until Frankie said, 'Hey, leave some for the rest of us, peasant!' and I could see the poultry instructor's slender back stiffen. Something nervy there, skittish, ready to run, unlike her large-boned friend who'd exchanged her usual military-style pullover for a newer-looking one in navy cable stitch. This had to be her idea of dressing up, I suspected. The other one had gone in for jeans and a junior lumberjack shirt.

They sat there obviously waiting for someone to serve them, laughable in a place like The Cross Fish, but eventually, give her her due, plump Lorraine who had been tending the friers behind the counter approached their table. We stared at her in shock for we'd never seen her like this before, and then Mad Marian ordered for the pair, voice booming out, rich and unrestrained, while we leaned that fraction closer craning to catch the younger one's tone, for she had definitely attempted some sort of soft comment, later described by Frankie as more of a coo than a cluck, for he really was hammering the hen-run imagery by this stage.

It was hard not to listen to them eat, so quiet had the place become. Even the normally boiling maelstrom in the chip pans seemed to have subsided, and Lorraine, ice-lolly stick in the corner of her mouth, leaned forward on the zinc counter gaping unashamedly as though two members of royalty had somehow just strolled in to grace the establishment.

At one point I remember a desperate Sammy broke silence with a whispered, 'Have you guys finished with that Burt Bacharach LP yet?' for we were heavily into Easy

Listening just then, scouring car-boots and jumble sales, having already amassed an impressive collection of our very own Greatest Hits by now.

Frankie looked at him, declining to reply. Poor Sammy. His name really *was* Sam, and when the sobriquets were being dished out he got the dirty end of the dipstick, you might say, for it would have taken a major leap of anyone's imagination to get even that fraction close to his namesake. Short, black, blind in one eye, you had to be kidding. Not even circumcised, either, as I recall.

And just then one of the Head Staggers sauntered by, catching us before we had time to do our synchronised, under the table, diving act. It was that red-haired young semi-skin, already extensively tattooed like his older brothers over in the social club right now, possibly planning their next drive-by, pipe-bombing venture. He grinned in at us, and I caught him taking in the two lady friends at the front table as well, and something about that second glance seemed to arrive at some connection in that pea-sized brain of his which made me go cold.

Next thing he had banged on the door, standing framed against the backdrop of the street and the parked jeep opposite. I could see Lorraine stiffen, for everyone knew he and his siblings were bad news, and he may well have been sniffing glue, too, for his mouth looked raw-ringed, always a sure sign of that old Evo-Stik in a plastic bag routine. For our part we tried to give the impression he didn't exist, which was a mistake, for he came out with this really loud, unpleasant laugh.

'Still gay are we, Brownlees?' his voice rings out, and across the table from me Frankie went pale. As I've mentioned, he had his back turned, but his face said it all.

Sammy and I, we tried not to look at him, even though we both knew the accusation had no truth in it, despite some of the graffiti and the fact he had gone through that one-man New Romantic phase which he had never been allowed to forget, not by that low-life bunch of scummy retards from the Loughview Estate anyway, represented by the one standing grinning in at us like some scalped, freckle-faced half-wit.

But then Head Stagger One, as we had christened him, as opposed to Two, Three and sometimes Four, in our worst nightmares, moved on, and we sat there, heads lowered to the empty plate in front of us. There didn't seem to be much to say after that, Lorraine and the couple at the table near the door quiet as well, as though silently digesting what they'd just heard.

Some little time later they finished their meal, and while the big one didn't actually snap her fingers, Lorraine moved smartly across to take the money laid out and waiting on the Formica. *Please, God,* I remember praying, *please don't let her leave a tip.* But then something much more mortifying occurred, oh, infinitely worse, for just as she got to the door Mad Marian shot a glance in my direction and, to my eternal shame, we heard her remark, 'Good evening, Brian,' the other one sliding this shy little grin in my direction, as if to say, *you don't know me, but I've heard an awful lot about you.* Of course that last part had to be an absolute load of poultry droppings, but I believed it, which was the important thing. I felt my face go cherry red and as soon as the door closed Lorraine tittered.

Now there had been a time when we had all rather fancied Lorraine in a sort of speculative way, for she had a certain voluptuous, sly quality in those early days, especially when she leaned forward over the counter in her less busy moments and we caught sight of that miraculous confluence of pale, squeezed flesh between the lapels of her tight, chippy uniform. She wore a neat little paper hat, too, like one of those quickfire waitresses in American diner movies. We even seriously considered co-opting her into the Clan as a possible Angie Dickinson figure, but then the weight started piling on, the spots appeared — just one French fry too many — and a mumsy apron replaced the snappy little starched number as the place began to go downhill like herself.

Hearing her laugh like that sent a ripple of distress through me, in much the same way I imagined the Head Stagger's crack earlier must have affected Frankie. But then, what does he do, that snake, but mimic, '*Brian?*' with a sissyish lilt to it, which coming from someone who had just been called a fruit to his face was, I considered, a trifle rich. I just could not get over the amount of damage that could be inflicted on hearing one's name spoken in that way and, of course, there was the other thing as well. When we were out together part of our private Rat Pack ritual was never to use our own real boring names, except, well, in Sammy's case. I was Dino, Frankie was always Frankie, and now he had gone and betrayed the code, and in public, too.

I had the entire weekend to brood on the matter. I kept hearing the woman murmur, '*Brian*', with a definite mocking inflection, I convinced myself, for if not, then why had Lorraine laughed the way she did?

On Monday morning even Gerry Mulrine seemed privy to my humiliation in The Cross Fish, and even if he wasn't, I wanted to believe it, for nothing or no one was going to stop me stoking the fires of resentment. He appeared to be grinning more than normal anyway, as though hugging some secret to that skinny chest of his, while gleefully drawing on one of his Free State cigarettes.

I was in such a state that by the time I was halfway through my deliveries I realised there was no mail that day for Prospect House and my two tormentors — well, one, actually, although could little Ms Buff Orpington really be as sweet and innocent as she appeared? After all she must have some steel in her character to stand up every day in front of all those big, mottled-armed farmers' daughters lecturing them on plumage moult or beak rot or whatever the frig your domestic fowl is prone to.

For three straight days in a row nothing for the folks who lived on the hill, not even a circular, although by now I had become ruthless about weeding out junk. There were always stories, of course, of postmen stuffing things down rabbit holes — your city mailman obviously being a much more dutiful and conscientious fellow — but then only a country man could ever know the aggravation of pushing a heavy roadster all the way up, then down, some farmer's lane only to deliver a two-for-the-price-of-one soap powder ad or pizza offer. To heck with that, likewise the charity appeals, the book club crap, credit card cons and plastic-covered catalogue rubbish. And wasn't I doing them all a favour, consigning a load of useless, glossy bumph, not to the darkness of some bunny's burrow, but the eternal, consuming flames of Sammy Senior's punctured oil-drum brazier in his back yard? It may not have been exactly Saving Planet Earth, but it was certainly sparing my legs and rear end a deal of needless grief.

On the Thursday no mail yet again and, Gerry Mulrine still

grinning like some nicotine-addicted ape, I became convinced in my head he had to be delivering the stuff himself, some sort of private arrangement, maybe even money changing hands. Yet I knew I couldn't confront him with it as he would only deny it and there was absolutely no way I could ever bring it up with old Hedley. The burden of it all began to feel as if I was carrying twice as much weight inside my head as on my back, so much so that on the Friday I decided to do something really stupid, even terminally disastrous, as regards the tenure of my summer job. Even though I had no cause to turn into their lane between those leaning pillars topped with matching, stone cannon-balls, I pushed on anyway, wheeling the bike up the stony incline.

The day was overcast, a heavy mugginess in the air, the cattle in the adjoining fields lying listless in the shade, haloes of flies about their heads. I was wearing jeans and an old Jim Morrison t-shirt, relic of a previous fixation with another dead hero of mine. Already it clung like a damp second skin and I was looking forward to the freewheeling ride home, the rushing air chilling my body like a refrigerator blast, but still I wouldn't give in and turn back.

Halfway, I decided to dump the bike — God alone knows why I hadn't hit on that particular wheeze before — laying it to rest in the long grass by the side of the lane, the thing being government property after all. Nearing the house I began hugging the hedge which I supposed would only make things worse for me discovered skulking empty-handed there like some trespasser, but I still couldn't help myself, not even at this late stage. I kept waiting for the dogs to go bananas, forgetting they were always kept indoors anyway. If they did start barking, I would turn back, I told myself. I would. Forget the whole thing.

There was an expanse of gravel in front of the house, worn bare in places, or heaped up in mounds in others by the tyres of their old jeep. Once I set foot on it the noise would give me away, no retreat possible, so I started making up excuses in my head like, *Oh, dear, wasn't I sure there was a letter for you today,* or, *I thought you might have had something you'd like to post,* for at the start the big one would sometimes hand over a sheaf of stuff for the old red post-box with its VR insignia set in the wall beside the church on Market Street.

With clammy palms I began edging forward, waiting for the first doggy rumble to break out. I got as far as the door, still no outcry, nothing, place silent as a graveyard. *Dead,* I remembered thinking, *what if they're all done for, dogs included,* like in one of those suicide pacts you read about, whole families taking the ultimate, terminal way out, in the mid-West states usually, for some weird reason. Well, maybe not so weird, considering farms where loneliness and the long winters get just too much, crop failure playing a pretty crucial part as well. Put it all down to an over-active imagination, but right then and there the notion that I might be first on the scene after some sort of mini-Jamestown Massacre of our very own did actually impinge like a bat on a window pane before sliding off and away into the bright day of reason.

Dry-mouthed, I got to the side of the house, and ignoring the two big front windows made my way around to the back, curious for some reason as to what might lie there, finding the usual knee-deep jumble of junk, old cookers, bedsteads, grates, wine bottles and the like, with a couple of geriatric apple trees long since run to crab thrown in.

By now the silence was roaring in my head and, with a battalion of cockle burrs clinging to both trouser legs, I stretched up towards the near window sill and peered in. I thought it might belong to the kitchen, reasoning, I suppose, if anyone was home that's where they'd be. But it turned out to be a ground floor bedroom, spacious and obviously feminine, which, crazily enough, came as a surprise, don't ask me why. The bed itself was massive, with a dimpled satin headrest, much bigger than the one in our upstairs room at home, the reality of that registering, not so much the size, but who shared ours back in my own house, setting off a series of shocks as I concentrated on what I could see on the far side of the glass.

Whoever had slept there recently hadn't bothered tidying the bedclothes much, if at all, some form of women's night attire dropped lazily where it lay, impossible for me to tell which of the two it belonged to, not being any sort of expert in that area. There were framed photographs on a bedside table, *two* bedside tables, with matching, pink-shaded lamps, an armchair piled high with magazines and books, a million pictures of dogs on the walls, but it was the bed I kept returning to as if there lay the key to something which, as yet, hadn't really hit home, stupid jerk that I was.

Then, over the back of a chair, I saw the shirt Little Ms Leghorn had worn to The Cross Fish, the red and white checked number, and draped over another, the navy sweater belonging to Mad Marian.

And it was then, finally, it felled me, the graphic evidence of something which had never crossed my mind, not once, not in any meaningful way, even though I don't consider myself a total greenhorn in such matters, certainly not like Sammy, who Frankie and I were constantly enlightening on the finer detail of exactly what goes where and how, 'down below'.

Well, I went reeling back from that window having stumbled on something I hadn't set out to find, not really caring any more about the mail or its absence. The couple weren't home, simple as that, and where they had gone, or when they'd be back was no concern of mine either, never had, nor should it be.

Yet going back down the lane to where that old red bicycle of mine waited among the bruised grass, I still couldn't get the pair out of my head, that damned bed continuing to haunt me, superimposed now on another, more familiar one, the big, double, mahogany relic behind my own parents' bedroom door at the head of our landing. And it continued to haunt me in the most awful fashion, for I kept visualising what might have been going on in those beds, *both* of them.

Eventually it got too much for me, my secret, I mean, and the following Friday night I opened my big trap, regretting it instantly when Frankie said, 'What you're basically saying is they're a couple of common or garden dykes.'

'Keep your voice down,' I panicked, feeling certain I saw Lorraine's ears prick up.

Sammy, as expected, looked sweetly bemused. 'What exactly do they *do*?' he whispered, and to my horror Frankie proceeded to fill him in, some of the details coming as much of a shock to me, as it did to our poor sap of a friend on the far side of the table.

Well, Monday morning came around, and with it an incredibly upbeat Gerry Mulrine.

'There's an extra bag of stuff for you over there,' cheerily he announced as soon as he saw me. 'Don't worry, it's all for the same address,' and the minute he said it I knew I had been right, he *had* been hoarding that couple's mail for them all along.

'Mind you, you might have to make two trips,' he couldn't help rubbing my nose in it.

But I told him, 'No sweat,' hefting the grey sack as I did so as if it held a feather pillow instead of at least a dozen books, a massive wedge of correspondence and, by the feel of it, a score or more of those rolled up chicken periodicals.

Setting off with the bike wobbling under all that weight, all that needless, bloody-minded bulk, my revengeful mood lasted right throughout the morning until those twin, leaning, cannonball gateposts loomed up. In my head I rehearsed how I would handle that first encounter with the one with the unruly ginger mane. Part of me wanted her to know I knew how she'd managed to humiliate me, but at the same time another part cautioned, *play it cool*, just the way my famous namesake would have done if he'd been in my place.

This time I persevered in pushing the bike all the way up the lane, working up a fine old sweat in the process, which helped to add to the impression of martyrdom I was determined to convey. The feeling was a good one, always is, in my opinion, but, of course, it evaporated the minute I got close to the house.

The dogs began barking, no typewriter today, I noticed, and I stood there already tongue-tied, holding the grey canvas bag like a peace offering, as though I was the one in the wrong, not who might be behind the door.

Then it opened and, unexpectedly, it was the poultry instructor. She looked tanned and relaxed as if she'd just returned from holiday, which, of course, happened to be the truth. Smiling, too.

'Hello,' she said, then, 'Brian,' as if we were old friends, her voice not flutey, or ultra-feminine, as expected, but confident, determined, even. 'That terrible old lane. You must be all in. The regular postman always leaves the mail in an empty milk churn down at the road, didn't he tell you that? Here, would you like something to drink, a cup of tea, maybe? You look as if you could do with one.'

I stood there like a total gawk clutching the mail bag, already falling under her spell, those dark eyes, hair cropped close Leslie Caron style, or that other actress I always fancied from Sinatra movies, Juliet Prowse.

Then she said, 'Marian's laid up with a tummy bug. I'm looking after her. Do you want to come in?'

And it was that image, that connection, that got to me, the big one sprawled on that unmade bed of theirs, feverish, sweating, and then this one standing before me band-box fresh and fragrant, for I could smell her from here, looking as if she couldn't possibly have emerged from those twisted sheets herself, yet me knowing all along she had. It was her secret and the thought that she had no earthly notion I was privy to it made me want to throw the bag of mail down on the gravel and just get out of there.

'Sure now you won't come in?' But already I was backing away. 'No? Well, see you Friday night then!' calling after me as I bumped the bike back down the lane.

Well after that I wanted to forget the whole thing, but for some weird reason Frankie wouldn't let go, gnawing and worrying away at the subject like a dog with a tasty bone. For me there was just no meat left to salivate over, not after having encountered those dark brown eyes and heard that voice coaxing me inside Rancho Notorious, as Frankie had started calling their place, after some old movie only he had seen. Somehow I had managed to build up a picture in his imagination that seemed to be getting more luridly technicolored by the minute and, God forgive me, just to keep him happy didn't I go on adding more ingredients to the stew, when in my heart I wanted to call a halt to the whole stupid, messy business.

'Now you're positive you saw them at it? I mean *really* at it?'
'Sure, I'm sure,' I lied.

He had beads of sweat on his upper lip. Who would have thought it, old Frankie a secret perve, and unable to resist I kept on feeding him these titbits of pure invention just to see the look on his face, Sammy's too, although he hadn't such a burning yen for the gorier details. Sometimes I would stop in mid-flow hearing my own voice saying all these things, and half of me would be sickened and disgusted, and the other half surprised at my own invention, as if I'd had another secret life somewhere in another and earlier existence with Peter Lawford organising orgies and the like.

Of course there had to come a reckoning and this is the way it came about.

One hot, throbbing evening Frankie and I allowed ourselves to drift off our usual homeward beat and foolishly found ourselves cutting through the old Protestant graveyard. Sammy had headed back on his own earlier, and so when we found ourselves ambushed deep in enemy territory among the church cedars, not by one, not even two, but five Junior

Head Staggers, who suddenly appeared as though risen out of the ancient earth like grinning apparitions in a Wes Craven movie, we knew we stood no chance, this was it, finally the moment of truth had caught up with us for all our past cocky, sneering misdemeanours.

One of the gang, Wilbur McCausland the glue-sniffer, seemed to have been promoted leader, which came as a surprise, for up to then we had always put him down as village idiot material. Here on his own close-cropped turf, suddenly he seemed dangerously in charge, while the rest of the bunch, two of them girls, incidentally, which only added to the humiliation, hung back in a semi-circle watching.

We stopped in our tracks for we both knew there was no way out, certainly not through that grinning bunch of pimpled zombies. Wilbur had a knife in his hand, holding it by the blade, and suddenly he threw it at one of the old cedar trees and we watched it flash, then bury itself up to the hilt in the soft bark. Dutifully one of the girls trotted forward, pulled it out, came back with it. Once more he repeated his party trick, for our benefit, obviously, and for a moment I thought Frankie was going to say something clever, but he didn't, just stood there looking paler than usual, which was pretty wan by anyone's standards.

'How about some target practice, Brownlees?' Wilbur said. 'Are you game?'

I couldn't tell whether he was stoned, or just charged up, you never could, for he always presented the same manic demeanour as if he woke up that way primed ready to go, boom, boom.

Frankie shook his head. I could detect his funk from where I stood coming off him in waves like a bad case of BO and I felt convinced our tormentors could sense it as well.

Then Wilbur said, 'How about you, Ritchie?' and I heard myself answer weakly, 'Why not?' stretching out a hand for the knife, one of those Bowie jobs, haft built up of alternate bands of brass and dark wood. Already I was taking an almost professional interest in the weapon, seized by a sudden crazed notion, I might somehow possess this up to now hidden circus talent which would strike all of them dumb with admiration.

But Wilbur only laughed. 'No, no, against the tree, dummy. Show him, Tucker,' and one of the gang stepped up to the old cedar and, stretching out his arms in crucifixion mode, prepared to be outlined by knife cuts, a look of manic adoration on his ugly, acned mug.

At which point, not having the stomach for any possible martyrdom, Frankie chose to back away, which anyone could see was a very bad move in the light of what was about to take place over at our ancient churchyard tree.

'Where are you off to, Brownlees?' said Wilbur. 'The two new girlfriends, is it? You and young Brian here? Wee foursome, is it?'

The girl laughed at that. She looked exactly like the others, that is if you didn't peer too closely, same clothes, same hairstyle, same nicotine-stained fingers, everything, except for the pathetic excuse for tits dimpling the Tommy sweatshirt.

'Think we didn't cop you in the chip shop all palsy-walsy like?'

Frankie said, 'We don't know them, I tell you. Anyway, they're not interested in the likes of us.' Wilbur laughed. 'Too bad. Bet you'd just love a go. Eh, Natalie?'

The girl's face split open at the sound of her own name. 'Yeah,' she said, 'in the back of their jeep.'

Frankie had a look of rabid desperation about him now. 'I tell you we're not their type!'

They were all laughing at him, but I knew it was the girl he was really upset about. He seemed to have lost his fear of the others, the knife, as well.

And then he came out with it, oh, God, didn't he just, and everyone went suddenly quiet.

'They're only interested in each other.'

Wilbur's face lost its smirk for the first time, and then, as though on cue, the others' expressions went dead on them as well, like lightbulbs losing power, shutting down one after another.

The forgotten volunteer up against the tree called out, 'Hi, what's going on over there?' and before he had time to duck or sidestep, Wilbur had hurled the knife, embedding it in the soft bark about a foot above his head.

And it was then that Frankie and I finally took off, expecting any minute to feel cold steel penetrate our shoulder-blades, the instant that crazy glue-head Wilbur McCausland managed to wrest the knife from the tree trunk.

'*Jesus Christ! Jesus H. Christ!*' Frankie kept repeating over and over.

He was hanging over a wall at the back of the Spar grocery on Market Street looking awful. I thought he was going to be sick.

'Those friggin' psychos. We might have been done for back there, you do realise that, don't you?' Then, 'Were you really going to do the big knife-throwing bit?'

'I don't know,' I told him. 'Somebody had to create a diversion.'

'Get Wild Bill Hickok.'

'You shouldn't have said that. About the two women, I mean.'

He looked at me. His hair was this unholy mess, first time I'd ever seen it in any kind of disarray. 'You were the one who started the ball rolling, remember? Anyway, that bunch of low-lifes wouldn't know a bender from a banana.'

I felt like saying, *well, they certainly sussed you all right*, but bit my tongue in time.

And that's where we left it, subject closed, end of episode, heading homewards our thoughtful, separate ways. But I still had a bad feeling about it, like a griping pain in the pit of the stomach.

The following Monday I left the mail inside the milk churn as instructed. It was a vast relief, for I didn't wish to face either of the two after Frankie had blurted out their secret like that, for, yes, I saw it in those terms now, something private, intimate, all to do with that bed, of course. And at night in my own room I found myself burying myself under the eiderdown until my head swam for lack of oxygen just in case I happened to overhear something shameful coming from the big double room at the far end of our upstairs landing, thankfully, my old man's snores all I ever detected above the hot red roaring in my ears.

Friday night had to come around, of course, no way of avoiding it, not now, not with Frankie at his most eager and quivering. Never had I seen him so highly-charged, drumming on the table, messing with the salt and pepper. Christ almighty, even blowing bubbles in his Fanta.

Sammy said, 'There's something up tonight. Haven't you noticed?'

We looked at him.

'Yeah, a whole gang of housing-estate retards roaming up and down all geared up for something,' the word 'retard' sounding strange coming from his lips, an expression obviously picked up from us.

'Oh?' said Frankie, trying to sound cool, but I knew he was thinking of that time in the graveyard with some of those same retards. 'What exactly are they doing?'

'Getting hammered, and not hiding it, either. Special Brew, and that other wino crap they drink. Buckfast.'

'Yeah,' said Frankie, with a flash of his old self, 'a contradiction in terms if ever I heard it,' and we were laughing at our own shared wit when Marian and her friend pulled up in the jeep across the street.

Brimming with good cheer they marched in, even the big, ruddy-faced one, who seemed to have shed her bout of indisposition, while the poultry instructor gazed about her with an expression on her face as much as to say, *isn't it great to be home among friends again*, and wanting everyone around to share it. No takers, unfortunately, for the atmosphere in the place had undergone this glacial change the moment they appeared. Even Lorraine appeared sulky and subdued, avoiding looking at the cheery pair over by the window.

They got their order, noticeably served with a distinct lack of charm. Frankie toyed with the salt, and Sammy with his plastic fork, until it snapped with a brittle crack that rang out in the silence. The poultry instructor giggled, and Sammy's face reddened, while Lorraine slammed a fresh basketful of frozen fries into the boiling fat with an angry, seething roar.

When they'd finished their meal and were sitting in a dulled state of digestive contemplation, this crazy urge came over me to do something to break the spell, I don't know why, make amends, maybe. But the moment passed, and they got up and left, walking out and across the street to where their old jeep sat parked.

We watched them climb in, the young one behind the wheel for a change.

Then we heard Lorraine mutter, 'Good riddance,' which made our heads swivel. She came round the counter and started stacking their emptied plates and cutlery, while managing to scrub the table top with a ferocity that was almost as shocking as her comment.

Events took a further, more horrific turn, for suddenly a ravening pack of young Head Staggers was milling about the place reeking of drink and mischief, just as Sammy had intimated, and it was plain they weren't there for takeaways, yet for some miraculous reason ignoring us completely as if we didn't exist.

'Well?' demanded Mister Knife-Throwing Man.

'Well, what?'

'Have they been in or not?'

And pointing to the empty table by the window, Lorraine told him, 'You've just missed them,' in tones not particularly cordial, yet not all that antagonistic either, we couldn't help remarking.

Wilbur leaned on the counter, his skinny backside hanging somewhere in the folds of his aspiring homeboy's Levis.

'No sweat,' he said. Then, turning as if noticing us for the first time, commented, 'Evening, ladies,' and his sidekicks creased themselves, laughing at the devastating wit and repartee of the man.

Under the table I could sense Sammy stiffen, his plastic fork going snap a second time. 'Fuck you, McCausland!' he said, half rising to his feet, and at that Lorraine came suddenly to life.

'No trouble!' she cried, flapping her dishcloth in the air as if it might somehow dispel potential mayhem like a bad smell. 'No bother here, you hear me? Take it out in the street where it belongs.'

But Wilbur held up his hands. 'We're not here for any of that, doll. Not right now anyhow. Other fish to fry.'

And the moment he said it I had this strange sensation that lurking beneath that red-raw exterior might be something I'd missed, something we'd all overlooked, a sense of irony, perhaps. But before I could pursue the notion he had ushered his merry gang of delinquents out into the street again.

At the door he turned.

'See you lot? High and mighty grammar school types? Well, maybe you are, but around here we don't like people like you, and people like you soon get to know it. Like those two stuck up lady friends of yours.'

'Yeah,' chimed in one of the gang. It was the girl we'd seen in the graveyard. 'I saw them looking at me. Eyeing me up. Lorraine, too. Right, Lorraine?' But by this stage Lorraine had vanished into the back regions of the chippie.

'Why don't you just shut the fuck up, Natalie,' Wilbur told her, which she did, almost gratefully, it seemed, and then they all disappeared, trooping off up the town in a swaggering, tight-knit clump.

After they'd gone Frankie whistled, saying, 'Talk about Bad Day at Black Rock,' but neither Sammy nor I were in the mood for any of his wisecracks, and soon after we all left The Cross Fish to make our separate, subdued journeys home, carefully avoiding any hot spots of sounds of breaking glass or drunken singing on our way.

The following Monday when I turned up for duty at the post-office Gerry Mulrine seemed to be in an unusually animated mood, obviously bursting with some revelation or other. But old habits being what they were, he still insisted on building up to it in a roundabout fashion by way of a lot of talk about his van needing a proper servicing and did I think Sammy's dad was up to it or not. Hadn't he once been in the Defence Regiment, maybe still was, and just maybe out on patrol on Saturday night when there was that bit of bother outside town?

'Bother? What kind of bother?' I said, rising to the bait.

'You mean you haven't heard?' says he, looking craftily at me through the curling wreaths from his cigarette. 'Well, I'll tell you one thing, young scholar me lad, there may be some mail for Prospect House over there, but if it were me I wouldn't be going to the trouble of trying to deliver it.'

That old chain-smoking buzzard, I felt like going for him across the sorting table.

'Tell me, tell me!' I heard myself shout, and at the sound of my raised voice old Hedley the postmaster poked his head in, blinking over his bi-focals like a sleepy owl.

'Tell you what?' he asked, and Gerry said, 'You know, that business on Saturday night. Them two poor women getting burnt out like that.'

'Aye, left homeless,' replied Hedley, shaking his head. 'Might have perished in their beds. Of course, no guesses as who the blackguards were responsible. Left their calling card in big letters, didn't they, the same crowd, as if proud of their handiwork. Another blow for God and Ulster. As if we needed it, or asked them, even.'

'I hear tell the polis have that young Wilbur McCausland already in for questioning.'

'A fat lot of good that'll do. Back in circulation, laughing his head off, before nightfall.'

I'd never heard old Hedley talk this way before, unguarded, passionate, and on a subject most people around here take care to avoid, for we all know how easy it would be to wake to the sound of breaking glass, and the heady aroma of unleaded four star, that's if we were lucky enough to roll out of bed in time.

'Aye, a desperate sorry business,' lamented Gerry, but with a gleam in his eye, for secretly he loved hearing 'that lot', as he referred to them, on the receiving end of one of their own.

Well, over the next few mornings the little isolated pile of mail for the house on Carntall Hill kept growing, then abruptly stopped as if at some mysterious signal. Gerry Mulrine mentioned something about a forwarding address, but before he could bundle everything into one giant-sized Jiffy bag, I slipped the entire lot into my own pouch when his back was turned. All that morning it lay at the bottom of the canvas bag under the other letters like a dead, accusing weight. I knew I couldn't explain what I'd done if I were to be found out. But, then, I couldn't explain it to myself either.

That particular day I rearranged my route to fit so that the bundle in question became the last remaining batch to be delivered. But who would be waiting to receive it? As the real import of that hit me, I braked, for up until then I had been running on instinct, brain shut down like a stopped watch. I was about a mile from the place at the time on a dry, dusty stretch of road straight as a lath. At my back lay the town and my final signing-off in the big navy blue, Royal Mail minute book.

Dropping down on to the slope of the ditch, I drew the fat bundle out for one last look, but with absolutely no desire to slip its rubber bands and go sniffing for evidence. All of that was over and done with. Case closed. One for the archives. Instead, the time had come to turn the bike around and go freewheeling home, allowing the rushing air to clear away any last lingering regrets.

But, of course, I did the opposite, didn't I, riding on until I came in sight of those familiar leaning gateposts with their stone cannonballs. Something there as well, a fresh For Sale notice sprouting out of the hedge, the shock of its bright lettering coming as a tremendous jolt, the suddenness, the haste of it, like fresh soil on a grave.

And there was more, the pillars daubed with the usual paramilitary initialling, and right across the width of the road itself, as if painted for an aerial overview in big, white, dripping capitals, the words PERVERTS OUT. At least it seemed to be that, until closer inspection revealed PREVERTS OUT, testimony to the midnight graffiti artist's dyslexia, and I caught myself thinking how Frankie would get a buzz out of something like that, while Sammy would have to have it explained to him, spelled out literally.

Before turning the bike around I took a last look in the old milk churn. I suppose I must have imagined I might find something there amongst the cobwebs, one last letter, perhaps, destined for the outside world, but lost now for good, unless I rescued it. But it was empty, the bottom dry as dust.

And that's how the business ended, me riding off on my old red roadster knowing I would never be this way again, or hear another word from the two wherever they might be.

That was last summer, *our* last summer, the junior Rat Pack's. Not exactly disbanded, with the coming of the shorter days and dark nights, more losing its adhesion like an old envelope shedding its gum.

The last time I saw Frankie he was a retro-Goth, piercings, black eye make-up, the works, in a graveyard green overcoat trailing the ground, while Sammy — and here comes the biggest surprise of all — Sammy got himself a job as junior reporter on the local rag with his own pop and country music column. 'Around the Gigs'.

As for myself, I'm still living at home in my room down the hall from my parents' big front bedroom, considering my options, which are still wide open, as I keep on telling them. Next year maybe I'll make a start on that novel. I'm thinking of calling it 'Rancho Notorious', even though I know the title has been used before. Then, again, who knows, maybe it's too early to commit to something still as raw and painful in the memory as that.

The Good Ship Lollipop

For an entire week he hadn't left the house, it seemed, except for trips to the local Spar grocery, wandering up and down the aisles, spinning out the time it took to fill his wire basket with all the tinned junk the old man lived on, Irish stew, corned beef, meat pies and gravy, luncheon-meat, chemical red salmon, cling peaches in syrup, with the whitest of white Wonder Loaf and digestive biscuits as ballast.

His own system felt as though it was slowly gumming up as well, all those noble intentions of changing that diet when he got here, or at least nudging it in a healthier direction, having ebbed away as the pair of them settled into a pattern of sloth together, with Bruce, his father's old cocker spaniel, lying between them on the rag rug in front of the fire leaking errant puffs of foul wind.

Finally, when he did rouse himself — he was beginning not to recognise this bloated stranger's face framed in the square of mirror in the freezing scullery each morning — his father looked up from the glowing coals, asking, 'Where are you off to, son?' as though faced with an act of desertion. The dog gave him the same reproachful stare.

'Bit of a walk to clear the head,' he explained. 'Get some air,' feeling fraudulent, for he had put on his expensive new leather jacket, the one he had arrived in off the plane, instead of the heavy Aran sweater he wore to the mini-mart. Already that smelt of a blend of fry-ups, chimney soot and Bruce, for he suspected the dog slept on it, irrational and all as that might seem. But then he was starting to feel decidedly irrational by now about everything connected with this house, another reason for getting out of it and away for as long as possible without the old man making him feel like a criminal. Him, and the dog both. They were like a double act, he told himself, Bob and Brucie, sharing each other's thoughts as well as food.

The time of year was late November, a raw mistiness in the air, no rain, a rare blessing. But then coming over now had been deliberate on his part, hopefully defusing some of the customary Christmas-time guilt he invariably experienced basking in the tipsy glow of family and friends back in London, with the old man sitting all those miles away toasting his shins in an empty house, Bruce between his feet. Would they have turkey, he wondered? Or would it be Smash and yet another tin of the Swedish meatballs?

As he walked from the house he tormented himself further with an imaginary menu, for he'd never have the courage to ask him straight out in case he received that brave, martyred look again. *Never go worrying your head about your oul' da. Tough as oul' boot leather, he is.* The reality was he looked like skin and bone despite all the canned crap he was putting away. Yet the dog seemed to be getting plumper as *he* lost weight, some sort of perverse ratio at work there, it struck him, like those couples with their metabolisms pulling in different directions. His mother herself could be said to have had a tendency to stoutness, at least in the latter years anyway. Regarding which, the old man definitely had gone downhill since she died, yet another of those intriguing anthropological equations, he supposed.

'Oh, fuck it,' he said, the thoughts getting far too depressing as he reached the foot of their terraced row, his father's house being the one right at the end with the extra bit of garden he no longer worked, a source of festering resentment with some of the neighbours, it lying fallow like that, while their own pathologically tidy allotments cried out for more space as they saw it. But then just how many frigging leeks and cabbages can a normal family put away in a year, not to mention all the spuds, onions, turnips, carrots, parsnips and Brussels sprouts? *Root crops*, he thought. *Land of the pale tuber.*

At the end of the row he turned right, passing the Primary School, yet eerily quiet, as though the pupils were a bunch of mutes, not like the screaming young dervishes who attended the one close to his own city avenue, hyper on additives from all that after-school crap they put away, some sort of lurid orange drink being the current suspect he was given to understand. He passed the Spar grocery with the blue Calor gas bottles stacked outside, then the Post Office, the chemist's, and, well, that was it, really, the place where he grew up all those years ago.

A woman in the passenger seat of a parked Cavalier stared at him as he strode by. He sensed her eyes drilling into him. Could it be the leather blouson, he wondered, that softly creaking, glistening newness which had attracted him in the first place, marking him out as pretentious somehow, affected, even, here in the sticks?

So far there was nothing firm in his mind regarding a route, simply letting his legs carry him, and so they led him across the road which marked the end of the village proper, and where the traffic hummed past at leisurely intervals. About a hundred yards further on lay the ancient graveyard and, on impulse, he turned in through its heavy iron gates, only the cries of the rooks in the barbered yews disturbing the quiet.

The path was freshly gravelled, sharp to the tread, so he moved on to the plushy grass verge. Ahead he could make out the old ruined crypt where he and the rest of the gang used to gather after nightfall daring one another to raise Baal, Prince of Darkness, or hoping, as least, to come across a human skull. It was their big occult phase, playing Black Sabbath at half-speed to decipher the hidden messages there, Ronnie McBride swearing he distinctly made out the words, '*Baby Kill*', over and over. But he was always the mouthy one of the group, eager to impress, even more than he was. He wondered where they all were. Why not ask the old man, he considered, but only for the briefest of moments, anticipating that look which continued to haunt him.

After his mother died he had arranged for the old man to have a phone put in so he could ring back on a regular basis. He'd pay the rental, and the bills would be forwarded to him, but scanning the itemised account when it arrived he realised he never used it, the thing gathering dust until his own dialling activated it each Saturday around teatime. Well, that had been the intention, but after a while he started putting off the dreaded call, leaving it for another week.

Then a fortnight would elapse, until remorse set in. This trip had been the culmination of all of that, getting him off the hook, as he thought, a week of penance in the land of the blanched tuber cancelling out perhaps a month, maybe two, of missed calls.

And while on the subject, just a day or so earlier when they were watching an antiques quiz show on afternoon television the phone actually did ring. He and the old man stared at it sitting there on the mock oak sideboard, then at one another.

'Well?' he said, as it continued to trill.

'It'll be for you,' said his old man.

'It might not be.'

And so they continued watching it until whoever it was rang off, which possibly had been the moment when he decided he really had to get out of the house and for longer than it took to cruise the aisles of the Spar supermarket scooping cans of Fray Bentos into a basket if he were to retain some grip on reality.

So now he had escaped, and to one of his old boyhood haunts, place of refuge for our four apprentice Goths, over the gate, still to be seen, the remains of a rusty lamp bracket placed there to deter body-snatchers, so the legend went, and they would squat on the dewy grass by the Templars' crypt hoping for their own Burke and Hare to materialise among the tombstones complete with bag of tools and orders for fresh cadavers. *Did they know Burke was born here? Well, Tyrone, actually. But close enough.*

That was Vernon Kincaid their resident brainbox, last he heard slaving in an insurance office. In his leisure moments he imagined him trouncing all and sundry at the local pub quiz. What's the capital of Turkestan? Name the largest freshwater lake in North America. How did marmalade get its name? And that old mate of yours, did he ever get to make a go of it in London?

Standing there among the tilting headstones, he had a sudden urge to mix with the living, and for the first time that day, a real, a proper destination came to mind, mentally retracing a route towards it by one of those private tracks he and his friends used to take across country. And the trail began right here, he recalled, at a gap in the wall where the stones toppled in, over some pasture land, then across other fields, bare of crops, or not, depending on the time of year.

Clambering up he saw that everything ahead of him was still, carpeted in a light ground mist. In the distance the woods appeared to be smoking slightly with a bluish tinge, and he started feeling excited again, some of that old sensation of being out in the open and exposed like that coming back after all this time. Once he remembered they had been chased by a bull, or it may have been a sexually confused bullock. Another time a farmer pursued them right across his land, standing up, steering one-handed on a tractor, waving his free fist in the air. On both occasions they escaped laughing into the woods.

But as he stood gazing out across the remembered landscape doubts were already starting to press in — someone like him, his age, dressed as he was, caught isolated out there in that bare and, let's face it, alien terrain. He heard the voice in his head telling him all these things, more specifically the one belonging to the person sitting hunched in his armchair staring into the grate watching the clock for his return the way he used to do all those years ago.

Another memory came back. First time he got proper, stinking drunk. Must have been sixteen at the time, staggering home with a churning ball of bile in his guts, all coming up in a rush into the sink in their scullery, him hanging over that chill rim retching while the old man stood patiently by waiting for the details, the how, the when, the where, most humiliating of all, with whom, for he was intent, oh, yes, he was, he said, on confronting those responsible for feeding his young lad the booze in the first place. Never touched the stuff himself. Old Archie Senior, his own father, had, and in a big way, from everything he'd been told, the usual business, skipping a generation.

But all this introversion was getting him down. He looked at his watch. Coming up to a quarter to four on a dead midwinter afternoon and no way could he face afternoon TV again, so he walked out from the village, past the new, upmarket housing estate, the Masonic Hall with those still mysterious hieroglyphs chiselled into the arch above its door, until he reached the big roundabout where the road branched off in three directions. Unhesitatingly he chose the one to the far left, for he knew where he was heading now, the connection having been made in his head the moment he remembered that episode of craning over the sink and spewing up half a dozen curdled Red Heart stout. He wondered whether that particular bottled brand was still served in the pub he was travelling to, old Maggie Steenson's place over in the next village. By his calculation he should make it in about a good thirty to forty minutes' brisk walking time.

Well, it took him closer to an hour, and it was growing dark by the time he passed under the first streetlights on the outskirts of the hamlet, it being barely more than a straggle of a few houses and a shop or two, one of the reasons they liked coming here so much, like a trip back in time for, in their eyes, the place and the people were definitely *backward*. That's how they were then, constantly grading things as to their degree of 'coolness'. In the case of Burnside, no argument, the place was pure Dogpatch.

Coming upon it like that straight out of the gloaming, it looked different, yet familiar, as well, a disturbing combination for some reason. One or two of the houses had been renovated, no thatched roofs any longer, and there was a new BP filling-station with a rack of newspapers outside. He passed by on the opposite side hoping not to be spotted by the girl behind the glass. She had her nose buried in a book, or a magazine, or maybe she was listening to a radio, although he could hear no music. Padding past, trying to act invisible, he caught the flicker of TV behind curtains and thought of the old man watching the same programme, and right there in the middle of that place he had a sudden attack of panic, thinking, *Christ, what have I done?*

Up ahead was a red phonebox. Praying it hadn't been vandalised, he pulled open the heavy, spring-loaded door, receiving a trapped blast of urine fumes and stale cigarette smoke, the mouthpiece of the receiver reeking of tobacco as well. Laboriously dialling with its old-fashioned finger holes, and holding it clear of his cheek, he heard the faint ringing tone on the other end of the line. On and on it sounded, until realisation struck it wouldn't be answered, for who was he kidding, he might as well be calling an empty house for all the good it would do.

Cursing that stubborn old man he slammed the receiver back on its hook. Through the smeared glass he could see the dead, forlorn street outside, and shivered at the thought of the long, lonely trek ahead of him along those country roads in the dark, the chill of the kiosk's concrete floor biting through the thin leather of his soles. Just what had got into him to set off on this crazy undertaking anyway? A rush of sentiment to the head, that's what, brought on by feeling pissed off at somebody sitting in a coal-gas induced trance listening to his phone ring and not bothering to raise a hand to answer it.

Backing out of the phone box, ahead of him he could see a wash of coloured light leaking out from one of the low buildings in the middle of the row. It came from the spot he remembered the old pub used to be. He and the gang would drink in the back kitchen, bottles lined up on top of the dead range. The place was like that then, drinkers spilling into all its private rooms, upstairs, as well as down, another reason why they enjoyed coming here so much, that air of illegality spiced with the reek of turf smoke a real turn-on as far as they were concerned.

Shivering, he continued to waver. Surely just one drink for the road wouldn't make all that much difference. No harm in taking a look at the old den of depravity, was there?

He passed a small church hall set in back from the street, the bluing poster behind the glass in the wayside pulpit looking as though it hadn't been changed since the time he and the other three caballeros had ridden past to stable their iron steeds in a tangled heap in the pub's back yard.

Maggie Steenson's was now The Ramble Inn, and the coloured light came from a Budweiser sign, the general impression being one of serious neglect and decay, a rusting, metal-meshed grille covering the window which had a diagonal crack down it, door tightly closed in a forbidding, *no outsiders, if you please*, kind of way. At least that was the impression he got anyway. A solitary car with a horse-box attached was parked outside. *To hell with it. It was still a pub, wasn't it?* And he pushed on the door and stepped inside.

Three men were at the bar with their backs to him. Two were wearing mud-spattered dungarees and woollen stocking caps. The third had on a suit. Nobody was serving behind the bar. The three turned as he entered, eyeing him as he came in from the cold. The man in the suit, he looked like a businessman, but without a tie, remarked, 'Wintry weather,' but he might well have been addressing his two companions who had gone back to staring into their lager glasses.

There was an open fire across on the far side of the room, looking a lot more inviting than the trio at the bar, so he went over to it, ostentatiously spreading his palms to its warmth. Behind him he could hear the man in the suit resume talking with the other two, but in lowered tones, which he took as reaction to his presence.

As his hands thawed he continued to check out the general look and feel of the place. He thought he still recognised the old proportions, just, although the bar did seem a lot bigger. The wooden tongue and groove ceiling had been sheeted in with grey acoustic tiles, with a single glaring fluorescent tube dead centre giving a depressing, clinical air to everything. The bar counter now was speckled blue plastic, and the old Dunville whiskey mirror decorated with harps and shamrocks behind it had gone. Other modern details filtered through. A battered looking dartboard, a cigarette machine, a television high on a shelf, mercifully dead, and all the stuff about the walls which certainly hadn't been there in old Maggie's day, Red Hands and loyalist insignia, a Royal portrait staring down at him from over the fireplace, team photographs of the entire Glasgow Rangers football squad spanning a decade at least.

Staring into Her Britannic Majesty's true blue eyes, he wondered how long it would take for him to get a drink in the place. But just then the man in the suit called out, 'Avril!', holding up his empty glass, and a woman appeared through a doorway at the back, not young, yet not so old, either, attractive in a rough, full-lipped way, wearing a navy sweatshirt with the J. Arthur Guinness logo across the front.

'Same again,' said the drinker at the bar fanning change out on the counter, the two silent giants in dungarees dutifully draining the suds in their straight glasses.

The guy ordering, the more he studied him, looked like a livestock auctioneer, or a cattle dealer, something like that, he decided. The suit had seen better days, especially in the region of the seat and legs, and his tan boots were caked with what appeared to be dried dung.

'I think this gentleman's first,' said the bar woman, and Mister Auctioneer turned around to look at him as if he honestly hadn't noticed him come in.

'My sincere apologies,' he said, smiling for the first time, while his two friends resumed staring into space. 'Do forgive my bad manners,' and the woman smiled at him as well, but with a deal more sincerity it struck him.

'A Bushmills,' he told her, moving to the bar.

'No ice, I'm afraid,' she said, as if he looked like someone who normally took ice in his drinks.

'Water, that's fine,' he told her.

As she turned to reach up to the optic, automatically he found himself grading the stretched curve of her well-packed jeans. It was the first real stirring of lust he'd had since he got here, and he felt himself relax, even before a mouthful of whiskey had gone sliding down. He paid the woman, and she smiled back, settling herself on a stool as though preparing to be flirted with, Mister Auctioneer being only too happy to oblige.

Standing at his own part of the bar observing all this, after the second Bushmills he began to get the impression he was being encouraged to join in their little ritual. The whiskey was making his eyes water, face burning up as well, and instinctively he pulled out his handkerchief, a spotted, green silk one from Liberty's his wife had bought him last Christmas, and the auctioneer glanced at it in his hand. The woman, Avril, did so, too, but with what he took to be appreciation, for he had always considered the possession of something as simple as that marked out someone with taste, even if it was only a handkerchief. In the same way his watch happened to be a Tag Heuer, and his shaving brush real sable hair.

At that moment a gust of wind caused a back draught in the fireplace, and they all listened intently as a metal sign out in the street somewhere banged and rattled.

The auctioneer said, 'Night like that there's only one thing better than a glass of the right stuff to keep the heat in, and that's a nice warm lady in your bed. Eh, young Avril?'

'Well, now, what would I be knowing about the like of that, Terry?'

'Believe that, you'll believe anything. Eh, young man?'

Finally the old rogue had reeled him in, both of them watching him now. He smiled back.

'Maybe it's the young lady's husband you should be asking,' he said, regretting it instantly, for it did sound a mite forward at this stage of the game, for that's what it was, a game, played out in a million bars between a man, or men, and the woman serving them across the counter, and one, if you happened to get lucky might play along too, at least until last orders were called and everyone went their merry, or not so merry ways.

'Oh, our lovely Avril's not wed. Has a boyfriend, mind. Well, last I heard, anyway. Big Earl. Where is he, by the way?'

'How should I know?' the woman said. 'I'm not his keeper.'

'Soon will be,' retorted Terry with a laugh, his name somehow suiting him, sportive, like himself, someone who would never give in to his age, which he reckoned to be early to late fifties, although people here generally looked a lot older than they actually were. A joke swam into his head, that old chestnut about the local census form and the population being broken down by age, sex and religion. The sparring couple nearby must have caught him smiling to himself, for they grinned back, the whiskey persuading him into thinking, age and religion aside, just maybe the last item on that list, or at least a spot of dalliance, might not be totally out of the question.

'Set 'em up again, Avril, honey,' ordered the Terry character, 'and while you're at it have a wee one yourself. And give the gentleman here whatever he's having as well.'

And so it began, that old, remembered, downward slide, the rounds bunching up on the bar in front of them, the place transforming itself into a hub of good cheer and fellowship, as the cold, dark night settled in outside. Tongue loosened, he began to do more than his fair share of the talking while the others listened. The two giants had still barely made a sound, save grunt or give a shuffle of their great feet, sliding their glasses forward for another refill. Yet he didn't begrudge a penny of it, for at last he was enjoying himself. He told them of coming to this same pub all those years ago, of drinking in the back kitchen with his three buddies, then zig-zagging home, making swooping, drunken passes on the country roads with their bicycle front wheels, and the more he talked the more details of those carefree nights returned to him. And, sure enough, didn't Terry, too, remember old Maggie, and the 'shenanigans', for many's the time hadn't he woken up in one of the back rooms himself with a sore head and the little birdies cheeping merrily away outside.

The woman, too, seemed fascinated by their stories, although more by his own, he flattered himself, noting how she would lean forward on her stool when it was his turn to speak. At one stage she climbed from her perch to go in the back, returning with lipstick restored, and hair freshly combed, a recharged whiff of scent there, as well, he convinced himself.

'Somehow you look familiar,' he heard himself suggest. Such a corny line, even in a place like this.

'Oh, now how might that be?'

And suddenly they were all looking at him.

'Well, maybe you have an older sister, then.' He was about to substitute 'mother', but, Christ, he wasn't *that* ancient.

'Take your pick, I've three. And, yes, I'm the youngest.'

Without being told she served them all another round while he wondered how to follow up his little gambit, for he couldn't just leave it hanging there. And then something did come to mind as he watched her top up the water jug for his whiskey, Terry being a strict three-star brandy and American Dry man. He recalled a night from all those years back when there *had* been a girl, and from this village, too. They'd run across her and a gaggle of her friends hanging around outside the local Orange Hall. There was a Young Farmers' hop on, but of, course, naturally, they felt much too worldly and hip to be caught dead at such a venue.

It turned out to be his lucky night, or, at least, he and she had paired off, leaving the others milling around exchanging wisecracks and insults under a street lamp. Casually, almost, they walked away, the two of them, and when the brightness of the village street ended abruptly, and the pitch dark of the real countryside began, they came bumping together in a clumsy clinch, more out of nerves than anything specifically amorous.

Looking back, it might well have been his first time, although nothing much happened. He was too awkward for that, as he suspected she was, although that night he convinced himself she was the more experienced, making a lie of it afterwards for the gang's benefit, telling them he had made all the right moves, while she had been the one to back off at the crucial point of no return. Of course he'd expressed it in far cruder terms than that, again for their consumption, but for some time afterwards he had felt romantic about her as though something emotionally charged had passed between the pair of them standing there, wordlessly grappling up against the cold stones of that old demesne wall in the dark.

'Her name was Beck,' he told them, and there was silence in the bar.

Of course he couldn't be one hundred per cent certain, but he recalled that was a common surname hereabouts, the place abounding with Becks, which only went to reinforce all those theories about how inbred the place was. And as though supporting the notion, well, perhaps not so much the incest element, Terry said, 'Aye, there's certainly a brave lot of people by that name in these parts. Eh, Avril?' winking across the bar at her while she studied her nails.

'Well, as I say, it was a long time ago,' he heard himself murmur, making light of his confession, for he couldn't help feeling the mood had taken a dip. Another drink was suggested, although, technically, it wasn't his shout, but Terry stretched and yawned while his two dungareed friends shifted their planks of feet, draining their glasses with sudden, new finality.

And then just as a kind of panic threatened to set in, being left on his own like that, despite the company of the lovely Avril, the door opened and a newcomer shouldered his way in, a bullish-looking individual with a stubbled scalp, wearing a t-shirt tight as a second skin despite the weather outside. Swaying, he stood gazing about him out of bleary eyes. Then, without uttering a word, he crossed to the dartboard, ripping out a dart from the badly stippled cork. As they watched he took a series of backward steps before sighting along the feathers at the target.

'Double top,' they heard him mutter before the dart left his mottled fist to execute his forecast perfectly.

'Earl!' said Terry. 'How's about you, big man? Where have you been?'

The bruiser in the t-shirt stared at him.

'Man about a dog,' he grunted, lurching forward to the bar where a pint stood already waiting. Putting it to his lips he drained most of it in one, wiping his mouth with the back of his hand after setting the glass down.

He nodded to the two silent ones. 'Charley, Todd,' before coming back to Terry.

'Get a winner today?'

'Newbury was off. Course abandoned.'

Another silence.

Then Avril asked, 'Where have you been?'

Earl looked at her. 'Same again. Mouth's as dry as a nun's twat.'

Terry laughed, as did the two giants. Standing on his own at the other end of the bar, he smiled, too, out of politeness, even though the crack scarcely warranted it, and the man in the dirty white t-shirt glanced at him, demanding, 'Who's this, then?'

Avril had her back to him as he spoke, fiddling with the spirits optic, and when she came around again she held a glass of whiskey in her hand. 'It was another Bush, wasn't it?' she enquired, placing it on the counter, with a smile perhaps just a shade too intimate for his taste.

Terry said, 'Just a weary traveller passing through giving us a bit of his crack.'

To which Earl replied, 'Never mind all that, I'm still waiting for my pint over here.'

Obediently Avril poured him one. 'He used to know your Rita,' she said.

Earl stared at him. 'My sister? When was that then?'

And suddenly he heard himself babbling, half his life story coming out, but in a much more drastically speeded up, edited version of the one he'd been offering earlier.

'He used to drink here in Maggie Steenson's day,' Terry explained.

'That oul' Fenian bitch,' said Earl. One of his lobes looked angry and raw as if someone had ripped an earring clear in a brawl. Tattoos, as well, running up both arms to coil about pumped up biceps.

'Did you hear your man on the News tonight, that fucker!' he demanded of the bar, mentioning a well-known MP of a similar persuasion to the pub's former landlady, although, to be honest, all those years ago he himself had never thought of her as anything other than one of themselves.

'Now, now, no religion, no politics,' said Avril, holding her arms across her impressive bosom.

'Hear, hear,' seconded Terry, while his two companions continued to study the ceiling.

Earl gave an angry snort. 'Scared of offending somebody's feelings, are we? Well, anybody in the present company has any problems with that up there,' pointing to the union flag pinned about the cigarette machine, 'they know what they can do.'

'Now, now,' scolded Avril, settling herself squarely on her high stool, 'there's no call for that kind of talk,' as though dealing with a fractious infant and, standing there outside their little arena, it came to him it was something she was good at. Oil on troubled waters. Whiskey, in his particular case, making him clearer-headed with each swallow, everything about him standing out in sharp focus.

For a start, our Earl had to be a lot drunker than he let on. How many pints had he sunk already? Two, three, was it? All on top of what he'd downed earlier somewhere else. He was running out of steam, that was becoming obvious. Menace, as well, Avril having seen to that, for despite all the diehard bluster he knew he would never actually come straight out with it, putting it to him point blank where his own tribal allegiances lay, all of that antediluvian crap. It wasn't the way things were done here, that much he did remember. More a case of curs sniffing each other's rear ends, pedigrees arrived at by stealth, dropped hints, references. Using that faulty hick antenna of his, quite possibly he had marked him down as one of 'the other sort' already.

Emboldened by drink he started to relish the prospect of

stringing him along, feeding him false clues, all of them, although he felt Avril had his number from the start. Anyway, what was she doing with a thug like this, too thick, or too drunk, or both, to realise his own girlfriend was being subtly flirted with while he kept squinting across at the dartboard, pleading, 'Ah, come on, Terry, throw a few arrows with me, for fuck's sake.'

But Terry only laughed. 'Now, you know well, Earl, that's not my game. Anything with a saddle on it, okay, but not darts.'

'Come on, I'll play you blindfold.'

But Terry wouldn't be shaken. 'Time to hit the road,' he said, finishing his drink. 'Right, lads? You and me have a stable to clear out in the morning first thing.'

Nodding acquiescence the two giants were already heading for the door.

'Night, night, Avril, don't be doing anything I wouldn't do. And goodnight to you, too, young sir. It's been a privilege conversing with you.'

And then the three of them were gone, a blast of chill air following after, and with it, in his case, the first real disquiet about the possible consequences of this night's adventure.

'Is that the correct time?' he said, pointing to the Budweiser clock on the wall.

'I should have told you about that,' apologised Avril. 'I've been meaning to get the brewery people come and fix it.'

'Well, can I get a taxi around here? Could you ring for one, do you think?'

She looked at him, then at Earl sitting now at the bar, fingers of one hand splayed before him, stabbing the spaces between with one of his darts. Laughing to himself he stepped up the tempo as they watched waiting for the first mishap to occur.

'Taxi?' he said. 'Taxi? What's that?' laughing some more.

'I imagine you've never heard of a phone either,' he heard himself reply in acid tones, for suddenly he'd had it up to here with these rustics. I mean, look at this retard here using the back of his hand for target practice like something from a bad movie. And Avril, wasn't she straight out of central casting as well, any instant now morphing into some axe-wielding harpy backing up her redneck boyfriend?

'Where's your toilet?' he demanded.

Without waiting for a reply he made for a door he remembered seeing the others use earlier, his bladder surprising him, holding out the way it had. Right now he felt it clench in spasm as he moved briskly for the great outdoors, recalling, as he also did, the way people would always relieve themselves in the pub's backyard in the old days. And even if there was a proper toilet, who was going to notice, or raise an objection? Besides, he quite liked the idea of having one last leisurely leak under the stars, sort of a parting, sentimental gesture, you might say.

He was standing there watching the steam rise when the back door opened, a bar of light pouring out, and there was Earl framed in the glow of the bare bulb in the passage at his back. *Well, let him join the men's club if he so wishes, it's a free country.* But when the other still made no move, simply standing there watching, he began to get uneasy. He felt he should say something, even though such situations were traditionally conducted in silence, embarrassed, or otherwise.

'Earl!' he called out in what he hoped were chummy, man to man tones. 'So how's it going then?'

Still no response, no movement, the clamour of his own piss an imposition on the still night air. But even if he had wanted to cut it short it would keep on coming, a full night's recycled booze pouring out of him in a not to be denied or rushed stream on to the dark, trodden earth.

'You were saying things about my sister before I got here.'

'What?' he said, turning.

Suddenly he had wet himself. He felt it down his front, then travelling hotly through the wool of his trousers.

'You were mouthing off about our Rita back there. My fucking sister.'

'I swear, I never —' he blurted, then stopped. Had he said, *fucking my sister?*

'Look, I think there's been a mistake, a misunderstanding. All I actually said was, a long, long time ago I went out with a girl from around here, just the once, mind, and her name happened to be the same as your own. Surname, I mean. It could have been anybody. Maybe she wasn't even from here, maybe she was a —'

At which point Earl came forward out of the light, confusing him, blinding him, exploding a blow bang on the side of his face. Perfect straight left, he decided later when he was going over everything in a reprise, the impact sending him careering back into a stack of beer crates, all empties, for he felt the round imprint of a dozen bottle-necks suddenly patterning the seat of his Prince of Wales checked Daks.

'Get up, fuck you!' Earl said, fists clenched, while he responded with the weak and utterly pathetic, 'I tell you you've made a mistake. I want no trouble.'

'Fucking taig! Fucking mick bastard.'

Squatting there on the beer crates from which he had no intention of moving, he thought, *okay, so maybe I was wrong about people sniffing each other out in some sort of leisurely, doggy fashion*, Earl obviously being a different breed entirely, a rabid one at that.

'Look,' he said, 'you've got that part all wrong as well.'

'Well, if you're not a pape, then you're a fucking queer. Either way, I hate both.'

It was the first time he'd been in a *proper* fight. Well, one like this anyway, and he'd always wondered what it would be like, especially the pain part. Right now his jaw felt reasonable, throbbing, but reasonable. He'd had worse toothaches. He wondered when it would really start to hurt, and by how much. A lot? A little? Something in between, possibly? He couldn't believe he was really thinking all this stuff, and calmly at that. Probably drink had a lot to do with it, and for one crazy moment it actually encouraged him to believe it might still help him talk his way out of this.

'Now, look here, Earl, there's no need for you and me to fall out over something as silly as a —'

Which is where he started losing count of which blow followed which and of what sort. Certainly not from any boxing manual. He managed to keep his hands up, protecting his face, but then took a deal of collateral punishment lower down, and more of the same when he was rolling about on the damp ground he had been so liberally sprinkling with his own piss moments earlier. Nobody had told him either that trainers could inflict damage of that order, for by this stage the whiskey seemed to have lost all its anaesthetic properties. *Jesus*, he thought, *how much more of this am I going to be able to take?*

At some point, somehow, he contrived to struggle to his feet, putting his fists up, but really only in defensive mode, at which Earl, instead of hanging fire, or taking a breather, even, came boring in with renewed ferocity, unleashing a flurry of haymakers which numbed his forearms when they weren't catching him ringing blows on either side of the head.

Now if this were the sort of story unconnected with real life, around about this point our hero's groping hand would have connected with one of the empties in the beer crates. It really should, and if there was any sort of justice or fairness in the world a bottle might have been the very thing to even the contest, perhaps bring it to a close.

However, what did ring the bell on the rout was the sound of Avril's voice.

'Earl, what's going on out there?' her call coming from the dimly lit passageway, and hearing his name, Earl turned his head, dropping both fists.

Later, when trying to reassemble all the fragments of that night's horror, our hero decided that had to have been the perfect cinematic moment to bring the beer bottle into play. The script cried out for it, for by this time it was like a movie running in his head, some often-played, old Bruce Willis or Sly Stallone video. Instead, reacting as any sensible coward would, he made a dash into the yawning dark where the yard's back wall appeared to have an opening, finding himself moments later in someone's garden trampling over what felt like a load of potato drills, falling a few times, then scrambling up and over a neighbour's fence. At least three more of these he must have scaled, fortunately all low and dilapidated, before coming out on the village street opposite the petrol station, black as a mausoleum now.

Bent over and hobbling at a half-run like someone prematurely, savagely aged in some way, he took off down the empty road he had travelled earlier that evening, away forever from this nest of horror.

But the journey back held more dread, diving into ditches, as he did, each time he saw the approaching lights of a car, for it might well be Earl, his thirst for vengeance still unslaked. And there was the pain too, for he started aching the moment he left the street lamps behind, like an animal postponing licking its wounds until it had reached the dark, throbbing all over and in places it didn't seem reasonable or fair to actually feel pain. The palms of his hands, for instance. Or inside his mouth. *The hair on his head, for God's sake.* As for his clothes, he could only imagine the amount of abuse they must have undergone, especially the new leather jacket.

Of course the worst part hung over him still, like a blade poised to fall, and when finally he limped up that deserted home stretch past the post office and the chemist's, before turning into his own row he checked his watch for the other bad news, but his expensive Swiss timepiece had stopped. He shook it. Eleven-thirty, he could just about make out, which must have been when Earl's blitzkrieg was at its height.

When he got to the house he saw the curtains were pulled straight across with no hint of a light within, which was the moment when he really felt as though his life was spooling backwards, and he was that teenager again terrified of being locked out, while being equally scared of the old man's reaction when he saw the state he was in.
    Leaning up against the door frame, he closed his eyes. There was a smell of earth with an overlay of dog-dirt in his nostrils. It came from him, he realised. After the third and more forceful knock, a light came on inside, with an accompanying growl from Bruce, as if, he, at least, was impatient to get the ball of blame rolling.

THE GOOD SHIP LOLLIPOP

When the door opened, face white with shock, the old man exclaimed, 'Good God, look at you! Were you run over?'

Not *where have you been*, or, *do you realise what time it is?* as he'd been expecting, like being sixteen again.

'Jesus, you might have been killed. The state of you! Are you all right, son? Are you?'

And for a moment he felt he might just get away with the line thrown to him of being in an accident, he really did, until catching that first glimpse of himself in the fireplace mirror, the black eye already puffing up in all its soon to be Technicolor glory, he decided he couldn't pull it off. How could he?

'Maybe I should ring for an ambulance,' said his old man. 'You could have broken something.'

Another shock to the system, him offering to use the phone. So then he told him, 'No, no, it's not as bad as it looks.'

Some joke, feeling as he did right now like he'd been trampled underfoot by a raging bull, or had his ribs squeezed in a vice. Even his toes felt the size of sausages, massively swollen, over-cooked ones.

'Take your jacket off. It's had it by the look of things.'

Slowly, gingerly, he lowered himself on to the ancient settee silvered with dog hairs.

'How did it happen? One of them joyriders, I bet. They come out of the city, tear along the country roads, then head back into town again, and burn out somebody's new car handy to where they live. The police? Too busy sitting on their fat backsides watching game shows on television with the barracks doors barred and bolted. This place has gone to hell, I tell you.'

Never had he seen him so animated, warming to his theme of how bad things had got of late, and he made it sound so real, so passionate too, that listening to him he wanted to be involved as well, part of it, another innocent victim, another statistic.

'Look, are you sure you don't want me to get Doctor Dinsmore?' again motioning to the telephone.

'No, no. I'll be okay. I'll just wash up first then get to bed. I'll be fine in the morning, you'll see. Honest.'

Only, of course, he wasn't. Not a wink of sleep or rest was to come his way as he lay waiting for the bedroom curtains to change colour from dark back to light again. All the rest of that long night he wrestled with his conscience over not telling the old man what had *really* happened, reminding him, the outline of his ruined clothes lying at the foot of the bed in an accusing heap. He continued to ache all over. Every part of him. One of his teeth was loose, and his ankle, the right, felt definitely sprained. But it was his ribcage and abdomen which seemed to have come off worst, the possibility of internal injuries passing through his head. But overlaying all of that, which was tangible, physical, he felt he could handle, given a day or two, was the still unresolved problem of the actual episode itself.

Twenty years earlier he had also lied when he had come home in a not dissimilar state, without the injuries, of course, although he had been a lot drunker then, reeking of beer, and not whiskey. Incidentally, just why hadn't the old man noticed, or even mentioned the smell of drink this time? Or had all that mysteriously evaporated on the way back under the influence of the panic running in his veins? That first time he had perjured himself, making up a story, and here he was about to do the same all over again as though the years between had taught him nothing.

THE GOOD SHIP LOLLIPOP

Lying listening to the dawn chorus, he decided to set the record straight. He would tell the true story, the full, unvarnished version of what had taken place, leaving nothing out, every last shaming detail. Stretched on his back under his mother's best eau-de-Nil eiderdown, suddenly he felt as if a weight was lifted from him, already rehearsing in his head the opening of what would be his great confessional coming of age, when he heard the old man in the living-room below. He had this early morning ritual of lighting the fire, after raking out the previous day's ashes, still warm, which ignited the screwed-up balls of newsprint, the kindling, then, finally, the carefully placed coals on top, all of it accompanied by a fugue of groans and wearisome sighs.

But this time a startling new sound came rising up, shocking in its novelty. For a moment he thought it must be the wireless, far too early for TV, someone crooning, male, certainly no professional, and then he recognised the voice. The old man was actually *singing*.

Coming bolt upright in spite of the pain, he craned to listen, the words of the song coming back to him from a long, long way off, from his childhood, that old number his mother would perform for him and his younger brother, ever associated with an ancient black and white musical and a curly-haired moppet belting it out in precocious, trouper fashion.

He found himself silently mouthing along to the words, '*On the good ship Lollipop, there's a great big candy-shop.*'

Then, in a further, even more surreal, twist, heard old Bruce below joining in as well, an accompaniment of howls as though he, too, was just as bewildered at what he was hearing.

Some short time later the aroma of frying bacon came drifting up, another first, for the old man invariably started his day with over-salted, lumpy porridge. And just when he was considering getting up, that's if his limbs would allow him to, there came a knock on the bedroom door, and the old man backed in bearing a tray, on it a full fried breakfast, the works, tea, toast *and* marmalade, and it was his mother's best china, too, the old blue and white willow pattern set kept locked up in the glass-doored cabinet in the parlour.

He laid the tray across his covered legs.

'You look as if you've gone the full distance with Mike Tyson,' he said, grinning. 'And don't be thinking of getting up, or going home, 'til you're back on your feet. Me and Bruce will look after you, won't we, Brucie?'

The dog had waddled in behind him and was watching him with a suspicious look in his runny brown eyes.

Then the old man went off downstairs still humming to himself, leaving the dog lying there following every mouthful he took.

And so it continued like that for another four days, him lying flat out like a pampered brat listening to the stranger below happy at his housework, once even hearing the bump and whine of a vacuum cleaner float up to him while he and Bruce exchanged shared looks of disbelief.

On the fifth day he rose shakily and went downstairs to a different living-room, dusted, clean, fire blazing, even a bunch of flowers in a vase on the sideboard. Shaved and changed into the blue and grey Viyella shirt he had bought him last Christmas, and had never worn to his knowledge, the old man greeted him, looking ten years younger.

'Well, son, and what would you like to eat for your dinner? How about a nice bit of boiled bacon and cabbage? What do you say?'

And to his eternal shame he heard himself reply in his newly acquired invalid's voice, 'Well, okay, but nothing too heavy or filling. Some stewed apple and custard for afters, maybe?' him back in his old junior plaid dressing-gown again, kept off school with the mumps, or was it chickenpox? being cosseted with a pile of comics to hand.

Later that day he rang his wife.

'Look,' he told her, 'there's been something of a tiny mishap here. No, don't get alarmed, nothing serious, just a minor argument with some hit and run young idiot's car, that's all. Don't worry, I'm all right, really. Just shook up, a bruise or two. I'm staying on another week.'

Eventually she got round to asking, 'And how's old Grumpy?' lowering her voice as she did so.

'Oh, he sends his love. Wants to know when you're coming over. The pair of us. Isn't that so, dad?'

And his old man, wearing one of his mother's flowered pinnies, grinned and waved back at him through the open scullery door.

Dining at the Dunbar

When our Cissie passed away, she left the house to me, the one we'd always lived in together the two of us, nothing remotely grand or 'desirable' about it, but still a wee palace as far as we were concerned, all thanks to Cissie, of course, for I'd never have the temerity to take credit for something that should have been written on her headstone — HERE LIES ONE WHOSE MOTTO IN LIFE WAS ALWAYS CLEANLINESS, CLOSE RUN THING TO GODLINESS.

Two days after the funeral I started drinking in earnest, up to then only having toyed with the stuff, and maybe Cissie had something to do with that for, although she wasn't one of your hosanna joannas, her disapproval was something I would never have risked, not while she was around anyway, even though she was only my big sister. Anyway the smell of drink in that house where air freshener reigned supreme would have been about as alien as incense in the Ebenezer Memorial Tabernacle down the far end of our street, so I shut myself away with a bottle —

a collection of bottles — blearily watching those dead soldiers take over the kitchen.

Where had they all come from?

The truth was I couldn't remember. I didn't remember to wash, shave, change my clothes, cook, or eat, either. The house began to resemble one of Cissie's worst nightmares, for I recall she used to get up in the middle of the night sometimes and start hoovering as if the dirt demons were after her.

Cissie. I can see her still. Heavy-set like me, with the same awkward stance and gait, although the last year or so because of her trouble she rarely left the house, sending me out to get the groceries and the Saturday night video, old musicals, mostly, for from an early age we both doted on those vintage stars of yesteryear, Kelly, Astaire, Cyd Charisse, Marge and Gower Champion. I bet no one remembers those two except some old-timer who danced the night away under one of those big revolving, mirrored glitter-balls. Cissie and me, we caught the tail-end of an era, foxtrotting with the snow-birds before Disco took over. John Travolta, I'm not. Nor was Cissie Olivia Newton John.

She would have laughed at that, for she was a great chuckler in her own quiet way, even when the pain in her legs made her reach for the high dosage Codeine. She suffered a lot towards the end, but forget hospital, would not be separated from the family brass bed. The house was everything to her, you see, the house and me, wrapped up in the same loving package, and here was I turning it into a tip, front door jammed by a foot-high paper drift of junk mail.

I had got to the stage where I had taken down all the family photographs, well, just her and me, for that's the way it had been ever since I can remember in that two-up, two-down, terraced kitchen house of ours. I couldn't bear any record of happier days. But, then, sitting staring at all those blank spaces on the wallpaper got to be nearly as bad.

And there I might have remained stewing in my own mess growing a beard like Robinson Crusoe, if help — if you can call it that — hadn't arrived from an unlikely source. From time to time, okay, neighbours had paid calls. In a street like ours folk go in for that kind of thing, rallying around, as they see it, but one afternoon whoever it was would neither take the hint, or no for an answer.

The letter-flap came banging in and through the slot I saw a pair of eyes regarding me as though framed by the slit in a balaclava, a voice crying out, 'Big Artie wants to see you! Artie Spence!' as if I didn't know who Artie was. For frig's sake everybody knew who Artie was. You jumped when his name came up, leapt even higher if ever he expressed a desire to actually *see* you. *Christ, Artie Spence wanted to see me!*

The two hoods hunkered at my front door that day were Growler Moore and Ivan Purdy, otherwise known as Hush Puppy. Our friendly neighbourhood heavies seem to have this thing about nicknames. Maybe it's because aliases come naturally in their line of work, even Mickey Mouse ones.

Of course, all this is in my head. Life with Cissie, you see, was like living in a fairytale world behind a safety curtain of double net, deaf, dumb, blind, the pair of us, to everything ugly and disturbing taking place on the outside. But all that was about to change the day those two tattooed lovelies in their matching, olive green, nylon bomber jackets came into my life and sat drinking tea in our kitchen while I had a quick scrub and shave upstairs.

'Fuck me, if it isn't Howard Hughes,' said Growler when I first opened the door.

'Fuck me, but this place smells like the monkey-house at Bellevue,' said Ivan. And more of the same while they put the kettle on, opening a packet of Rich Tea digestives for themselves.

Well, I came downstairs, face tingling from the unaccustomed kiss of the razor, and stood there watching them make themselves at home. For the first time I noticed both were wearing poppies, so it must have been early November, which only goes to show how far I had lost track of everything, including time.

'Do you know what Artie wants to see me about?'

They looked at me. My voice didn't sound right, as if it belonged to somebody else, someone who'd been abroad a long time, losing touch, as well as his ear, for his native tongue.

'That's for him to know and you to find out,' said Ivan brushing crumbs into his saucer. 'Jesus, your sister would do her absolute nut if she could see all this.'

'Yeah,' said Growler, 'a right friggin' midden and no mistake. Now, get your coat on.'

Outside the air hit me like a slap from a wet facecloth, making me totter, legs wobbly, as if, like myself, they'd been out of circulation far too long as well. We passed some of the neighbours making a big deal out of brushing their front steps, but I knew they were there purely for the purposes of speculation, I hadn't been away that long. Everything looked hard-edged and very, very bright, including the freshly-painted red, white and blue kerbstones, probably for Remembrance Day, although every day around here seems to be like that. You only have to read what's written on the walls to realise it.

At one of the houses a woman was buffing her already gleaming windows with a new chamois leather, its exceptional yellowness startling to the eye. As we approached she stopped what she was doing, putting a hand out to touch my arm. She was wearing Marigold gloves, same sunshine shade as the chamois.

'Kenny,' she said, 'Kenny, dear, I'm awful sorry for your trouble. Poor Cissie,' and I felt a lump rise in my throat, my two escorts looking heavenwards as though embarrassed, possibly even displaying some delayed respect for the bereaved, but somehow I didn't think so, next minute moving me roughly on towards my showdown with Mister Wonderful. That's Artie Spence's nickname, by the way, although people never say it to his face.

At the foot of our street one of the houses has been left derelict, deliberately so, it would appear, sandwiched as it is between two perfectly sound, lived-in dwellings. Growler and Ivan marched me up to this abandoned looking site, even though the door was clad in graffiti-free, reinforced, steel plate, knocking three times. All the time I kept thinking, what had I done to get on the wrong side of Artie Spence, for a summons to the Dunbar Supper Club, as it was known, usually meant one thing, and I didn't wish to dwell on anything as seriously debilitating as that.

My two goons pushed me through and into a short, dim hallway, still with carpet underfoot, even flowery paper on the walls. Up ahead was this great big room with booths around its rim. I could see a pool-table, a bar, cigarette and gaming machines. The place looked empty even though it had a twenty-four hour, members' only licence, or so I'd been told.

'Stay here,' ordered Growler.

He didn't actually growl when he spoke, but then a lot of people's nicknames would appear to be based on things that are pretty obscure anyway, Hush Puppy being a case in point. He leaned up against the pool table idly rolling balls into the far pocket while I stood there like somebody waiting to be called into a doctor's surgery. Some doctor. Some surgery.

'Okay, he'll see you now,' said Growler.

Artie Spence was sitting behind a new looking desk, so clean, so cleared of everything as to look positively eerie. Not even a paper clip.

'Close the door behind you,' he said, and Growler did as he was told, even though it was clearly obvious he didn't wish to leave, at least not yet anyhow. This, after all, was the fun part as far as he was concerned, watching me get what was coming to me. But just what exactly was that? I didn't feel too hot, nauseous in the stomach. Couldn't recall when I'd eaten last, not even a biscuit with my two visitors earlier.

'Pull up a pew.'

For the first time I realised a dog was in the room. At first I'd taken it for a hairy rug spread out alongside the desk. Then I remembered Blondie, Artie's Alsatian. People said it had been a police dog in an earlier existence, a typical Artie jest. It was also rumoured he liked to walk it on a chain past the patrols out with their own animals, him with his renegade Shepherd with the studded collar, or, sometimes, a Red Hand bandana knotted about its powerful neck. It was amazing, really, just how much a recluse like me actually knew about Artie Spence.

'Forgive me for saying so, old hand, but you look like absolute shit. I know you've been through a lot, but you shouldn't let yourself go like that.'

One thing more. Artie Spence always looked like he'd just stepped out of a fashion pull-out, every mother's dream of what her boy should be. On the outside, that is. Underneath, another dimension entirely. Today he had on a beautifully faded denim shirt with pearl buttons, and although I couldn't see under the desk, ironed jeans with creases, too, I'd hazard a guess.

'What weight are you anyway? Fourteen? Fifteen stone? Look at you. Your sister would be ashamed of you. Speaking of that good woman, that's why you're here, for we have a wee problem, you and me, now that's she's gone. To put it bluntly, we're talking about outstanding debt, never a nice topic.'

And he took a small spiral-backed notebook from the desk drawer and read out a figure that made me go even weaker at the knees. The shock must have showed, for Artie got up, spreading his palms flat on top of the desk while Blondie gave a low, warning growl in case I might suddenly decide on freaking out.

'She didn't tell you? Benny Armitage the wee Shylock was into her for near enough two grand, just like a lot of other people around here, over their heads, until we made him an offer he couldn't refuse, if you see what I mean.' At which he allowed himself a wintry smile which only made me feel worse.

'To cut to the chase, we're servicing all Benny's financial affairs and commitments from here on in. But not at sixty per, not even fifty, even forty. Let's say, twenty-five, shall we? I mean, a quarter's reasonable, wouldn't you say? We're not bloodsuckers. Neither are we a charity. This club, Ken, I tell you, this fucking place, you would not believe the overheads, not to mention all the people we have to take care of.'

There was a pause.

Then he said, 'Look, ask the lads to pour you a wee scotch. On the house. I can tell you need time to get your head around this. Ken, we're not fucking animals. You and me were raised in the same street, went to the same wee school, remember? Now, we all know you kept your head down and your nose clean when the rest of us we're out there doing our bit for the Cause, some of us paying a heavy price for it, but then some people are just not cut out for that. *I know that*, but there's others who're not so understanding, or forgiving. Do I make myself clear?'

He came around the desk then, and I had been right, he *was* wearing pressed Levis. His belt buckle read G — for Gucci, I imagine, or Gap, maybe. How would I know?

Growler and his mate were shooting pool in the other room, the intense clack of the balls banging in my head.

'Well that wasn't so bad. Or was it?' said he cheerfully, chalking his cue.

'Yeah, still got your kneecaps,' said Purdy, and they both laughed.

As I moved to leave Growler called out after me, 'Don't be a stranger, you hear me now, Kenny?'

Walking home in a daze I felt like somebody who'd just risen from a sickbed only to be told what he'd got was incurable. I still couldn't take it in. How had she kept it from me? *How?* But then she'd always protected me from things anyway, ever since I was a youngster, then all the way up and into manhood. Yet I didn't *feel* like a man. Not a proper one. Not in the context of what that was supposed to mean around here. Not as it was understood in the Dunbar Supper Club.

That afternoon I walked and walked further and further and through areas I hadn't ventured into since Cissie and me, we used to go downtown together on Saturdays to the big shops, the cinemas, Woolworth's top floor cafeteria, Smithfield, places like that. People didn't do that kind of thing any more, not since the bad days of the Troubles, I told myself, the two of us sitting there in our matching plaid slippers watching *Singin' in the Rain* and *Gigi* and calling out the choicest bits if one of us had to get up to put the kettle on.

That day my world was turned upside down, inside out, just the way it happened in so many of those old movies round about reel one. But, in my particular case, I couldn't see any happy ending before the final credits rolled. And, yes, people were thronging the big stores, laughing and smiling, hordes of them, darting in and out of pubs, carols already playing inside every shop, the City Hall illuminated like one gigantic Christmas cake, the tree, a gift from the people of Norway, lit up in front of it. I kept getting bumped into, or maybe it was the other way round. Everybody seemed to have a purpose, a destination in mind, all except me. For a long time I stood up against a shop window watching them climb on and off buses. One of the single-deckers had the name of my own area across the front of it, but I wasn't sure how you paid — was it before, or after you got on? — so I walked back all the way home again.

It was properly dark by the time I got to our street. I could see the bluish play of TV screens showing through the curtains of every house I passed, people inside eating and talking, families, number thirty-four being the odd man out.

Pushing hard against the tide of correspondence covering the inside mat, I let myself in, and for a long time sat in the dark too nervous to go near a light switch. The place smelt stale and airless like somebody else's house. There was an even worse smell coming from the kitchen.

Then the questions started arriving in a swarm, the ones I'd managed to keep at bay all day by dint of exercise. How had she allowed it to go on as long as it did? And when exactly had it all started anyway? Why hadn't she told me, not even at the end, knowing it would all blow up in my face, me sitting here now like a bomb victim?

I knew there was a bottle of sweet sherry in the cupboard under the stairs. With drying mouth I sat there visualising its every detail, the yellow and gold label, the uncut foil still gripping the neck, the dimpled base, the entire, green glass gleam of it. The torture lasted for about twenty minutes, then I rose and went to the glory-hole. Inside it smelled of wax polish and cleaning fluid. One of her old flowered aprons still hung on a hook behind the door. As I reached for the light pull it brushed against my face. The bottle of Empire Cream was on a shelf up near the sloping ceiling, but I held myself back before reaching for it. It was the smells, you see, all of her scent contained and concentrated in that confined space, so, instead, I dropped to my knees, reaching deep into the lowest and darkest recesses where the stairs began.

Back there was a cardboard box, thick with dust, the words COSSOR MONARCH printed across it. Maybe that was what she'd spent the money on, I thought to myself. But not all of it, surely. Then, again, hadn't that old valve radio been bought when I was still at school?

Blowing the dust away I carried the carton into the front room and laid it on our leather inlaid coffee table. Taped across the joins with ancient, yellowing Sellotape, it made my hands feel filthy just looking at it, but I had to continue now I had begun. Anyway Cissie wasn't around to stop me, not now, not ever. I always knew, you see, that's where she hid away her most private, secret possessions, and being the sort of person I was, not once had I gone against her wishes and pried inside.

And I suppose that says a lot about me, my character, I mean. Big, fat, biddable, home-bird Kenny. Still, to be honest, I had never really given a lot of thought to what other people did, or didn't think of me. At school, maybe, but then that was ancient history, like something that had happened to someone else, a stranger. No, I had managed pretty well to get by without ever running up hard against someone else's unflattering opinion of me. Not until today, when I had seen myself reflected in the eyes of Artie Spence and his buddies, with every shop window from then on throwing back the same mocking image. Sitting there with Cissie's holy of holies in front of me, I wondered if maybe she, too, had seen me in that same light. I would never know, and there and then I had a little weep to myself, and after that I tore off the dried strips sealing her old box of tricks.

A deep top layer of musty papers was what I found, which I went through looking for something else, bills, receipts, bank statements, a Co-op book, anything that might help solve the mystery of the debt she'd run up with that wee moneylender, and which now, I discovered, *I* owed Artie Spence. Right at the very bottom I came upon this cache of mementoes, a still curling whorl of blonde hair in a little silvered box, a pair of tiny baby bootees, a perished pink rubber dummy, a teething-ring. I began to feel I was turning over Cissie's grave. Just who had all these infant keepsakes belonged to anyway?

DINING AT THE DUNBAR

I might still be sitting there staring at them, no wiser, if I hadn't gone back to sorting through some of those old documents again, and in the middle of that sheaf of mildewed stuff came upon a folded page in an envelope that answered my question in such a way it felt as if someone had slipped a noose about my neck and was tightening it bit by bit, as I took in what was written there.

Looking back on that day, it occurs to me that just maybe you can experience an entire existence's worth of hurt inside one twenty-four hour period. I really believe that. Well I do now, after coming across my own birth certificate in that faded buff envelope. Bad enough discovering that somebody had got your age wrong, five years out, and actually older, but the real bombshell lay in the section under MOTHER'S NAME. The space above had been left blank, but, then, so, okay, I *was* a bastard, something I'd always suspected anyway, then taken as read. Cissie always avoided the issue, and I never pressed. Just occasionally I might have asked myself why she hadn't wanted it brought up. Well, now I knew. MOTHER'S NAME: *Cecilia Moore. Spinster.*

There it was, folks, in black and white, three little words, like the song says, that were to turn my world upside down like a dropped cake.

Back inside the box went everything, including that great big secret of hers she'd taken to the grave with her, or thought she had, for it was mine as well now. I sealed up that old radio carton with new tape, then put it back where it belonged, where it should have stayed, under the stairs.

As regards the rest of that night, I can't remember how I got through the hours. One thing I do know, I didn't open the bottle of sweet Empire sherry. It's there in the glory-hole still, along with Cissie's box, for, yes, I continue to call her that. The other more formal, official one would be unthinkable. Even voicing it in my own head I'd feel as if it could be seen stamped on the outside like a brand for all to see.

The next day was a Saturday. It seemed I was coming out of my coma, for I actually checked it against the Littlewoods' calendar hanging behind the kitchen door. It, too, had a premature picture of Christmas, just like all those shop-window displays I had passed the day before. Of course it meant nothing to me, the religious, the festive bit, I mean. For all I cared it might have been Ramadan, or the Jewish one with the other funny name. I had stopped believing a long time ago, and even if I hadn't, what had been dumped on me twelve hours earlier from a great height would have made anyone a sceptic, I imagine. That's the way I felt anyhow, cold, angry and very, very bitter inside.

After I got up I washed and dressed carefully. A white poplin shirt — it had the scent of mothballs clinging to it, which gave me a momentary relapse: smells were going to be hard to handle, I was beginning to realise that — a pair of dark green corduroy trousers, a double-vented, tweed sports jacket. To be frank, I didn't even know I had such a thing in the wardrobe. In the mirror I looked like a schoolteacher, or a scoutmaster in civvies, somebody pretty square anyway, even though I could have done with a haircut. That, too, had been Cissie's department, me in our old bentwood chair, and her going snip, snip, snip, then clip, clip, clip.

The kitchen was still a mess, but I didn't care. Anyway I had no interest in the state of it, any part of the house any more. My head was clear. As far as I was concerned the entire place was now only four walls and a roof, windows and a door, wood, brick, slate, with inside a lot of somebody else's useless old junk, particularly the stuff stored away in a cardboard box under the stairs. I had this picture of someone running across it one day, maybe pondering on what was inside for a moment or two before giving it to the rag and bone man, or burning it in the backyard, something I had thought of myself, but I needed more time, needed to get my mental breath back.

First things first, I kept telling myself, *first things first*, repeating it like an incantation all the way down our street right up to the reinforced, grey, metal door I'd been brought to the day before.

Trying to recall the magic sequence, I rang the bell three times, two long, then one short, plus a fourth one out of nervousness. There was a peephole, barely a pinhead in size, I hadn't noticed before, and I tried not to stare too hard at it and whoever had their eye pressed against the cold steel on the far side.

Eventually that someone did open up, sticking his head out, then glancing rapidly up and down the street, before enquiring, 'Who're you, mate?'

I told him, somebody I hadn't seen before, quite a bit older than I expected, and extremely jumpy, I could see that, like somebody who had been given a job he didn't think he was up to. His name was Bo Bo, and later we were to become friendly, sharing the same general unease around so many hard cases, Bo Bo Blevins, this stocky wee guy with a bad leg and a stutter, as if one of those wasn't bad enough to be going on with, the stammer becoming even more evident when he tried to quiz me as to my business.

'I'm here to see Artie,' I told him, 'he's expecting me. Needs my signature on something.'

Well, why not? Mightn't it come to that?

'Call back in an hour's time. He's out at the minute. Okay?'

'Okay,' I said, and went walking off, feeling conspicuous in my old-fashioned get-up, like somebody who'd gone to a lot of trouble for nothing, so as to complain, maybe, about something, the electricity, or the gas, or the refuse collection, or a faulty item, say, bought the day before.

Sitting on a park bench some time later killing time, the notion would not leave me. I mean I actually started picturing that fictional product, a clock-radio that wouldn't work, not a peep, nothing, even when I opened it up. Not that I told the salesman that. I mean I'm not a total chump.

Just before noon I went back to the club, and this time Bo Bo let me in straightaway.

'I've told big Artie. He's expecting you.'

He still sounded nervous though, as I followed him up the badly stained, carpeted passageway, adjusting my pace to his. The left leg was the bum one, and not the result of a punishment shooting, either, unusual whenever you saw someone with a limp like that around our parts. Polio, Bo Bo told me. When he was twelve. We were around about the same age, but he looked like my father, that's if I ever had one.

'The lads are watching last night's big fight,' he said before we got to the bar. 'On satellite.'

Then he pushed open a door which must have been closed the first time I'd been there, sound-proofed, or reinforced, maybe, like the outer one, for the instant Bo Bo opened it the noise hit me like a blow, the commentary on the cantilevered TV high on one wall screaming at fever pitch, the place dense with craning fans roaring abuse at the screen, every table covered with pint glasses, bottles, chaser shorts, even though it was still early in the day.

Clumsily Bo Bo threaded his way between the closely-packed tables, me hugging his heels. This was truly hellish, the din, the heat, the smoke, the sweating faces of the punters, their weight-lifting girth, all of it. One or two heads turned in my direction, for everything about me must have screamed *outsider*, but somehow Bo Bo steered me safely through to that far door marked PRIVATE, the very word itself reaching out to me like precious balm.

When it closed behind me the silence in Artie Spence's office was such a shock I felt certain I could hear the blood hammer in my head.

'Well, that was quick,' said he, not looking up from an open ledger on his desk.

Today he was wearing a burgundy crew neck. It had a miniature golfer over the left breast teeing off. I could also see an expensive-looking black leather jacket hanging on a hanger in the corner.

'I'm going to sell the house,' I said.

He lifted his head at that, steepling his fingers. They looked pale and well cared for as if he might be one of those compulsive hand-washing types, whereas his face appeared lightly tanned.

'Now why would you want to go and do a thing like that for?'

I stared at him. This wasn't the answer, or the question I had been expecting. At the same time I could hardly say, *because it means nothing to me any more, that's why*. Not since yesterday evening about seven o'clock, to be precise.

'Look, there's no need to get premature. Anyway, I

wouldn't want it on my conscience. As I said, we're not into ruining people. We look after our own.'

'But I can't pay up. All I have is the house.'

'Ah,' said he, 'ah,' as if something had gone suddenly click.

Then, 'What about dole money, benefits, that sort of thing? I mean, have you ever been in work, Kenny?'

Suddenly my head felt like it was bursting. I hadn't come here for this. In, then out, that's what I had in mind, not this social worker crap. Anyway wasn't Artie Spence supposed to be someone who'd *killed* people? Served time for it? I mean was nothing in this world the way it was supposed to be?

'Let me make a suggestion. One thing I've learned, there's always a way round things. Don't look so serious, nobody wants to see you out on the street. Anyhow, where would you go? This is where you were brought up. And you don't look like somebody who might easily fit in with strangers. Am I right?'

Then he said something that threw me completely. 'Tell me, Kenny, can you cook at all?'

He laughed, teeth pearly white, capped like a movie star's.

'No, I don't mean like one of them guys you see on daytime TV. Your basic stuff, fries and things, burgers, chips, steaks.'

I said, 'I don't follow you, Artie.'

He threw his head back, staring at the ceiling, sighing.

'Look, you see that wee guy who brought you in here? Bo Bo, he's called. Maybe you know him. Bo Bo Blevins. What maybe you don't know is Bo Bo used to have a serious gambling problem. Horses, dogs, cards, you name it, he's done it. In over his head like your Cissie. But, worse. Oh, a lot. Know what he's doing here? He's working off his debt, that's what. A bit at a time. Here in the club. Now he might well be drawing his old age pension by the time he's clear, but then it was a real big wedge the bookies were into him for. And he likes it here. Keeps him clear of temptation. If he goes near that one arm bandit next door, well, he knows the score. One arm, one leg, it's up to him. So, now, I'll ask you again, Kenny, can you cook, or can't you?'

That was Saturday. The following Monday I was standing in the club's kitchen, only a sliding hatch separating me from the action in the bar beyond, all togged out in white trousers, double-breasted catering jacket, even a chequered handkerchief about my neck, staring around me at my new place of work. I mean, what could I do? Turn Artie Spence down? Tell him I had other plans? I had none, as a matter of fact, all my brave resolutions having leaked away over the course of the weekend.

Bo Bo Blevins was with me wearing a Rangers apron.

'Are you sure you know what you're doing?' he was saying. 'I mean you don't look like a chef. Then, again, you *are* big and fat. The wee woman who did the cooking before you left to go to her daughter's in England. We've had to make do with takeaways ever since. You'd be surprised how hungry some of them galoots out there can get. Especially after they've come in from a job.'

I tried not to think of that last observation of his. In fact, for me, it would be three monkeys' time from then on as to what went on behind that peep-holed, armour-plated door at the bottom end of our street.

'Just what exactly are the meal-times?' I asked.

He laughed, first time I'd seen his miserable kisser crease up since we'd met.

'*Exactly*, is it? *Meal-times*? Like at *home*, you mean? For fuck's sake, we're like a Seven-Eleven here. Closer to Seven-to-Seven. Right around the clock, that's us.'

Well, of course, he had to be exaggerating. Nobody could be expected to be on call that length of time, nobody human, that is, and, besides, there were only the two of us. Anyway, Bo Bo didn't seem to have a home to go to. I was convinced he slept on the premises. He was always about the place whenever I turned up in the morning, yawning after another late night. He spent a lot of the time cleaning tables, washing dishes, mopping floors, and when he wasn't doing that he was leaning in the open hatch gazing longingly at the one arm bandit machine like some brightly-lit altar he would never be allowed to worship at. Every time he heard those revolving fruit click, then line up, he would give a little shiver. But if a jackpot ever rang out, followed by a silvery cascade, he would start to shake all over. It was a new experience for me. I'd never known an addict before. He also studied form, marking up the races in his paper without ever placing a bet, like some nicotine junkie never without an unlit fag in his mouth.

Bo Bo Blevins and me, what a combination. And it became just that, a team effort of two, me dripping sweat on to the hot plate, chip pan smoking like a volcano, the microwave going *ping*, and him calling out orders through the hatch.

'Cheeseburger twice with fries, double mushy peas, four pie and chips, cod in batter, another pasty, extra portion of spicy chicken legs, pop tarts, two, fillet of plaice, grilled, not fried, coleslaw!'

That last order was for Artie by the way. He rarely ate at the club, and if he did then it was always something strictly dietary or health-conscious. Bo Bo would carry it into him on a tray, folded paper napkin and all, with his very own condiment set. Inside the bar it was Colman's mustard, brown vinegar, ketchup and Daddy's sauce. Not that I minded all that much what they doused their food with, not at first, anyhow, when it was simply a race against the clock and Bo Bo's cries of, 'And another plate of chips for table fucking five!'

Once during a lull when I was sitting on the floor with my head back and eyes shut I heard Bo Bo say, 'Know something? You're the right mystery, you are.'

'What do you mean?' I replied, continuing to enjoy the respite behind closed lids.

'Don't come the little Bo-Peep. How come you can do all this stuff?'

'Stuff?'

'Yeah, somebody must have taught you how to cook.'

'Call this cooking?'

But I knew what he meant. I hadn't developed a flair simply overnight. But at the same time I wasn't about to tell him Cissie had been my teacher in the kitchen either, as in a lot of other areas I also preferred not to dwell on any more. So I just laughed and hoped he would let it go. At that moment, luckily, somebody jerked the lever on the fruit-machine and his attention wandered.

One of the unexpected blessings of working where I did now was it did seem to take my mind off all that other business, Cissie and me, I mean, for even if I wasn't slaving in the steam and the heat and a permanent blue haze, at home I was too tired for anything but switching off and crawling into bed still reeking of cooking fat. After a time, of course, you don't notice it yourself, the smell, I mean. Other people do. Any time I ventured from the kitchen into the bar to grab a

Bounty or a Boost from the chocolate machine, or snatch a fleeting glance at the TV, I'd hear cries of, 'Watch out, here comes the oil-slick!' favoured comment of Dingo McClean one of Growler's buddies. Right from the start he had it in for me, I'll never know why, complaining about the grub, sending it back to have it re-cooked, re-heated, changing the order, things like that. 'Pansy Potter' was another of his chosen jibes and, of course, 'Mammy's boy', which really hit a nerve.

Naturally I started spitting in his food, that age-old, retaliatory kitchen tactic, and Bo Bo added his own contribution as well, for he, too, was Dingo's butt, enduring 'Hopalong' and 'Limpalong Lesley'. Of course, those pricks, they never know what you've done to their steak or lamb chop after you've dropped it, *oops*, then kicked it around the floor a few times, so revenge is never really as sweet as you would like it to be, powdered glass being the ultimate in satisfaction, I imagine.

Together, through the hatch, we would watch him wolf down what was put in front of him, for there was always the outside possibility he would catch on. But he never did, and usually he was pretty well plastered anyway. Besides burning me up inside, he had begun to have an effect on me in other ways as well, to do with my keeping such a close watch on him any time he happened to be in the place, for it was then I started paying a lot more attention to all the other things that were going on there.

If you can imagine that single booth with Dingo, Growler, Ivan Purdy and a couple of their cronies as being the still, hard centre of my surveillance, and then, radiating out from it, all those other slightly less interesting circles of attention, that was the world I observed. Over in another corner would be grouped the muscle brigade, pumped up on steroids, shaved heads, tattoos, bulging biceps. The Michelin Men, I called them. A lot of the time they stuck to their own catering, although they did like the occasional steak, bloodier the better. Then there were those other looser, less well-defined groupings, tapering off in pecking order right down to your basic bunch of hangers-on and barflies. The more I watched the more I was learning, with Bo Bo filling in additional details from his table-clearing operations.

'Expect a late rush tonight,' he'd mutter out of the side of his mouth, returning with another trayful of dirty dishes. 'Take a ton load out of the freezer. The word is Artie's sending his top team on a job. Big heavy number.'

Acting the innocent, then I would say, 'Lorry load of smokes, is it?'

'You'll hear all about it on the News tomorrow. Bang, bang, okay?'

'Really?' I'd reply as if the only thing of interest to me in what he had to say was whether I had put enough sirloins aside.

I could see Bo Bo was excited, almost as if he'd pulled off a treble in the 3.30. But, then, maybe I was as well, in my own muted fashion, for I, too, was beginning to feel the tug of this unsettling new world, even from a distance, and through a two foot square, wooden-framed opening in the wall. It was like watching a performance every night, sometimes several at once, in different parts of that big, roaring room, the ebb and flow of people getting drunk, then heated, then taking offence, then calming down again, then maybe passing out. Sometimes the entire sequence going through its cycle in the time it took me to return to the stove, or the grill, get involved there, then come back to the hatch once more.

Foolishly I began believing in the fantasy that there was this transparent, one-way curtain between me and all that action that kept it in full view and me invisible. I had this actual picture in my head, like in one of those thriller-type movies with the good guys on one side of the glass and the baddies on the other. And, after all, who pays any attention to the sucker in the dirty white jacket bobbing back there like some red-faced apparition? Me and Bo Bo Blevins, we might as well have been a couple of shadows flitting about. It's true. What we got up to in the kitchen was our business, period. What they were about out there, another affair altogether.

But, unfortunately, someone took it into his head that those two separate concerns might be starting to converge in some way, and that someone had to be a right sicko bastard by the name of Dingo McClean.

I first began noticing the way he would keep glancing my way if ever I was framed in the hatch, as though his eyes were drawn by movement there and, in another unsettling development, he stopped hassling me verbally whenever I came into the bar, just that baleful stare following me like a creeping laser dot trained on my shoulderblades. No one else in the place seemed to have a similar problem, and gradually I tried ignoring it, as well as him.

Then one night, late, there was a commotion over in his booth. He was shouting something which couldn't be heard above a European football semi-decider on the box, pointing in the direction of the hatch, while at the same time, bent over, clutching his stomach. The others with him looked like they were trying to pacify him, but he happened to be a lot bigger then they were, and no amount of exertion on their part could keep him from kicking up a fuss.

Bo Bo, who was in the kitchen at the time, started getting agitated.

'I better go out and see what's eating that bastard,' he said.

'Why?' I asked.

'Well, for one thing, he's been holding his guts all night, and, two, he's been in and out of the bogs like a fucking yo-yo.'

'Then maybe you shouldn't have pissed on his chips the way you did, instead of the vinegar,' I joked, for I must have been in a rare, daredevil mood that evening.

'You didn't, did you? Oh, Christ!' Bo Bo's face was suddenly paler than death. 'You don't fucking know him like I do. A joke's a joke, but he's a right crazy cunt. Should be on a fucking leash.'

'Look,' I told him, 'we've done nothing. Not this time anyway. Let him suffer. That's his problem. Anyway, I'm tired of his cracks.' *Get me*, I thought, *Kenny Millar the Karate Kid.*

The next thing we knew Dingo was on his feet, still bent over, and heading for the toilets at a stumbling run yet again. We watched from the hatch, Bo Bo and me. It was the moment we'd both been waiting for, except we hadn't had a hand in it, not this time, anyway. Still, I was determined to enjoy the show while it lasted from my look-out in the wall.

Putting the cooking on hold for the time being, I hung in the hatch waiting for Dingo to reappear. Nearly five minutes elapsed before, finally, he came out of the door marked Gents, even though there never was a Ladies. He looked pale, a lot paler than when he went in, but no longer holding his gut. But instead of heading for his mates in the far corner, he came lurching through the centre tables where the not so hard men sat, the booths being reserved for the elite, those like himself with reputations to uphold. And that night in the

Dunbar Supper Club I was to receive a stern education in just exactly what that meant. I watched him coming for me feeling like a hypnotised chicken trapped in my own back-lighted coop.

'Oh, fuck, oh, fuck,' I heard Bo Bo moan as he dived for the back door leading to the yard where the bins were kept. *Well, thanks a bunch, Bo Bo, mate. Always knew I could depend on you.*

The TV still roared — someone had just missed a shoot-out — but everybody was now watching what was happening in their own immediate neighbourhood, or what was about to happen, as if some sort of sudden intense heat was coming off Dingo like radiation, a sensation, as opposed to a noise. Coming right up to the bar he leaned on the counter, beefy, bare arms livid with blue tattooing. He also had an earring, something which I had never really noticed before, quite small, and surprisingly delicate, the kind of pointless observation a condemned man might make before the trapdoor drops open.

Our eyes met. Rather, his locked on to mine.

'You,' he snarled, 'you, fucking Delia Smith,' and without thinking of the consequences I heard myself enquire, 'How was your meal? Okay, was it?'

Later I was told my off the cuff comment was to enter club folklore. My reputation as a joker had become fixed in that moment by accident, just the way other people get nicknames that are to stay with them for life. The truth, of course, was the words had sprung spontaneously to my lips as though from the half-remembered depths of some old movie, one of those lines where the tablecloths in a restaurant are always chequered black and white because Technicolor wasn't invented yet.

'You've fucking well poisoned me, you fat cunt, you know that?' And here a spasm crossed his face as if to illustrate his complaint.

'Think it's funny, do you? Get your fat arse out here. Pronto!'

The commentator on the TV was handing us now back to the studio, his voice human again, and up on the screen came the panel of four wise men paid to fill the gap until the next programme arrived. I must have been in a very peculiar state, for in that moment I remember praying there would be a sudden newsflash cutting into the transmission, the more horrendous the better. A bomb, maybe.

Somebody in one of the booths — I think it was one of the bodybuilders — called out, 'Pick on somebody your own size, McClean!' and there was this big laugh, which only seemed to enrage my tormentor further for, to everyone's consternation, he suddenly pulled a gun from under his Red Hand of Ulster sweatshirt, laying it flat on the bar counter.

I looked at it lying there, out of curiosity more than fear at this point, for I had never seen one, not in real life before. I have to say it looked enormous, much bigger than the trim-looking, designer affairs on TV or the movies, sort of a blue black *Dirty Harry* number with a heavy looking, scored, wooden butt.

People started shouting then.

'Get a grip, McClean! Put it away, for fuck's sake, man! You'll have us all lifted, wanker!'

Now I'll never know why I did what I did, for instead of doing a dive, like quite a number of the punters at the middle tables, I came away from the hatch at that point, around the corner of the bar and into the lion's den, even though my legs were shaking, with the strong likelihood of a damp trickle as a follow-up. Everybody in the place seemed to be holding their breath and looking at me.

By now the TV was running a penalty replay, but no one was paying much attention, least of all me studying the gun on the bar as if it might go off under its own volition. More to the point, was this crazy character in front of me just maddened enough to use it?

We stood there facing one another, me in my soiled whites, sweat cascading down my face, and him in his cut-off muscle shirt with the bloody hand emblem across its front.

'Well, well, well,' he said, 'if it isn't the fucking Naked Chef himself,' and everyone started relaxing as though the crisis point had passed.

'So, tell me something, fat boy, what are you really like with no strides on, eh? Come on, let's have a dekko, drop 'em.'

The entire club was now transfixed all over again, not a single man there slackening his gaze, as the moment stretched, me standing there feeling stripped already by the scrutiny of all those watching eyes.

'Don't keep me waiting, Oliver Hardy, I fucking well mean it.'

And then he said, 'Otherwise it'll be one sissy down and one to go,' and I heard someone shout, 'Holy Christ!' as, feeling the blood cloud my eyes, I went for the gun lying on the bar.

In my grasp it felt heavy and ungainly as I brought it up, trembling a little, trying to recall that two-handed grip I'd so often seen on *NYPB Blue* and those other cop shows. It carried a smell of 3-in-One Oil about it, too, which I remembered from the tool shed in our backyard.

Now to say that scent brought back a sudden memory of

my Cissie — for she was always the one who fixed things around the house when they needed it — would be maybe just too coincidental, following on, as it did, hearing Dingo say her name like that, or what to me sounded like her name, but, whatever the truth of it, I continued feeling murderous towards this man who had been my enemy ever since I got here. I wanted to kill him. I was ready to kill him with his own gun if necessary. Forget powdered glass, this was a lot more instant.

I kept wondering if I should thumb the hammer back or not. According to all those cowboy films, that was what you did, and this looked like one of those same Colt 45s, certainly a revolver of some kind. Later I was to learn it was a Webley, and an ancient one at that, possibly not fired since Dunkirk or El Alamein, despite smelling of oil.

Everything and everybody around me seemed to have gone into a state of slow motion, frozen, still, but then I heard someone say, 'Okay, okay, fun's over for tonight. Put it down, Kenny, there's a good lad,' and Artie Spence was standing in the open doorway of his office, lit from the back like some rescuing angel, or John Wayne, maybe, without his cavalry hat.

The gun still felt awkward in my hand, but not as much as before, and Dingo's face was certainly a picture, anger, yes, but fear there, as well. If I put the gun down that fear would evaporate, I told myself, and wrath would take its place. Did I want that?

'For the love of Christ are youse two goin' to dance with one another or not?' came a voice from one of the back booths. It belonged to 'Hoppy' Hopwood, half-drunk already, baseball cap swivelled back to front on his bald, tattooed dome, and instantly all tension in the room eased.

'How about that double beefburger I ordered about a fortnight ago?' rang out another voice.

'Yeah, I'm fucking well starving over here! And where's Bo Bo with them drinks?'

'How about some service? Like waiting for fucking Godot!'

In the midst of it all, Dingo and me, we continued standing there like a couple of actors enduring a severe bout of heckling, only ourselves to blame because of a real hammy performance, and suddenly the gun felt alien in my hand, oily, disgusting, too, and looking down, I thought to myself, *just how the hell did that manage to get there?*

Then I heard Artie say, 'Stick to cutlery and the kitchen stuff, Kenny. Shooters don't suit you. Now let's have it.'

But before I could hand it over, vastly relieved, Dingo cut in. 'It's my rod, so it is.'

'Not in here, it isn't,' said Artie, walking across and taking it off me. 'No weapons on the premises. You know the rules.'

By this time I had got myself across to the bar ready to go behind, then back into the kitchen where I belonged, for Artie was right, none of this was my affair. I never should have got involved, never, not even for a nano second.

'It's my fucking rod, I tell you,' repeated Dingo standing his ground, murder in his eyes.

For a moment Artie held the pistol up to the light examining it before spinning the chamber. Nothing fell out, and everyone in the room seemed to give this big collective sigh of relief, all except Dingo who came stepping forward fists clenched by his side.

Artie looked at him. 'You're barred,' he told him calmly. 'Don't come back.'

Dingo swung his head in the direction of his four buddies

hunched in the far corner. Growler had risen to his feet. He was swaying a little because of the booze, but the other three gazed down at the table of drinks in front of them.

'No shooters,' continued Artie, shoving the gun in the back pocket of his chinos. 'We don't need the aggro. This is a club we run here, not some fucking Wild West saloon. Do I make myself clear?'

'Oh, absolutely, Sheriff!' some wag called out in a high, sissified voice, and Artie grinned.

'Big man. Big, fucking man.'

Still Dingo wouldn't give in, and we all tried hard not to stare for it was becoming painful to watch, even if the same scumbag was only getting what he deserved. Finally, though, he made for the door, lurching slightly as though the drink had reared up in him again.

'I'll be back and tooled up,' his parting shot.

'Be my guest,' Artie told him. 'We can settle this outside right now if you like.'

But Dingo decided to walk and live to fight another day knowing, as we all did, about Artie and his judo black belt.

After the door closed there was this sudden, relieved outburst of joviality. Somebody switched channels on the TV to the late night, soft porn movie right in the middle of a sweaty, writhing clinch, and a tremendous roar went up. Artie looked more affable as well, and if this had been a movie stand-off for real with a bunch of proper cowboys instead of our own home-grown variety he might well have called for drinks on the house, but he didn't, calling me into his office instead.

This time he didn't offer me a chair so I stood in front of his desk twisting my chequered handkerchief behind my back. My palms still felt slippery from the butt of the gun, which was a curious sensation, seeing as they were used to dipping in and out of grease and suds all the time.

'I'm sorry, Artie,' I told him, 'about losing the rag like that. It won't happen again. My nerves got the better —'

Right there he stopped me with an upward sweep of the hand. 'Don't be,' he said, 'you did us all a favour. I should have bumped that loony-toon into the street a long time ago. One dangerous head-the-ball, spaced out most of the time. No hardware, no pills, that's my rules. Speaking of which, you don't drop the occasional tab yourself, do you, Kenny?'

I looked at him in shock.

'The odd wee upper to get you through? It's a long day, after all. You're under a lot of pressure. Which is what I wanted to talk to you about.'

Then he stopped. 'You all right? Here, sit down. You look a bit white all of a sudden.'

I lowered myself into the bucket chair facing that perfect desk of his.

'This is what I have in mind. Let me run it past you. A decent menu instead of all that junk you've been dishing up, 'cause it's disgusting, so it is, an insult to the system. The very smell would turn your stomach. That's why I keep that door closed there all the time. Maybe you've noticed. I mean, wouldn't you prefer cooking something decent for a change instead of all that pig swill? Frankly, I think your talent's wasted, because don't imagine I haven't been keeping tabs on you, for I have. Look, here's something I've drawn up.'

And he passed across a typewritten sheet sectioned off according to the days of the week. Monday, I read, Dish of the Day, Grilled Salmon with New Potatoes and Broccoli. Tuesday had an Italian flavour, Spaghetti Bolognese with a

Tomato and Onion salad. Wednesday was Indian-themed. Thursday, Chinese. Which was as far as I got.

'Well? Think you're up to it?'

'It's not me you have to worry about, Artie,' I told him. 'It's that lot outside.'

'What do you mean?'

'Well, do you think they'll go for it? It's a wee bit ambitious, wouldn't you say?'

'And what's wrong with that, eh? You're looking at a great believer in moving on, so you are. Ten long, wasted, fucking years, marking time, like a good few of those characters out there you've just mentioned.'

Leaning back in his chair, he put his hands behind his head.

'And let's face it, we're not the only ones, are we, Kenny? How many years, is it? Ten? Twenty? You and Cissie in that private, wee, locked-away world of yours. Don't look so surprised, I make it my business to know what's going on. Like on the other side of that door there, for instance,' and he pointed a gizmo at what I took to be a dead, grey TV screen high up on the wall, and suddenly the inside of the bar came up in living black and white, everybody having a good time in energetic mime.

'Don't worry, it doesn't reach as far as the kitchen. Just the till.'

He laughed. Then he became serious again.

'Kenny, one other maxim of mine is, we are what we eat, and looking around me, I'm not too impressed with what I see. Clogged arteries, diabetes, the big C, you name it, ticking away like a time-bomb. And just as important, what must the outside world think of us when they see a bunch of overweight couch potatoes instead of lean fighting machines? Where's the respect? Where's the example? Who'd want to put their trust in an army of Mister Blobbys, answer me that? So, are you with me on this or are you not?'

'I'll change the order at the Cash and Carry,' I told him. 'I'll send Bo Bo down.'

'No, do it yourself. And while you're at it tell our jolly little Asiatic friends there to get their act together. No more BSE burgers, no more battery broilers, no more sawdust sausages. Otherwise, I'll be getting annoyed and cancel our standing protection package and take our custom elsewhere.' Another laugh.

At the door I turned. 'What about your man? Dingo, I mean?' for I was still concerned there might be unfinished business there, with me ending up as some sort of sacrificial pig in the middle.

'If the same guy's any sense in that fucked up head of his he'll be on the Liverpool boat a.s.a.p. Otherwise, well, I don't need to draw a picture, do I? Speaking of which, one final and very important piece of advice, Kenny. Anything that goes down from tonight here on outside your kitchen, far as you're concerned, might as well be happening on Venus, or maybe Pluto. Got that? *Star Trek*? Science fiction? And you know something? I envy you. I really do. You're a lucky man, master of your own wee universe in that kitchen of yours, nobody or nothing to worry your head about except cooking up a storm for all your loyal customers out there. And me, too, don't forget. So, here's to good health, Kenny, the most precious gift any of us can ever have.'

Well, I left that office floating on a cushion of air, buoyed up, eager to go, ready, steady, cook, as the television programme has it. But then that's the sort of effect Artie Spence has on people, otherwise he wouldn't have got where he is, famous in his own way, without ever going on TV, unlike all those other former hard cases you keep on seeing every night of the week spouting off. Now, certain people, I know, have called him a psycho, not to his face, mind you. But the way I see it is — one, he is highly intelligent, and — two, he happens to be *our* psycho.

As for that revolutionary, groundbreaking cuisine of ours — for it wasn't just Artie who came up with all the bright ideas — after some initial groans and grumbling, soon everyone in the place appeared to take to my recipes, even the bodybuilders, the ones who look as if they're wearing Puffa jackets when they aren't. Appreciation became a new experience. I was beginning to enjoy it. In a very short time, expecting it, too.

'Absolutely terrific seafood risotto there, Kenny, if I may say so ... How ever did you manage to get those duck breasts as tender as that? ... Any more of that spinach and ricotta ravioli left? ... '

Well, okay, so maybe that's going it a bit strong. I should dream. But at least Artie always made a point of complimenting the chef.

Looking back, the whole business began to get a trifle out of hand, well, more than that, an obsession, you might call it, in, as well as out of the kitchen, for Bo Bo and me would sit watching all those afternoon food programmes on the box scribbling down recipes between us.

'How the fuck do you spell fricassee?' he'd say, sucking the pencil he used to mark his form sheet with.

Everything was going just fine. I was even trying out new

dishes at home, when one morning Bo Bo met me with a troubled expression on his face.

'Dingo McClean's back. And shooting his mouth off. Says he's going to sort Artie out once and for all. Him and a few of his friends.'

'Didn't know he had any,' I said. 'Anyway, Artie could eat him for breakfast.'

Which only goes to show how far I had lost touch with reality, feeling immune to any sort of unpleasantness beyond the boundaries of my kitchen.

'I'm not so sure,' said Bo Bo. 'This could be mega serious.' He was very sensitive, was Bo Bo. Sensitive, I mean, to what was going down outside on the street. 'Expect a bit of bother.'

'Maybe so, but it's not my affair,' I told him.

He looked at me. 'I've seen this situation before. You haven't. We might all be in the firing line.'

Even so I shut it all out, even when I began noticing the new mood in the club, the secrecy, the tension. And Bo Bo didn't make it any easier, for he would keep on telling me things I didn't wish to hear as I sweated over the pots and pans, the nastier details that hadn't yet made the papers or the News. Artie, too, seemed different. He barely spoke to me now, not even when I produced something extra special for him, a quite sensational duck à l'orange one time, I remember.

For the first time, too, guys could be seen going into his office in twos and threes, those with the reputations, emerging later, grim-faced, to leave by the back way, padding past me in the kitchen like commandos without their make-up on, all very different from the happy, whooping drunks I'd seen in the bar earlier.

In the small hours they'd return, changed men, bursting with jokes and horseplay, straight into the hard stuff. I stayed up late to serve them, big, substantial, filling dishes like chilli and Irish stew, for whatever they'd been up to out there in the darkness, the appetites they had on them were awesome, all scrubbed clean as well, hair still wet, like a football team fresh from the showers. Bo Bo said something else as well, I recall, about their Hotpoints at home going all out on heavy-soiling, and boiler suits being burned, me pretending, of course, I didn't know what he was on about. But then I was just following Artie's advice, taking care of number one, wasn't I?

One night, however, my resolve took a knock when a police presence arrived in the shape of a big, beefy inspector and two equally bulky flat-foots bringing the sheen and the smell of rain on their uniforms into the club with them. They stood there idly gazing about them at everything and everyone like a small delegation of sightseers. Artie came striding straight out of his office — obviously, the CCTV must have been on and working that night. He looked relaxed, as did the inspector.

'You've done the place up. Are those new carpets?' says he, casting a cool, appraising eye around. 'Mind you, I still see most of the same old faces. Evening, lads!'

One or two of the drinkers at the tables gave embarrassed ducks of the head, but the bulk of the club's membership stared hard at the TV on the wall even though it was showing a toilet-roll commercial at the time.

'Tell me, what's that terrific smell?' continued the inspector, sniffing the air, while the two constables dutifully wrinkled their snouts as though following orders.

'Look, I know you guys are on duty, otherwise I'd offer you a drink,' said Artie, 'but are you hungry by any chance? I guarantee you won't taste a better cassoulet west of Toulouse.' Then he called out, 'Chef! Come and meet the Inspector!'

Wiping my hands on my apron, I came out of the kitchen.

'We're all very proud of him, so we are. Aren't we, everybody?' said Artie, looping a fatherly arm about my shoulders. He smelt of some sort of cologne.

'He doesn't look very French,' said the inspector. 'More local, I'd say. You're Cissie Millar's young brother, aren't you? Kenny, isn't it? A decent woman. I don't know whether she'd be all that thrilled to learn you've hooked up with this crowd.'

All three cops were now studying me hard that way they have of making you feel you've done something wrong and they know it but are just saving up the knowledge for a rainy day.

'Sure you won't try some?' persisted Artie.

The inspector laughed.

'Catch yourself on, Artie. I'm not here on a social visit, or a food-tasting evening, either. This business on the street has gone on far too long. You know fine well what I'm talking about. You all do!' he said, raising his voice, even though everybody in the place had their ears tuned like transmitters to everything being said.

'Enough's enough, okay? No more, or the consequences will be dire, believe me. I hope I'm coming over loud and clear.'

'Crystal. An accommodation, as they say, has been reached by all parties. As from today.'

'Good. I'm glad to hear it. Just keep it that way,' said the inspector turning on his booted heel and heading for the door where big Gerry Burnside, one of the resident bouncers, was poised to let him and his boys in blue out.

'Still why don't you just come down to the station in the morning, there's a good lad, Artie. For a wee chat about this and that. Okay?'

After they'd left to go back to their Land Rover deliberately parked outside under a street lamp for everybody to see, Artie led me into his office, arm still draped about my shoulders.

'You all right?' he asked.

I was shaking.

'Hey, come on, don't let that big ape get to you. Kojak, we call him. That's how out of touch he is. Has nothing on anybody, and well he knows it. Anyway, remember what I told you that first day? About not getting involved? Well, you're not, so cheer up. Okay? Here, have a wee brandy,' and he crossed to a cabinet and took out a bottle of Courvoisier and two glasses.

I watched him pour a couple of stiff ones, and felt my anxiety balloon instead of recede, for I hadn't put a drink to my lips in months, deliberately so. Still there was nothing else for it but to do Artie Spence's bidding and keep him company. After all, that seemed to be the pattern in this new life of mine, and so the three-star slid down like sweet, liquid fire.

'Here's to good times, Kenny. No more aggro. No more turf wars. From here on in there's only one game in town and you, my son, are going to be part of it. Now, how does that grab you?'

And in that moment, with the brandy spreading through my veins, I really wanted to believe him, and gradually it did seem to be coming true, just as he said it would, the club and my cooking combining to form a happy fusion.

Artie Spence and me, we would share a good bottle of Chilean red late at night, just the two of us, when the place was quiet, Bo Bo having now a home to go to, unbelievably, spending more time there as well. Man to man we would talk about life and the future and his plan to broaden out his business interests into running a proper restaurant, maybe even a chain, for as he said, now that things have settled down big time, not only in the immediate neighbourhood, but everywhere else as well, a lot of money is to be made with people hungry for all the good things in life they've missed out on. Like top notch cuisine for one.

Listening to him talk I'd feel this sudden wave of warmth pass over me, mixed with gratitude, too, for this man sitting across from me in his black executive leather chair had saved me from depression, he had, I saw that now, over something I could never hope to change, Cissie and me, I mean, our secret, for it's taken me all this time to realise it had been a two-way, shared thing all along, the pair of us tied together in that way. That particular debt has been repaid in full, just like the one to Artie Spence.

And now and then it does strike me, as some sort of ironic footnote to all of this, in my own wee, private way it might be said that I, me, Kenny Millar, played no small part in bringing that business with Dingo McClean and his associates to a head the night I served him with a decidedly dodgy turkey-burger well past its sell-by date.

Just like Dingo himself, you might say.

Albatross

Sprawled drinking Drew's best Black Bush in that big, south-facing lounge of his with the really tremendous views, even in the dark — it now being two in the morning — they're listening to Fleetwood Mac, all that electronic sea-wash making them even more woozy, while upstairs Drew's wife Georgie is in that king-size bed. Possibly even emperor-sized, reflects Gary. Like nearly everything else in the house.

'For God's sake, can't you play some other track?' she'd begged, but got shouted down, so she left them to it, Gary Boy not having been back since '72, everything, but everything changed, especially his two old buddies, Drew, a sizeable pot on him by now, balding with it, and Colin, well, Colin, not nearly so, save for a touch of snow on top and a little more of the stoop, although he was never the bookish one, our Gary having that distinction. Or, curse, as he recalls.

Colin looks, well, *careworn*, frankly, in a washed-out old sweatshirt and frayed cords, casual, but maybe just a shade too casual, whereas Drew has on a canary yellow Pringle turtleneck, cashmere, almost certainly, Boss jeans, and those moccasins with the gold chains bridging the instep.

Musing on all this, as he does now, Gary suffers a twinge of something. After nearly a week of hard drinking he still can't help himself, still can't throw off old habits, detached, beady-eyed as ever. He wonders if the others have noticed. Georgie certainly has. Earlier in the kitchen, the pair of them coming together in a fleeting, vaguely adulterous clinch, she'd murmured, '*You* certainly haven't changed,' which he'd taken as a compliment, not having put on a pound since he'd seen her last. But then she went and spoiled it by saying, 'Watching, watching, all the time.'

Back in the old days when she was this blonde Jane Fonda lookalike, always hanging around the three of them wherever they went, he and Georgie had a minor thing together. At least *he* saw it that way. Then, again, maybe *she* didn't. And to be perfectly honest, he did feel a pang when he heard she and old Drew had got spliced. Georgie and Drew, for Christ's sake! Like Barbarella and Ted Turner. Being out of the country he couldn't make the wedding, but harboured this sneaky notion of turning up looking disgustingly tanned and fit. Juvenile, wishful-thinking crap, of course, but then it's the sort of fantasy everybody has at one time or other. Right?

Still, the years have been kind to her, he has to admit. Golf, tennis, gym, the sunbed. Still musing, recalling that trim, toned torso up close, he feels the unmistakable stirrings of a semi-boner coming on as he stretches out on one of Drew's big leather club settees, one of three, in rich, lustrous tan, facing the giant raw stone fireplace. 'Six grand's worth. Imported. Like the fucking mason.'

To which Colin nods assent, like he's been in on the deal, which he probably has, being Drew's works manager these days. Wife Deirdre, who he hasn't met, but will soon, is on the payroll also, so he understands.

Drew pours all three of them another generous shot of cask-matured, fifteen-year old, mercifully refraining from costing it this time, for ever since he's got off the plane Gary feels he's been subjected to a running cash inventory, money, money, money — like the song — airport car park jammed with top of the range Mercs, Saabs, BMWs, the smell of easy assets hanging ripe and heavy in the air like expensive scent on a whore's fur coat. Welcome to the Klondike, and him, old Gary Boy, only prospector in town without a claim or pan to his name.

Drew aims the remote at the Bang & Olufsen and, finally, after about a hundred or so plays, Fleetwood's big, monster number one dies in mid-gulp. In the subsequent silence they hear the moan of the wind outside, followed by a soft pattering of what looks like snowflakes on the pitch black, floor-to-ceiling windows.

'White Christmas, eh, guys?' observes Gary in the pause, the other two turning a look on him as though he's just voiced something embarrassingly effete and citified, which now, he is, he supposes.

Then out of the blue Drew says, 'Remember those old Daisy air rifles we used to have?'

'The rat hunts,' recalls Gary.

'At the dump,' says Colin, keeping the ball rolling.

And for a moment all stare deep into the amber swirl in their Waterford tumblers, each with his very own personal snapshot of that acrid-smelling, old killing-ground.

'The way we used to talk about going on a proper shoot one day? Remember? With proper guns?'

Suddenly Colin and Drew are laughing together, at him, his face.

He grins back. 'So? *So?*'

He is most decidedly drunk, the alcohol snaking through his veins as though a hot tap has been turned on inside somewhere gradually eclipsing the cold supply.

'*What*, for fuck's sake?'

'Show him,' orders Drew, and obediently Colin gets up and goes into the other room. He comes back carrying three waxed green zip-up cases, like musical instrument cases, only long and tapered. He lays them flat on the polished, granite-topped coffee table.

'Happy Christmas,' says Drew. 'What you always wanted, but were too afraid to ask for,' and Colin unzips one of the cases and there's the dull cobalt gleam of gunmetal and polished hardwood inside.

'Go on, don't be shy, take her out.'

It's a twelve-bore, chased breech, twin hammers, smelling of 3-in-One Oil, and feeling the slick film coating his palms, Gary suppresses the merest shiver of distaste.

'Christ, guys, what's all this? What bank are we planning to rob?'

Colin gives a laugh. 'The Allied Irish, I'd say.'

'No fucking way, man, that's where all my money's stashed.'

Drew laughing also, as, unzipping his own gun, he trains it on the blackness outside as though at an invisible prowler.

'Look at that workmanship,' says Colin. 'Fantastic, eh?'

And so they sit there, Gary feeling under no obligation to enquire any further, as if what's in front of him has simply no other function than to be admired, like the Mona Lisa, or the Three Graces, say.

After a time Colin rises and goes across to peer out of the sliding windows overlooking the invisible York stone terrace.
  'We should be going,' he tells Drew, tapping his watch.
  'Okay,' the other agrees, standing up, the pair of them looking down on Gary Boy stretched out lazily on his big tan settee.
  'So, we *are* going to rob that bank after all,' he jokes up at them.
  'No, just something you always promised yourself you'd get around to one day. Come on, there's some gear of mine you can borrow in the garage.'
  But Gary is feeling it hard to renounce the wraparound comfort of that big old soft leather couch.
  'Look, you guys, no harm to you, but at my time of life I'd feel no end of a dick taking pot-shots at a bunch of rodents in the dark somewhere.'
  'Fuck rats,' Drew tells him. 'We're going on a duck shoot.'
  Which some short time later leads to all three of them travelling in Drew's big Cherokee Jeep through the night. Or what remains of it, Colin having pointed out that first sliver of pink low down where the horizon should be. In his heavy proofed parka and waxed trousers Gary feels the way a spaceman must feel on Mission One, olive green rubber boots bolstering the illusion. He's in the back seat staring out between those two heads in front, the dashboard lights throwing both outlines into vaguely sinister relief. Like two kidnappers, he catches himself thinking, with him the victim being driven to the hideout.
  'Here,' says Colin, passing back a freshly opened bottle

between the seats and, taking a swig, Gary feels it going down, reigniting, and leaning forward, asks, 'Just exactly where are we heading, chaps? Some kind of a mystery tour?'

By now the four-wheel-drive is bumping over a narrow, gravelly track, pale in the dipped headlights. Out here it could be anywhere, any place, in the darkness of a countryside Gary once knew well, but now finds forbidding, foreign, even. Another nervous fit takes hold at the possibility of being marooned here. How would he find his way back?

All this time that knife-edge of rose shading into cerise is strengthening ahead of them. They seem to be racing into it, racing *it*, until, finally, the Jeep topping a rise, he feels the floor beneath his thick-soled boots switchback, but in almost luxuriant slow motion, their headlights shooting straight out across an expanse of something dead flat with the faintest silvery sheen to it.

'We're here,' says Drew. 'Now where's that fucking boat?'

'There,' says Colin, pointing, and the Jeep bumps over more shingle, travelling on some little way before coming to rest.

'Okay, everybody out,' orders Drew and Gary climbs down, rubber space boots sinking into shifting pebbles. Not moon dust. Shivering, he looks around. Off to his right, the Lough, for, of course, he knows where he is now, its surface ruffled black silk, stretching off and away to what he always considered infinity even in daylight. Now, in the dark, the illusion has become real, palpable. He hears the soft lap of fresh water breaking against the pale crust of dried foam and bleached driftwood.

Wrapped in Drew's parka, gloved hands thrust deep in its pockets, he experiences a moment of private calm, remembering, as he does, times past along this same stretch of shore, foraging, wading, or simply skimming stones across the table-flat surface watching them hop, skip and jump like those Second World War bouncing bombs on old black and white TV footage. He's still racking his brains over the name of that boffin bloke — it *was* Barnes, wasn't it? — when Drew starts opening up the back of the Jeep.

He watches him take out the cased shotguns. Maybe it's the alcohol, but he still hasn't allowed the fact he has never handled one before to seriously bother him. When the time comes, it'll be fine, he tells himself. *He'll* be fine.

'This is yours,' Drew tells him, handing over one of the cases, slamming down the rear end of the Cherokee, and reading the raised chrome nameplate on the back for the first time like that, Gary takes it as some sort of personal sign, our merry little band of braves kitted-out, tooled-up, ready to ride. Geronimo.

Their boat, a paint-blistered old dinghy with about six inches of rainwater inside, is upended to let the bilge run out, Gary standing by while the others take charge, piling in the gear, fixing the oars in place, dragging it to the water's edge. He has no problem with any of it — again, why should he? — sitting in the stern now, facing Colin as he rows them out across the inky expanse, a tremendous chilly calm all around, soft creak of oars only sound to be heard.

Their so-called 'island' is little more than a bump on the surface of the lake, a few impoverished alder bushes breaking its crown, barely room for the three of them to lie alongside one another after they've beached the boat, half in, half out, of the water, Gary following the others' lead as they stretch out, bedding down on a thin, crackling layer of driftwood. Bone-dry, brittle, it smells of absolutely nothing, bleak midwinter having squeezed the living juice out of everything all around.

After a time the bottle makes the rounds again. They drink from it in turn like kids on a Sunday School picnic, Gary recalling cake crumb sediment lying at the bottom of the lemonade in that way which you always steeled yourself not to think about. For some reason the whiskey tastes sour, bitter, or maybe it's his mouth. He's beginning to feel hungry too, and wonders if there's anything edible in that game bag.

'Okay, so here's the drill,' Drew tells him. 'Hold everything until they come in to feed and hit the water, then, bang, do as we do. Okay?' and he nods back even though feeling ever so slightly miffed at being taken for a total greenhorn, which he is, he supposes, but that's really not the point, is it?

'And break your gun now to be on the safe side,' instructs Colin. 'And don't 'til the very last minute. Got it?'

'Yeah, some of us have this sentimental attachment to our balls,' says Drew, getting a laugh, Gary foolishly trying to top it with, 'I'm sure Georgie wouldn't be all that chuffed, either.'

It's funny how a feeble little crack like that can cause damage, or perhaps it was waiting to happen all along on account of the whiskey, notoriously mood-altering at the best of times. Then, again, Gary had forgotten what a touchy creature Drew could be in his younger days. No great change there, it would appear, for after that he goes all cold and distant on them, concentrating murderously instead on water, land, sky.

After some time Colin asks, 'Shouldn't they be here by now?' receiving only a growl in reply.

Gary is getting jittery himself, face and feet icy cold, hands, too, which raises the question whether he'll be able to pull the trigger when the time comes with his gloves on. Should they be? Alongside, on the driftwood, hinged open, lies the shotgun, disabled looking. He tries to recall the actual mechanics of the thing, the precise action involved in discharging it, knowledge only gleaned, now he realises, from movies, or photographs in an old *Field & Stream* magazine. Drew has doled him out a handful of fat, brass-ended, crimson cartridges. Surreptitiously, in his pocket, he counts them. Six. Three for each barrel. He'll be lucky if he gets off one.

Without really thinking he reaches across and takes hold of the whiskey bottle jammed in the shingle, putting it to his lips. For an instant the others stare at him, then look away, as though he's no longer part of the plan, an embarrassment. *Well, fuck that*, he tells himself, and takes another swig, about four inches left.

'We should have brought a dog,' Colin says. 'I did tell you. Gerry Madden's retriever,' and muddled by the drink, he thinks, *instead of me, does he mean?*

'What the fuck for?' says Drew. 'They're not showing, I tell you.'

'Come on, give it another wee while.'

'Total fucking washout.'

'It happens.'

'Does it?'

Suddenly Gary's feeling he's the one being blamed for the situation, not in so many words, not straight out, him, the outsider, bringer of bad duck karma.

'Maybe they decided to give it a miss,' he chips in, attempting to lighten the mood. 'I mean, wouldn't you, if you were a duck? At Christmas?'

There follows an unpleasant silence.

'Know something?' Drew tells him. 'You still have that big mouth on you.'

'Well, pardon me for thinking we came out all this way for a bit of sport, not have ourselves a nervous breakdown over a few fucking waterfowl with no sense of direction.'

And the instant he says it, he's thinking, *Christ, we're actually having a barney, the way it used to be.* Football, motorbikes, records, girls, capital of Baluchistan, any topic would do, and old Colin on the sidelines trying to smooth things over like now.

'Look, the odd straggler does fly in. Maybe a brace, even.'

'There's fucking three of us,' snaps Drew, reaching for the bottle. He drinks, then corks it without handing it across.

Away on the distant, still dark shores of the Lough, Gary sees a prick of light sharpen, then another, and another, as if an entire village of shift workers have all stirred at the same time. It's a genuine revelation. He's stunned by it registering like that, a personal message to him and him alone. And then a lot closer to home, suddenly, revelation number two, for there, hugging an islet nearby, barely a spit of shingle, he catches sight of something white bobbing in the shallows, and most definitely feathered, too. Even more miraculous, the others seem unaware of it.

Instantly his breathing becomes soft, quick and shallow, and he draws a pair of cartridges from the depths of his poacher's pocket, their brass caps frosty to the touch. He stretches out his other hand to the broken shotgun, all the while keeping what he's doing concealed by the outline of his body. Then, going by feel, he eases the cartridges home, one, two, with the ball of his thumb, closing the breech, snicking back both hammers, muffling the action with his cupped, gloved hand.

Shakily he draws a bead on the kill, floating, unsuspecting, on the swell under its reedy overhang, a lot bigger than expected, plumage all fluffed out on account of the cold — *like a duvet*, he thinks to himself, *duck's down* — which is as far as empathy takes him before he lets off the first and what turns out to be his only barrel of shot.

The report is deafening, recoil an even greater shock, the water where the duck was rocking seconds earlier a sudden boiling broth flecked with white.

By now Colin is on his feet shouting blue murder, while Drew lies still, hands covering his ears.

Next thing Colin has grabbed the gun off him.

'You fucking lunatic, didn't I say not to play around? Didn't I?'

Still coming down from the blood rush Gary stares back at him. Had he actually said that, *playing around*? He doesn't think so somehow. It strikes him as grossly unfair to be lying at a time like this.

Then it's Drew's turn.

'You might have killed one of us, you know that?' He shakes his head as if trying to dislodge something.

'Right in my bloody ear, too. What the fuck got into you?'

'The crazy bastard probably did it for a laugh.'

Suddenly Gary is feeling genuine outrage, both of them turning on him in this way.

'I got a duck,' he tells them — it sounds funny like that, so he elaborates — 'one of your famous fucking mallard what-you-me-call-its. Go on, have a gander.' He couldn't resist it. 'Over there, in the water. Blown to blazes, unfortunately,' both of them staring now at the crime scene, water strewn with fallout like somebody's just ripped open a pillowcase.

'I don't believe it,' says Drew, plunging in.

He's wearing khaki, thigh-length waders. They watch as he lifts up the reedy overhang, groping around in the dark water.

'I told you we should have brought Gerry Madden's dog!' Colin calls out to him. He sounds angry still, but more at himself now, Gary suspects, at having lost it back there like that.

Drew comes wading back. He's empty-handed.

'So, where is it?' asks Colin.

'Duck all, to coin a phrase. Mister Magoo here just shot a fucking swan, that's what.'

'Oh, Christ,' says Colin dropping to his knees, 'now we're for it.'

'Not if we get rid of it and clean up the rest of the crap before the water bailiffs make their rounds.'

'Even on Christmas Day?' not so innocently Gary enquires.

There's a pause like a hole opening up, enough contempt there to last a lifetime. Oddly enough the shock of hearing that word *swan* hasn't filtered through yet, not even the fact of having *murdered one*, for that *is* the word, he tells himself. It is, isn't it?

Only when they're back in the boat and pulling for the shore does it really hit him. Rather, its dead presence does, lying close to his feet like that. At first he tries not to look at it, the long, coiled, snakelike neck, the jet black poll, the yellow beak, those amazing webbed feet. But then he finds he can't drag his gaze away, held fast by that congealed stare. He begins to feel sick, something curdling in his stomach, and when he leans over the side to throw up, the others laugh, even Colin.

Soon as the boat scrapes ashore Drew jumps out and heads for the parked Jeep, returning with a plaid rug in which he proceeds to wrap the carcase.

'Georgie's mother bought us that,' he tells them. 'She'd go fucking spare if she saw this. They both would.'

'What about just burying it out here?' suggests Gary, the nausea by now having subsided helped along by another fierce slug of Black Bush.

'And have the foxes come and dig it up? No, we're stuck with the fucker. I'll put it in the freezer in the garage until I think of something.'

'The dump, maybe?'

Colin grins at him. 'We've got an incineration plant now. State of the art.'

'Yeah, we've come a long way from tank tops and kipper ties,' says Drew.

'Don't remind me,' Gary sighs. 'Don't even *dare* remind me.'

Which, of course, is what they proceed to do on the journey back, dredging up several other best forgotten wardrobe nightmares, so that by the time they're pulling into Drew's driveway the corpse in its Royal Stewart shroud behind them is almost forgotten, a rapidly fading blip on the chart of the night's other disasters.

Piling out of the four-wheel, three unshaven wrecks in all that ridiculous outdoor gear, they look at one another, then laugh, before Drew puts a warning finger to his lips miming someone asleep in the house in front of them. And while he's disposing of the evidence in the garage, Colin and Gary tiptoe on ahead, letting themselves in through the big, silent, dark kitchen, everything for the festive blow-out laid out in moulded, gleaming tinfoil.

By now Gary's brain appears to be functioning normally. For the first time he's feeling relatively sober, too, and gazing about, finds it difficult to reconcile the Georgie they all once knew and loved with this model housewife and her amazing Möben kitchen.

And then, some few hours later, after they've showered, shaved and dozed in front of the freshly tended fire, the lady of the house herself appears.

'So,' she enquires, 'where's that lovely, big, free-range duck I was promised?' gazing down at the three of them stretched there all reeking of her hubby's aftershave. Dolled up in a powder blue trouser suit, sexy as hell with it, she, too smells of something expensive and citrusy.

'What you reckon?' asks Drew. 'Break open the bubbly now, or wait for Deirdre?' and at the mention of his wife's name Colin stirs uneasily.

'I'll ring her now,' he tells them, taking out his mobile and going off into the kitchen, closing the door behind him.

'Right, you two wrecks, so how was it on our big bad boys' expedition? Or aren't we supposed to ask that,' says Georgie settling herself on one of the settees, thighs clam-tight as if she's wearing a skirt instead of trews, even though, in actual fact, they're not, it's just that Gary enjoys *imagining* the word so much, associating them in his mind, as he does, with a pair in Black Watch she used to favour in the old days.

Getting up, Drew crosses to the drinks cabinet.

'Better ask your man here that,' he says with his back turned.

And suddenly for Gary it's crunch time, go for it, and to hell with the consequences, or supply the edited version.

A few days later, going home on the plane, a generous gin and tonic on the pull-down tray in front of him, he decides the first option might well have spared him a deal of needless anxiety over that thing solidifying in a block in the garage, while back inside they were all getting plastered together.

But then all that is way, way upstream.

Right now the three of them are clinking flutes together, Moët, of course, while old Colin is still in the kitchen out of earshot.

He comes back in again, sweat beading his brow. 'She's on her way,' he tells them, gulping down an offered glass of champagne. 'Her people, you know.'

Cheerily Drew claps him on the back. 'Well, we did try to warn you, old sport. It's what you get when you will go off and marry the wrong sort. Not so much marrying a wife, more the entire bloody tribe.'

'For God's sake, Drew,' cautions Georgie, 'today of all days.'

Most of this is arcing way over Gary's head, not helped by the fact he's starting to get plastered all over again, and feeling devilish with it, distracted by Georgie's thighs outlined so fetchingly through the fine, expensive material of her slacks. Already they appear to have parted the barest fraction, convincing him it might turn out to be that crucial gap between wifely rectitude and the compliance of someone game for a re-run of last night's little encounter up against the kitchen draining-board. Well, he can dream, can't he?

By the time Colin's wife arrives they're all of them experiencing the aerated rush from the champagne, and Deirdre is a big surprise, not the dour, disapproving character Gary was expecting for some reason, but a tall, freckled, rust-haired stunner in a fur-collared topcoat. Radiating intense feminine heat she comes breezing in, and almost instantly she and Drew lock horns, but in playful mode as if it's an old, old ritual.

'So what kept you?' he greets her. 'Early mass, was it? Wafer a day keeps the big bad bogeyman away, eh?'

Georgie says, 'Drew, now what did I tell you?'

But Deirdre only grins. 'Sure everybody knows he's only an old bigot. Aren't you, Drew?'

She's got these terrific teeth and a baby's healthy, pink, inner mouth when she laughs.

'Here, I've gone and left all your presents in the car,' she tells them, going back outside, returning with an armful of shiny, wrapped parcels, old Colin all the while watching her with a look veering between nervous awareness and idolatry.

Observing all this from his settee, Gary experiences that old pang again, the one he felt when he first saw Drew and Georgie together. Now it's Colin's and Deirdre's turn to leave him depressed, comparing his own situation, the messy divorce, maintenance bleeding him dry, the 'studio' flat. No kids, at least. Just like this lot. So, why is that? But does he really have a hankering to go browsing through other people's bedroom drawers, even Georgie's? Viagra, suddenly he's thinking, marital aids, handcuffs, blindfolds, delay creams.

By now all four of them are on their knees gleefully ripping open their gifts, even the deliciously cool Deirdre, and Gary gets to wondering if all this *stuff* might not be some kind of kiddy substitute, all these treats spread out on the giant rug. At least he and Miriam did *try* for a family. He gets up and helps himself to some more of Drew's champagne.

But then Georgie says, 'This is for you,' taking something small, square and tastefully wrapped from her bag lying on the coffee-table. 'I hope it's the one you like.'

Feeling a louse because of all the disloyal thoughts he's been having, he tears open the package, aftershave, Paco Rabanne — how did she know? — and, smiling, Deirdre glances over at him, really for the first time, it strikes him. Going across to Georgie he gives her a swift brush on one glitter-dusted, peachy cheek.

'You shouldn't have,' he tells her. 'Really.'

'Yeah, really's the word all right,' says Drew. 'His big, proper present's all wrapped up out in the garage. Right, Colin?'

It's a heart-stopping moment, both women shooting curious glances back and forth between husbands.

'Come on, don't be such a creep, give us a clue,' pleads Deirdre. After only one glass of champagne she seems to have relaxed considerably, a definite, mischievous feyness revealing itself there.

But Gary is still hung up with Drew and what he's just said.

'Wouldn't be the Jeep, would it?' he says, and everybody laughs, especially Colin, who then asks Georgie, 'What time do we eat? I'm starving,' Drew unable to let it rest with, 'Yeah, duck shooting can certainly give a man an appetite, eh, Gary?'

At which point the two women get up to go off into the kitchen together, releasing this terrific smell of cooking as the door swings open.

'Mind you don't go missing the Queen's Speech, Deirdre!' Drew calls out. 'You know the way you always look forward to it!'

She looks back over her shoulder at him. '*Your* Queen, not mine.'

'You reckon?'

Then, going across to open the wine, he tells Colin, 'God, I love that wife of yours. What she sees in you, mind.'

'Why don't you give it a rest? Nobody's finding it all that funny, you know.'

'Well, Deirdre does. And Gary here.'

They look at him straining with the corkscrew — a dozen bottles at least lined up, red, white, rosé — in his Royal St Andrew's clubhouse get-up, coral pink cardigan, matching Lacoste polo shirt, Prince of Wales checked slacks, the big chunky watch Georgie has just given him throwing off tiny shards of light. Rolex, possibly.

'One more dig about religion or politics, and we're out of there, okay? We don't need it, even from you.'

Colin on his feet suddenly, old Colin with his abiding concern about his blood pressure, now nudging the danger mark, by the look on his face.

'Hey, everybody,' Gary says, leaping in, 'how about a top-up? No offence, Drew, but this stuff's starting to taste like cat's piss.' And without waiting for a reply he takes up a glass and a freshly opened bottle of the red.

'Here's to the old team, the three musketeers!'

'Speaking of muskets ... ' says Drew.

Just then Georgie pokes her head in. 'I need a big strong

man straight away,' she announces, and grateful for the reprieve Gary heads for the kitchen.

Bent over the low-level oven Deirdre is prodding at the spitting brown beast within, taut backside a symphony in moulded gabardine, possibly the result of many hours at the same fitness centre her friend attends. Visualising the pair of them in sweat-soaked Lycra, Gary feels his throat drying.
'Be a darling and give us a hand,' she says, turning her head.
'Twenty-five pounder,' says Georgie, looking equally fetching, all hot and bothered from her culinary efforts.
For a moment they study him, eyes zeroing in like those laser pens that are supposed to cause no serious damage as long as you don't stare back. Which, no fool he, Gary heeds, stooping down and taking a two-handed grip on the rim of the oven tin.
'Where do you want it?' he asks, and Georgie points to the table and a white china serving platter the size of a satellite dish. Without spilling a drop of those rich, bubbling life juices, he manhandles the turkey out on to it, and Georgie drapes a tea towel over it.
'It needs to rest now,' she tells him. 'So why don't you go back inside and do likewise.'
'Yeah,' laughs Deirdre, 'up all night reliving your misspent youth, I hear.'
'And don't forget, buster,' says Georgie, jabbing him in the chest, 'I've still a crow to pick with you. Or should that be duck?'

Back in the living room Colin and Drew seem to have patched up their little differences, well, Colin, anyway, Drew never having really lost his cool in the first place, both of them well into that really good bottle of Beaune. Gary joins them. He's enjoyed his brief interlude in the kitchen, realising just how much he's missed the dangerous, knowing company of women, and possibly because of it indulges in some serious showing off when the great burnished bird finally arrives on the table, even volunteering to carve, napkin tucked into his shirt.

By now the mood is one of loud, whooping merriment and, gazing around in a haze of good fellowship, Gary feels moved by it all. He has a paper fez on his head, the crackers having been pulled, mottoes read out.

After which things get a trifle blurry. He recalls a good-humoured shouting match over the choice of music, the women winning the day, Fleetwood Mac getting the push in favour of Van Morrison's throttled vowels. Sitting in the honoured guest's place between Deirdre and Georgie, he ponders why it is women, women, in general, never really seem to experience nostalgia in quite the same way, or to the same extent, as men. Surely there must have been something a lot more moving, musically speaking, in their teenage years than that ugly little fat guy in the hat with the frog in his throat.

But then, suddenly demolishing his grand theory, doesn't Deirdre sing herself, something in Irish and most definitely nostalgic, the rest of them sitting staring into their drinks and feeling oddly bereft somehow, even old Drew, despite his well-known aversion to what he terms 'fiddley-dee fucking music'.

Later they smoke a little dope for old times' sake, passing a joint around, Georgie the only one declining, not Deirdre, strangely enough, and then as it starts getting darker and darker outside the big, wall-sized windows Deirdre goes off to the bathroom, returning with her face done and ordering hubby, 'Let's go. Don't forget we're expected over at my Uncle Eugene's place,' dragging him to his feet. She's going to drive, she tells them.

Jesus, what a woman, thinks Gary, *lucky Colin*, finally managing to get himself a little birdie on the lips, her telling him, 'Come back soon. That old London. I lived there for a year once. Hounslow. Hated it,' and for a moment he has this colossal rush of regret thinking of the two of them in the same great city and the terrible tragedy of them not even knowing it, or each other.

After they leave everything seems to slide into slow motion, Drew half-asleep by now, the weed having done for him. Looking over at the slumped figure, head lolling, on the sofa, Georgie sighs. 'I suppose I'll have to get him upstairs, otherwise he'll just crash out down here.'

'I'll give you a hand,' Gary volunteers, and between them they manage to wrestle the limp somnambulist up the stairs.

'No, not in there, here,' orders Georgie, resting for a moment on the landing, Drew having put on the old avoirdupois over the intervening years. He also stinks of booze, fags, as well. *Do I smell like that*, Gary can't help worrying? But, hey, he was right, they *do* sleep in separate rooms.

Like a felled ox, down goes mine host. Believe it or not, the bed has a Batman duvet cover, touching in a way, seeing him flat out on one of his old youthful icons. But before things can get any more marital, Georgie peeling off his pants for starters, Gary retreats downstairs.

Back on the settee again — already it feels like part of his own furniture at home — he pours himself another glass of something, doesn't matter which, staring into the leaping flames in Drew's big, roughcast, stone fireplace. Like something from a ranch-house movie-set in a Western, for the first time, it strikes him. Or one of those snowed-in cabin jobs in a Rock Hudson, Doris Day feature. Looking outside he sees all the white has disappeared as though mysteriously hoovered away while they were busy whooping it up. From upstairs the sound of the loo comes drifting down and moments later Georgie descends smelling of mouthwash.

'Beats me how you lot still smoke that stuff,' she says waving her arms about.

Then, sitting down opposite, thighs all prim and proper once again, she says, 'So, what are we going to talk about, you and I?' Which, of course, only creates one of those awful silences, Gary visualising it stretching across the polished floorboards between them like this slow-moving, treacly tide.

Then she says, 'First real, grown-up chance we've had since you got here.'

'Yeah. Boys will be boys, I'm afraid.'

'You're right. Not a lot changes.'

'Think so?'

Then tiring of all this cat and mouse, pussy-footing stuff he decides to come out with it. 'Look, about that duck business.'

But she interrupts him. 'It's okay. Drew's told me all about it.'

'He has?'

'Sure. About it all being a washout. Still, you did have *some* fun.'

He stares at her, trying to read something deeper, more meaningful there.

'And that was *all* he said?'

Like an idiot he has her intrigued now, he can see it in her eyes, so he's back-pedalling fast. 'No, no, it's just that Drew seemed to take it, well, so personally, those stupid wildfowl not showing up and all.'

She looks at him. 'Drew's that way about a lot of things.'

'You and me, for example?' *Oh, Christ, he can't believe he just said it.*

For a moment she actually seems to relax, thighs appearing to loosen slightly, but then with a soft, silken snap they come together again.

'Poor Gary,' she says with a laugh. 'You'll never grow up, will you?'

Then, yawning, 'Well, heigh-ho, I'm off to beddy-byes. Nice long lie-in for all of us in the morning. And, please, *please*, don't go playing that depressing old record down here, you hear me? What's it called again?'

'Albatross,' he tells her. 'Look, I'll be shooting off early. Need to check out a few people. The long-lost relatives, you know.'

'But we will be seeing you before you go?'

'Oh, yeah, sure, just a couple of days taking in the green, green grass of home.'

'Judging by the smell in my living room, I'd have thought you'd have had enough of the other sort to be going on with,' she says with a laugh, planting a fleeting, goodnight kiss on his cheek before heading off up that big, see-through, Swedish pine staircase of theirs. Yet, for some odd reason, this time he has no compelling urge for a last, lingering look after that perfect backside as it vanishes off and up out of view.

The following morning early, nursing his hangover, he creeps from the sleeping house with no real plan in mind, having lied about visiting relatives. Even if he had, those he had left were hardly the sort he wanted to hook up with anyway.

At a loose end of his own choosing until his flight takes off, over the next couple of days somehow he manages to put in the time, staying in a gruesome bed and breakfast on the coast, the wind howling in off the Irish Sea rattling the glass. Still, he manages to survive it all, telling himself he needed the time to think anyway, work out a few things, even seeing a patch of clear blue opening up for him and some of his more pressing problems back home.

'So how was it, then? Get a chance to check out the old homestead?'

Once more he's in the Jeep, heading for the airport this time and his three o'clock flight, Drew behind the wheel, Colin in the back as before, the pair of them in their casual gear still, for the holiday period continues arching over everything like one vast extended hangover, from which, lucky old Gary, he has recovered by now.

'Never got the chance,' he lies. 'All those deadly aunts and uncles, you know,' wary still, unable to relax, not until he's in his window seat looking down at the diminishing patchwork of green, a stiff drink in front of him.

Then Colin, who has been quiet all along, enquires, 'Well, did you enjoy yourself, or not? Go on, tell the truth,' good, old, soft, dependable Colin, and suddenly he's feeling incredibly guilty. These guys really are the salt of the earth, he tells himself. He's the one who has lost that precious gift of innocent candour and openness.

'It was great,' he confesses, meaning it, too.

'Just make sure you don't leave it so long next time,' says Drew. 'I mean, I don't want Georgie giving me a hard time.

And, Deirdre. Know what *she* said? Why were we hiding you all this time? No kidding. She did, didn't she, Colin?'

But Colin seems preoccupied, staring out at the bare fields racing past on the long straight run to the airport.

'Still has what it takes with the ladies. The boy certainly hasn't lost that, eh, Colin?'

But Colin still seems somewhere else, and minutes later they start slowing down before pulling into one of the terminal's set-down bays. His bag is on the back seat. Colin reaches it across to him.

'Well, you guys,' he tells them, 'don't be doing anything I would do,' incredibly trite, he knows, but what the hell, he's entitled.

But then Drew says, 'Hey, Romeo, hold on, we've got something for you,' climbing out and going round to the boot, coming back with a big, bulging black, plastic bin liner.

'Going-away present,' he says, handing it over with a grin. 'Don't worry, it should keep until you get home.'

'What is it?'

But Drew only laughs, climbing back up into the Jeep. 'Well, now then, it wouldn't be a surprise, would it? Have a good trip.'

Gary stands there watching the big cherry red four-wheel drive accelerate off in the direction of the Exit sign, Colin's face looking back at him through the rear window. He raises a hand to wave, but before they can make eye contact Colin has turned away.

All around he hears the sound of cars arriving and departing, shouts, laughter, couples, whole families embracing, him standing on his lonesome looking down at the plastic sack at his feet. Alongside his pigskin travel bag it seems shockingly out of place somehow, the sort of thing some poor emigrant might carry on board. He looks up as an Airbus comes in low over the terminal buildings. Even this close its windows seem incredibly toy-like.

Fifty yards away a guy in a uniform with a walkie-talkie appears to be checking him out, more critically, his 'present', so grabbing it by the neck, along with his real luggage, he starts walking in the opposite direction, past the hiss and suck of the Departure doors and inside the queues of people in front of the X-ray machines, his brain taking one careful, nervy step at a time, on the lookout for a rubbish bin. But, of course, he has forgotten, hasn't he, where he is, those being almost a relic now because of the bomb scares.

Starting to sweat a bit he visualises himself out in the sticks somewhere still searching, missing his plane, anywhere as long as he can dump his not so 'little' souvenir. And it's actually beginning to feel like he might be stuck with it, when at the back of the Avis rental car park he spots one of those big commercial dumpster things. Sidling up to it, trying to give the impression he's searching for his hire car, he feels like a real terrorist.

But just as he's about to lift up that heavy, dented, rubber lid everything seems to stop dead for him. Hemmed in by all those latest model Vauxhalls and Fiestas he freezes, smitten. Another plane passes over, taking off this time, and under cover of the roar he unties the cord pulling open the neck of the sack. At the bottom there's something wrapped in an old, stained, grey sweatshirt. He prods at the wrapped mystery, even though by now he knows what it is. Yet it doesn't feel the way it should somehow, not lumpy, nor softish. More a hard, solid slab of something. His fingers tell him more. Finally, his eyes. A thick pile of magazines, ancient, mildewed, yellow *National Geographics*. Ballast. The one on top has a Masai warrior on the cover. He stares at him for an instant before gathering up the bin liner and dropping it into the darkness of the dumpster to join all the other useless, forgotten trash lying deep down inside there.

Back at the airport the monitors tell him his flight's on time. Passing through the X-ray arch, he has his brush-down, checks in, heads for his gate. High above the escalator is this big blue and green panoramic blow-up, entire width of the facing wall, what else but that famous scenic shot of their very own geological ninth wonder of the world — or is it tenth? — across it the invitation, COME BACK AND SEE US ALL SOON.

But, too washed out and jaded to react, even in a cynical way, he refuses to give it the satisfaction of rising to the bait.